TRIUMPH OF THE WOLF

MAGNETIC MAGIC
BOOK 6

LINDSAY BUROKER

1

"I HAVE THREE INTERVIEWS NEXT WEEK AND A JOB OFFER I DON'T know if I want to take." My niece's voice came through tinny over the speaker of my phone, which balanced precariously on a landscaping boulder while I raked up sodden needles and broken branches. "It doesn't sound meaningful, fulfilling, or like it'll enhance my skills for my résumé."

"Doesn't pay enough for you to move out of your parents' backyard, huh?" I tossed pine boughs into the cart I'd driven onto the lawn.

Sun beamed from the morning sky, but a wicked windstorm the night before had left debris all over the grounds of Sylvan Serenity Housing. Most of the time, I appreciated how much verdant acreage the apartment complex sprawled across, especially given its suburban Shoreline location near the busy freeway. This was not one of those times.

"Not even close," Jasmine said. "I'd make more pouring coffee drinks at the bikini-barista espresso stand."

"Those girls earn a lot for standing in the damp Seattle climate while so scantily clad. You can't expect a job that competes with that."

"I'm halfway to a master's degree and have been working in the field with my mom for almost ten years."

"I've heard they can make six figures in tips alone."

"Oh, please." After hesitating, Jasmine asked, "That's not true, is it? Because if it is, I may need to rethink my job hunt. I'm trying to prove myself to the world through my great work ethic and the power of my brain, but... I'm super hot in a bikini."

"I have no doubt." Lower back sore, I stood straight to massage it. "But I'm not actually sure what they make. Oddly, I'm not compelled to visit their establishments that often. I'm more drawn to..." Movement in the woods bordering the property caught my eye. Leaves stirring. In the wind?

"Scantily clad penises?"

"If they're attached to charming, intelligent men who make me feel good about myself, yes."

"How *is* Duncan? There's a rumor going around the pack that he might put himself forward as a candidate to be our next alpha. Lorenzo is pretty old, and the young upstarts are always talking about challenging him. But I doubt they'd challenge someone who can turn into an old-school, two-legged werewolf with superpowers. And did your mother *give* him that magical medallion that the male alphas in the pack historically wore?"

Focused on the woods, I only half heard my niece. Though I was more than a hundred yards from the trees, I thought I *sensed* someone out there. Someone with magical blood.

Had the pack sent a relative to spy on me? Or on Duncan? Or, more likely, had Lord Abrams—pissed off that we'd killed his scheming business partner, Radomir—sent spies? Or potion-enhanced thugs with rifles loaded with magical silver bullets that could kill werewolves such as me?

"Aunt Luna?" Jasmine prompted.

I picked up the phone and leaned my rake against the boulder. "Yes, I'm still here. Duncan hasn't said anything to indicate he craves leadership of the pack—I'm not sure he even *likes* anyone he's met in the pack besides me. As for the medallion, he's borrowing it while we deal with our mutual challenges."

As I focused on the woods, I grew more and more certain that the being out there had a *lupine* aura. Another werewolf.

"I have a visitor," I said. "Let me call you back."

Gardening tools set aside, I grabbed the magical sword sheathed in the cart next to the branches. It had been a gift from Duncan, one I'd recently recovered from Radomir's lair. Technically, it had been in his armored SUV with him, a vehicle that my truck and I had a lot of reasons to hate. Fortunately, the SUV was as mangled as Radomir's body, last seen at the bottom of a ravine along a remote mountain road.

Now armed, I strode across the lawn toward the woods. Nothing moved among the trees, aside from a few bare branches and fir needles stirred by a breeze, but I continued to sense a werewolf. Someone watching me.

Halfway to the woods, I halted, now close enough to recognize the aura.

"Lykos?" I asked, the face of the eight-year-old boy who happened to be Duncan's clone brother popping into my mind.

Maybe his presence shouldn't have surprised me. He'd been here once before, just a few days earlier. Duncan had gone out to attempt to befriend him, but that hadn't been fruitful. From what I'd heard, the kid had hidden in the woods while Duncan tried to lure him out and explain his hobbies of metal detecting and magnet fishing. Duncan had mentioned wanting to practice being paternal in case he was ever inspired to partake in parenthood, but a half-feral werewolf kid wasn't the easiest subject to father.

My senses told me Lykos was backing away. Maybe he'd wanted to spy without being noticed.

Well, that was too bad. I didn't want to be spied on, not by some vengeful scientist's pawn.

Since Abrams was the one who'd created the kid, and who'd presumably been housing and feeding him, Lykos might have come because his master had ordered it.

I looked toward the parking lot, thinking Duncan would be the logical one to deal with our visitor, but his modified Roadtrek camper van wasn't there.

"I'll have to confront him myself."

I contemplated finding an evergreen bush to undress behind, turning into a wolf, and going out to challenge Lykos, but Duncan hadn't given up on befriending the kid. And I had no reason to hold a grudge against him either. The last time we'd faced off, Lykos had realized I was bigger and stronger than he, at least for now, and he'd fled.

Though I kept the sword, I detoured to my apartment for another type of weapon. Since I hadn't purchased any salami logs lately—it had been a while since I'd felt the need to bribe the young werewolves in my family—there weren't any in the fridge, but I did have some sandwich meat. As a semi-carnivorous type myself, I was rarely without such staples.

I peeled a number of slices of salami from a package and walked back out to the woods. A mossy stump just past the property line—where my landscaping obligations ended—was flat enough to serve as a table. Aware of the kid watching—I couldn't see him, but I continued to *sense* him since he had an aura as powerful as Duncan's—I laid out the pieces.

The pungent scent of cured meat wafted up to my nose, making me aware that the lunch hour approached. Nobly, I resisted the urge to eat the salami myself.

About forty feet away, a head leaned out from behind a tree. With tousled brown hair, curious brown eyes, and a lean face with less baby fat than one would expect in a kid that age, Lykos looked exactly like what he was: a young version of Duncan.

I waved at the salami, trying to indicate that he could have it without any strings attached, and backed up. Realizing the sword had to make me look threatening—more like I was baiting a trap than providing a friendly offering—I leaned it against a tree.

"I'm expecting Duncan before long," I called over the rumble of nearby freeway traffic. "He'd like to see you. He's curious about you. Are you curious about him?"

The kid blinked a couple of times. Thus far, I hadn't heard him speak and wondered if he was verbal at all. Might being raised by Abrams have traumatized him? Kept him from learning to speak?

"It didn't traumatize *Duncan*," I muttered.

Well, that wasn't fair. It probably *had*, but by fifty years old, he'd had time to get over his childhood—and learn to be exceedingly garrulous. Still, the shackle scars on his wrists were a reminder of his past.

"He's pretty fun to hang out with too," I called, groping for ways to entice the kid to establish a relationship with Duncan. And to come over to our side. Abrams wasn't worth working for, damn it. "Did you ask him to show you all his magnets and what they can do? He's got a huge collection for a guy who lives in a van."

"Uhm," came a man's voice from behind me. "Are you the property manager?"

I spun, grabbing the sword. Because of the traffic noise, I hadn't heard anyone approaching.

A man with a large digital camera around his neck and a drone in his arms skittered back, almost tripping over his heels in the damp grass. He fumbled the drone but didn't drop it.

"Sorry," he blurted. "But the kid in the leasing office said I should talk to you about... er." He eyed the sword. "*Are* you the property manager?"

"Yeah." Behind me, I sensed Lykos slinking away. "I'm head of security too."

As if that would explain me waving around a sword in a twenty-first-century Seattle suburb. I lowered it to appear non-threatening, though my hackles wanted to rise up when I realized who this was. He'd been here once before to take photos of the property for the real estate listing. As I was reminded every day, my employers were trying to sell Sylvan Serenity, my home and place of employment for more than twenty years.

"What can I do for you?" I kept my tone level, not bleak and full of distress at the reminder that I needed to join Jasmine in seeking a new job.

Going to one networking event that had resulted in me turning into a werewolf to battle the host's werewolf sister in his bedroom closet... probably didn't count as job hunting.

"The Sylvans want some new photos of the grounds and of a unit I guess you just cleaned but that is still vacant. I didn't realize the storm yesterday had brought down so many branches though. Is there any chance someone will be by to tidy up in the next hour or so?" He looked toward the cart I'd already filled with branches.

If he thought it was a mess now, he should have been here at dawn when I'd started. Given how many boughs had come down near the parking lot, the tenants were lucky none of their cars had been taken out. We had a lot of tall old trees in the Seattle area, and I'd seen them snap in windstorms and flatten cars, gazebos, and even houses.

"*I'm* cleaning the grounds," I said, "and I'll get it done as soon as possible. Why don't you take a lunch break and come back?"

Or take a lunch break and *don't* come back, I thought. Unfortunately, there were already a number of great-looking photos of the place, and the listing had prompted a lot of interest. Since an apartment complex of this size had a limited buyer pool—not many people could scrounge up millions and millions of dollars to pay what it was worth—it wouldn't sell overnight, but I had little doubt that it *would* sell.

"How long do you think it will take?" He looked at my sword as if to imply I'd been screwing around instead of working.

I bared my teeth at him, not hiding my extra pointy canine—*lupine*—teeth, and contemplated using the blade to give him a buzz cut.

Eyes widening, he skittered back and fumbled his drone again. "Never mind. Take your time. I've got another property I can do first. I'll come back this afternoon." He eyed my teeth. "*Late* afternoon."

I kept myself from telling him not to come back at all. Barely. As a dutiful employee, I would do my best, as I always did. Though I sometimes wondered what it would be like to work for myself and be my own boss. I looked forward to the day when I had enough money saved for the down payment on a four-plex and could live in one unit, rent the others, and have the tenants to pay off the mortgage... until the debt was gone and I could retire on the income.

As I traded the sword for the rake, my phone rang.

The name that popped up on the screen made me groan. Chad Schneider. My ex-husband.

2

I didn't answer Chad's call, nor did I check the voicemail that he left. Whatever he wanted, I wasn't interested.

My ex-husband was the one who'd originally propelled Duncan into my life. Even though that had turned out better than expected, it wasn't due to anything Chad had done. He'd hired Duncan to steal the magical wolf-lidded case from my apartment. That was *after* years of cheating on me, rarely contributing anything to the family's finances, and even, before his final departure, leaving me in debt he'd created and wiping out the kids' college funds. If he ever showed up in Seattle again, I might tear his throat out—whether I was in my wolf form or not.

My frustrations fueled my energy to clean up the storm debris, and by the time Duncan showed up in early afternoon, the lawn looked good again.

He gave me a cheerful wave as he headed across the grass toward me, his aura noticeably similar to that of the boy's. The sun highlighted his twinkling brown eyes, the three days' worth of beard stubble framing his strong jaw, and the only slightly creased forehead that looked extra appealing now that the scar he'd had all his life had disappeared. When it had linked him to that control device Abrams had held, I'd worried if I could trust Duncan not to turn on me. That had, more than once, kept me from inviting him to my bedroom, even though I often woke up in the night, wishing for his company, stirred by urges that I'd thought I was, at almost forty-six, past having.

"Greetings, my lady." Duncan paused a few feet away to bow. "I do love it when you gaze at me with avid lust and longing in your eyes."

"You're imagining that," I said, even if that was *exactly* the look on my face. I couldn't admit it to him. He was already full of himself.

"That can't be. Over the course of my life, I've bestirred lust in many a woman. I know the look well."

"You're awfully cocky for an itinerant treasure hunter who rarely discovers more than rusty shopping carts and bike frames."

"You know I've found more than *that* during my adventures." Duncan winked and lifted a chain around his neck, pulling a medallion with a wolf head out from under his button-down shirt. Despite the brisk January air, the top couple of buttons were unfastened, and I glimpsed the swell of his pectorals. My libido hummed with renewed interest.

Hell, he was right. I *was* lusting for him.

Duncan smirked at me, released the medallion, and unfastened another button. His eyelids drooped, and he gazed invitingly at me through his lashes. He read me all too well.

"Didn't you only find that because of a vision my case and my mom's medallion gave you?" I asked, trying not to feel flustered. Or horny.

"Not *only*, surely. I was hot on the trail and only slightly aided by those events."

"I see."

"Though your intervention most certainly made my life easier and quite interesting as well." Duncan beamed a smile at me and waved at his forehead.

"I hope you're not talking about how I, in a huff of lupine frustration, destroyed that control device, which resulted in you being cursed to die."

"That was more alarming and distressing than interesting. Fortunately, all is resolved, and I've been feeling quite fit and hale these last few days." Duncan gave me the lids-drooped, bedroom-eyes look again, then lowered his voice. "I was admiring you from around the corner for a few moments before you noticed me." His gaze descended toward my chest to suggest exactly which parts of me held some fascination for him.

That turned me on more than it should have. He'd essentially been ogling me while spying on me from a distance. I should have been affronted, but damn if it didn't feel good to be ogled, especially at my age.

Oh, I'd been feeling fitter, and even *younger,* since I'd stopped taking the potion that sublimated my magic, but that didn't mean I didn't look my age and have two grown sons. Having someone drawn to me made me feel young and hot again. And Duncan... He'd been at my side, helping me with all my problems—and all my *enemies*—since realizing he liked me a lot more than he did my ex-husband. That alone was enough for me to want to invite him to my bedroom... or behind the nearest rhododendron.

Only the fact that my mother, every time we visited, kept trying to urge us to *mate* so Duncan could get me pregnant made me hesitate to do exactly that. Each time Mom had brought that up where he could hear, he hadn't looked thrilled. Even if his near-brush with death had prompted him to reconsider fatherhood, what kind of guy wanted to be manipulated into a relationship by his potential girlfriend's *mother*?

"You did sneak up on me," I said into the silence, aware of his brazen gaze roaming over me. "Like a stalker."

He lifted his gaze to my face—checking to see if I minded his perusal? "You've admitted before that me stalking you doesn't disturb you as much as it should."

"I know I have. And it doesn't. I want..." I lifted a hand. I wanted *him*.

His eyebrows rose.

"To let you know that if we were to do anything right now, we would have a spy." I shifted my raised hand to point toward the woods. "Did you notice?"

His brow creased. "Did Abrams send men? I've worried he would bother you."

"Sort of. Your half-sized doppelgänger has been lurking among the pines." I waved toward the stump where I'd placed the slices of salami. Since my heritage enhanced my eyesight, even from a distance, I could see that the lunch meat had disappeared.

Had Lykos gotten it? Or the crows? For that matter, Duncan might have smelled it and helped himself. Werewolves had *excellent* noses—and voracious appetites.

"Ah. I haven't yet sensed him, but if he saw my van arrive, he would have a good idea about how far away I can detect paranormal beings, so he could have slinked off, roughly out of range." Duncan scratched his jaw. "Actually, he knows *exactly* what my range is."

"Must be weird having a clone."

"It is, yes. Let me go see if he's out there and wants something. Later, perhaps, we could..." His gaze swung back to me, lust lingering in his eyes.

"Go on a date to a nice restaurant?" I asked.

"I... was thinking we could skip to getting horizontal, perhaps in a romantic setting, but I do enjoy eating and am always amenable to doing so with you."

"Would the horizontal romantic setting be the twin bed in the back of your equipment-stuffed van?"

"It could be."

"In the crowded presence of SCUBA gear, metal detectors, and enough magnets to short-circuit your genetic material?"

"Such things definitely put *me* in the mood. And I've told you before that magnets aren't a threat to our virility." Duncan winked at me, but his head swung toward the woods. He must have caught the aura of Lykos. "Keep that in mind. I'll be back soon."

"Keep your... virility in mind?" I asked after him.

"Always."

I snorted and finished the last of my clean-up, then walked toward the parking lot so I could get my truck and haul the debris-filled cart to the composting facility for disposal. On the way, I ran into Bolin heading from his SUV to the leasing office with two coffee drinks in his hands and his leather man purse draped over his shoulder. He'd had the strap repaired since our last parking-lot battle against hoodlums.

"Is Jasmine coming to visit you?" I nodded toward the whipped-cream-covered and caramel-drizzled mochas, thinking one might be for her, though she hadn't mentioned coming by.

"I wish." Bolin glanced at me. "Though I wouldn't invite a friend or even girlfriend to come visit me during work hours, of course."

"Of course. That wouldn't be professional." I avoided looking in the direction that Duncan had gone.

"These are both for me. I was up late practicing..." Bolin glanced around, spotted a tenant with a laptop bag cutting across the lawn, and lowered his voice. "My art."

As if those vague words had needed to be delivered in a whisper.

"You didn't get your usual pair of giant caffeine bombs first thing this morning?"

"I did, but I already drank them, and the caffeine has worn off.

Like the resurgence of animals and vegetation surrounding Chernobyl after the meltdown, my natural state has returned."

"Interesting metaphor. Is that the kind of poetic imagery that Gen Z women dig?"

"You mentioned bombs. Naturally, I thought of exploding power plants."

"Naturally."

"The grounds look good." Bolin sipped from the left-hand beverage. "The real estate photographer will be pleased."

"I do ache to satisfy him."

Bolin choked on his beverage.

I waited to see if he needed the Heimlich Maneuver—he did not—then pointed toward my truck.

Before I could walk away, Bolin raised a finger. "My father wanted me to warn you that some new prospective buyers will be coming for a tour this evening."

"Great." I bared my teeth to let him know that it wasn't *great*.

Bolin didn't skitter backward or fumble his drinks. He'd either grown accustomed to me—and my grumpy streak—or his burgeoning druid powers gave him confidence that he could handle himself if my wild instincts overtook me. And maybe he *could*. Not only did he have a collection of potions that he always carried in his bag, but I'd witnessed him calling up vines from the ether—technically, the parking-lot pavement—to halt a two-ton van. He was halfway on his journey to turning into someone badass, the gilded-leather man purse notwithstanding.

"Do you need any more invitations to networking events?" Bolin offered. "Even though *I* look forward to moving on from my internment in Shoreline, I know you like this area and might want to continue to live in your unit here."

"Internment? It's not a concentration camp. It's a beautiful apartment complex that hasn't been pestered by crime in almost a week."

"It's not horrible, but..."

"I know, I know. You want to manage your parents' complexes in more exotic areas. Even though Jasmine lives happily here." I waved toward the east.

Her parents' home was in Redmond, not Shoreline, but it wasn't too bad of a commute for a dating couple.

Bolin opened his mouth, then closed it. At a loss for words? That was rare for the former spelling-bee champion.

"If we get, uhm, serious..." His cheeks flushed red even though, as far as I knew, they hadn't done more than hold hands yet. Maybe kiss. "Maybe she would like to travel *with* me. My parents could even hire her, and she could assist me, er, my family with our real estate endeavors."

"Werewolves aren't the *assistant* types. We're strong and independent and very hard to shoehorn into traditional employment positions." I didn't mention Jasmine's brief flirtation with the idea of a career as a bikini barista. "Especially for our boyfriends' families." I didn't have to ask Jasmine to know that was true.

Bolin sighed. "I suppose I've sensed that about her. She's a free spirit and very independent. And *so* beautiful." He sighed again, oozing the longing of a Wordsworth poem. "Maybe it wouldn't be so bad if this place didn't sell right away. I could keep working here while we explore our compatibility."

"That sounds like a good plan." I sensed Duncan approaching from the woods and nodded across the lawn toward him.

There was no sign of Lykos. Had the boy let Duncan find him?

"Especially the part where I don't have to find a new home for a few months," I added.

"You wouldn't continue to live here? I'm sure a new owner wouldn't kick out the existing tenants. Though... I suppose your rent wouldn't be waived if you weren't working here." Bolin hesitated, looking like he wanted to ask if I could afford to live here if it wasn't a part of a compensation package.

"Probably not. The rent isn't that high, but it would be hard not to... keep working on the place. After all this time, I'm used to being the one on call."

"You do do... *everything* here."

"Yup."

"The new owners might find it odd if one of the tenants started replacing the toilets of the other tenants."

"I would assume so, yes."

As Duncan joined us, apparently having heard a portion of the conversation, he asked, "Have you ever considered buying this place yourself, Luna? That would solve a lot of your problems."

I laughed. "You might not have guessed this from the Goodwill clothes I wear, but I don't have a family fortune that would allow me to fork over tens of millions of dollars for a real estate investment."

"Your clothing is lovely—" Duncan smiled as he glanced toward my shirt—or maybe my boobs, "—but I did assume you would need backers."

"Nobody's going to *back* a middle-aged woman with no college education, no rich connections, and no existing real estate portfolio who gets furry and howls at the full moon."

Bolin knew about my heritage, but he still raised his eyebrows at the imagery.

"You wouldn't necessarily need to mention that last," Duncan said, "though it would earn *my* buy-in as a backer."

"Uh-huh. Would you be putting one or two wheelless, rusty shopping carts into the pot?"

"Oh, five or six, I should think. This is a quality property with an excellent manager. Why don't we discuss it tonight on our date?"

"Shopping carts do get me in the mood."

"*I* find them quite appealing."

"Because you're odd."

"A trait you've admitted you adore."

"I don't think that's the exact word I used."

Bolin must have decided we needed our privacy—and that I wasn't on the verge of submitting an offer for the property—because he slipped away, drinking from the right-hand cup as he continued his walk to the leasing office.

"I was able to get close to Lykos," Duncan said, growing more serious now that we were alone. "I offered to take him magnet fishing."

"He didn't immediately jump at the invitation?"

"Apparently, he's here on business."

I waited for Duncan to expound. He looked thoughtfully, or maybe pensively, toward the woods. My earlier concern that Abrams had sent the boy for nefarious reasons came to mind. Maybe I didn't want more details.

"Does Lykos speak to you?" I asked.

"He's on the laconic side, but yes."

"Has he admitted he finds you charming and affable and that he wants to spend time with you?"

"Actually, he said he's here to kill me."

"I guess the affability isn't genetic."

Duncan's smile was bleak, but he couldn't be worried about Lykos succeeding at killing him. Both as a man and as a wolf, Duncan was twice the kid's size. At least. I presumed that would hold true if they turned into the bipedfuris too, though I seemed to remember hearing that even the werewolves with that ability didn't gain it until puberty.

"Abrams sent him," Duncan said.

"To kill you?"

"To study me, learn my weaknesses, find a way to exploit them, and *then* kill me."

"Are you... concerned that he could do that?"

In a fair fight, Duncan could fend off Lykos, but was it possible the kid was smart enough to do what Abrams suggested?

I growled. If the old bastard wanted Duncan out of the picture, he ought to be man enough to take on the task himself.

"Not too concerned. While Lykos admitted these things to me, he was eating your salami and watching me pull a fender out of a pond." Duncan tapped a pocket in his jacket, the outline of what had to be a rope wrapped around a large cylindrical magnet visible. "He looked intrigued."

"Fenders are pretty fascinating."

"*I* think so. I believe this one was off a 1970s Volkswagen beetle. Such a fun little car. That fender must have been down there for decades." Duncan touched his chest and took a moment to gaze into the distance as he cherished the find.

Less moved to cherishment, I asked, "So, you don't think Lykos is a real threat?"

Duncan lowered his hand. "I'm not that worried about him, but I do believe he'll divulge anything he learns about us to Abrams, who, it sounds like, is feeling vengeful."

As I'd feared.

"We're going to have to deal with him at some point," I said.

"I know. I—"

My phone rang, and Duncan paused.

Worried that Chad might be calling again, I grimaced and almost didn't take it out of my pocket. But my youngest son's name popped up on the screen, and I tapped the answer button without hesitation. Austin hadn't called since he'd sent that letter, admitting he hadn't known what to do or say since seeing me turn into a werewolf. Respecting his need for time, I also hadn't called him, but I'd written a letter back and said I would be here to answer questions whenever he was ready.

"Hi, Austin." I strove for a casual tone, though I desperately wanted him to say he was ready to talk. After so many years of withholding that secret from my sons, I longed to come clean and also explain why I'd made the choices that I had.

Duncan backed away to give me privacy for the call.

"Hey, Mom. I've only got a minute before I need to take my turn as duty officer, but, uhm, I wanted to warn you about something."

"What's up?"

"I, uhm, think I told you that I talked to my brother about... that night."

"You mentioned it in your letter, yes."

"I guess Cameron talked to Dad."

I grimaced.

"From what Cam said, Dad was going to be in the area for work, so they're both heading up there."

"In the *area*?" I stared at the phone, thinking of Chad's call. He hadn't been calling from *Seattle*, had he? "Like *here*?"

"Seattle. I'm not sure where they're going to stay. Cam left his camper in Texas, I think."

I hadn't even known he was in the South. The last I'd seen on Cameron's socials, he'd been cruising through the Everglades, searching for the meaning of life. And, I hoped, gainful work he could do from the road since he showed no inclination toward settling down.

"What are they going to do here?"

"Some kind of work that Dad got offered. I didn't get many details. I just thought... you might want to know."

"Yes. Thanks." I looked toward the woods, as if Chad might be out there spying on me right now. No, his methodology relied on hidden cameras in my bedroom, not skulking behind trees. The creep.

"Sure. I gotta go. Talk to you later."

Austin hung up before I could tell him I loved him. I sighed, feeling bleak. And more worried about Chad—and what he wanted—now that I knew he was in the area.

Off in the grass, Duncan stood with his hands in his pockets, waiting. He raised his eyebrows toward me.

I didn't know what to say, but if Chad showed up here, I wouldn't hide Duncan—or that we were attempting to have a relationship... when the world allowed it.

The phone rang again, and I winced, certain that was Chad calling now. But Lorenzo's name appeared on the screen.

"Hello?"

"Luna," he said, his voice grave. "Your mother would like you to visit."

"Is she... okay?"

She wasn't, not with her cancer advancing, but I didn't know how better to phrase it.

"It hasn't been a good week for her."

I swallowed around a lump, wishing some of the magical artifacts we'd tried on her had healed her malady. The Taint, as the wise wolf called it. But it seemed magic was better at healing wounds than curing diseases.

"Okay," I said. "I'll head up there soon."

It wasn't as if I wanted to be home if Chad showed up anyway. Since he'd lived here with me for most of the years of our marriage, however itinerant he'd been during his career as a traveling software sales rep, he well knew how to find the place. He didn't know much about my lupine family though. I'd never visited them in the years we'd been married—in the years I'd been taking the sublimation potion. He shouldn't find me up there.

"Maybe I can hide out at Mom's cabin for the week," I muttered after hanging up, thinking of the potential buyers and real estate photographer that would also be around over the next couple of days.

"Need a ride somewhere?" Duncan offered, joining me again.

I started to say no, but if Mom was noticeably worse... I could use some moral support. Besides, did I want Duncan to be here if Chad showed up? That might start trouble. Even if Duncan had once agreed to find the case for Chad, they'd parted ways, and I'd overheard one rant-filled phone call where Chad had threatened Duncan.

"Yes. I adore sitting on the equipment stacked all around your passenger seat, with my knees to my chin."

"I have other things you can sit on." Smirking, Duncan pulled out his keys.

"Is it strange that I'd rather spend time with you than my ex-husband?"

"No, that's normal. I'm a delight."

"That word may not mean what you think it means."

"We can consult your etymologist later." Duncan waved to indicate Bolin in the leasing office, then led me toward the Roadtrek.

I followed more eagerly than I otherwise might have, given our grim destination. But leaving didn't keep me from worrying that I would have to deal with Chad sooner or later.

3

"Things have gotten worse for your mother?" Duncan asked as he drove us toward Monroe.

"That's what Lorenzo said."

"That's unfortunate. She's still sharp and seems like she's kept herself fit most of her life."

"Oh, she has. Disease isn't fair about who it strikes down." Glum, I gazed out the window at the traffic, sun glinting off car frames and windshields. Cold rain would have felt more appropriate, but the weather was determined to be nice in the aftermath of the previous day's storm.

"I suppose you won't be in the mood for that date I suggested," Duncan said.

"I... might need a distraction."

"Some dinner then? Followed by a drive-in movie?"

"A *drive-in*? Are there any theaters left around here that do that?"

"It's a bit of a commute, but there are a couple. I looked them up. Don't you find the privacy of one's vehicle much more appealing than a crowded theater?"

"After we helped the local theater owner—Harold—he might be willing to put together a private showing for us," I said.

"That could be appealing, but he would probably frown upon us having an intimate moment, were we moved in such a direction by the story unraveling on the screen. Whereas if we were in my van at the drive-in..."

"What's playing right now that you think would be so moving?"

"The drive-in is currently offering a chainsaw-massacre thriller and an alien-invasion movie."

"Two options that are sure to put feelings of intimacy into a woman's mind."

"You don't think so?"

"If you want to hang out in your van, we might as well have our date in the parking lot at Sylvan Serenity. We can watch the ghost hunters set up for their evening search for the paranormal."

"Excellent. I'll bring popcorn."

"I was being sarcastic."

"Imagine my shock at such an uncharacteristic tone from you." Duncan winked, never offended by my snark. "I'm amenable to whatever evening activity will allow us to spend time together. I fully expect it'll be the company more than the venue or entertainment that moves you to a desire for romance." After giving me an easy smile, he focused on navigating out of town and into the foothills toward Mom's cabin.

"*You* might not be moved after chatting with my mother. You know what she always focuses on when you're in the room."

"I remember her complimenting my fine physique on one occasion."

"Your abs specifically, as I recall. They managed to convey old-world power and virility."

"They are talented muscles."

We passed the last of the farm properties and headed up the winding road into the woods that had remained largely untouched since my family had moved into the area generations ago. When we reached the frog pond less than a mile from the property, Duncan shifted in his seat.

"I sense a number of werewolves."

"That's... not uncommon here."

How many times had I arrived to find half the pack lounging around Mom's property in the aftermath of a hunt or shedding their clothing in preparation for one?

"They're on the move." Duncan cocked his head. "Chasing something?"

I couldn't yet detect anyone with a magical aura, so I couldn't tell.

"I can't sense whatever they're after," Duncan mused, continuing up the road, "so I guess it's not anything or anyone paranormal."

"I've not seen a lot of magical elk or deer in these woods."

"Just the critters with glowing eyes near that cave?"

"Well, yes. *You* had glowing eyes briefly after drinking from the pool there."

"There was natural power in the place. It's no wonder your mother was drawn to live near it."

I sensed what he'd detected and didn't answer as I contemplated it. As he'd promised, there *were* a number of werewolves. My family members. And they were on the move.

Was that Jasmine among them? And Emilio? Oddly, they were running beside or maybe even *on* the road in their wolf forms. Before long, they would reach us.

"A deer wouldn't run down the road to escape predators." I supposed it was possible, but they always seemed to shoot off into the depths of the forest when being chased.

The roar of an engine reached our ears before any wolves. An SUV and a truck came into view, barreling down the gravel road toward us, the vehicles bumping through ruts and potholes without slowing.

Duncan veered to one side, inasmuch as he could. The road lacked a shoulder unless one wanted to park on a log.

Even seeing us, the drivers didn't slow down, and the reason soon came into view. As I'd sensed, numerous wolves ran behind the vehicles, some surging forward to nip at the tires and fenders. One young male leaped and landed in the bed of the truck. Another tore off a tailpipe and held it triumphantly in the air, prancing like a proud stallion rather than a wolf. Was that Emilio?

Duncan stopped his van, and we stared as the strange caravan roared past us, the white-knuckled drivers not glancing in our direction. I recognized the SUV, a sign for *Logan's Real Estate* on the side.

That was the guy who'd put a neighboring lot up for sale, wasn't it? Or maybe he'd been the one who'd visited Mom and asked her about *her* lot supposedly being for sale. The last I'd heard, Jasmine's mother had gotten to the bottom of that, and it wasn't listed on the market anymore.

A wolf in the rear of the pack, with a saucy tilt to her tail, glanced at us as she passed. Jasmine. She swished her tail, either in a greeting or because she was having a good time, then continued after the others.

"Those are your family members, aren't they?" Duncan sounded amused as he watched the scene receding in his side mirror.

"Yes. That's what passes for fun up here."

"Chasing off real estate agents?"

I shrugged, not knowing *what* had prompted the attack, and hoped someone wasn't pestering Mom about selling her property again. Could those vultures have gotten the word that she had a terminal illness? And they were circling, thinking they would get their hands on her land afterward?

"Fat chance. Mom has numerous children and all sorts of other kin."

Duncan looked at me.

"Just musing." I waved.

He pointed in the direction the car chase had gone. "Do you want to go after them? In case they need help?"

"In case my family needs help? Or the real estate agents do?"

"From the way things were going, it appeared more likely the real estate agents would need it."

"That's what I think, but I'm not terribly inclined to help them." I pointed up the road. "Mom and Lorenzo can fill us in."

I didn't think this was what Mom had wanted to see me about, but I didn't know. Maybe real estate agents had been up here all week, and this was the culmination of some harassment.

"During one of our previous visits, you said there's nothing back here that anyone—any *human*—would necessarily value, right?" Duncan looked over at me. "There are old mines but no valuable ore was found in the area?"

"As far as I know, yes. It's just woods."

"And the magical cave."

"Yeah, but normal humans wouldn't know about that and wouldn't be able to see the glowing mushrooms or anything."

"Could they see the red eyes of the animals who've drunk the water?"

"I don't know, but, even if they could, that wouldn't be a *selling point*. It's creepy."

"I suppose that's true. Maybe that frog pond has some appeal. Is that on the property?"

"I wouldn't think so," I said. "That's quite a ways from the cabin. Besides, *ponds* aren't exactly a rarity up here in the rainy Pacific Northwest."

When we reached the long driveway, Mom and Lorenzo weren't standing at the end of it this time. I sensed them in the cabin back behind the trees. Whatever was going on with the pack, it couldn't concern them too much.

Or... My stomach knotted. It might be that Mom was too weak to walk down the driveway, even if something *did* concern her. And would she be too proud to ask Lorenzo to carry her? Likely.

After we parked in front of the cabin, Lorenzo stepped out onto the porch. This late in the day, it lay in shadow, despite the blue sky. With tall trees looming on all sides, the cabin didn't get a lot of natural light, but Mom probably preferred it that way, the scents of mossy fir, cedar, and pine all around when she opened a window.

Lorenzo lifted a hand toward me, nothing on his face suggesting he was surprised by or objected to Duncan's presence. We hadn't had a chance yet to see if the rest of the pack would accept Duncan wearing the medallion, but Mom and Lorenzo had said they didn't mind.

A distant howl came from the direction of the road, the direction those vehicles had been going. Others joined in. It sounded like the wolves might have stopped where the forest ended and the more civilized—and more densely populated—farm properties began.

"They must have succeeded in driving those men away." Lorenzo gazed in that direction as we joined him on the porch.

"They seemed to be enjoying themselves as they did so," I said.

"It was an opportunity for them to take out their frustrations."

"What's been going on?" I asked.

"More properties that are owned by the pack have been listed for sale. Renata has said she's felt like she's been playing, what was it called, oh, a game called Whac-A-Mole to follow the legal process of alerting the listing agents that they've been fooled and the parcels are *not* for sale. Numerous agents have been involved, not all the same one, but she believes a single entity may be behind the listings."

I looked at Duncan, wondering not for the first time if Abrams might be behind this. But *Radomir* had been the businessman. Abrams wasn't from this country, and I doubted he was even here legally.

"With Radomir gone, would Abrams be making real estate plays?" I asked Duncan.

"I think Radomir was the mastermind behind the attempt to try to get your property. Unless this was all set up before his death..." Duncan waved at the surrounding woods, then tilted his palm toward the sky.

"You have property?" Lorenzo asked.

"No, not me. Duncan meant the apartment complex where I live and work. I don't have a financial stake in it, but it also had some schemy stuff going on recently. We resolved that though." Again, I thought of Radomir dead at the bottom of that cliff. A most definite resolution. "I'm skeptical that it was related to this."

"We're confused about *why* someone wants the properties back here," Lorenzo said. "They are large in acreage, but the often-steep terrain would make development difficult, and the existing homes are very rural and rustic. The timber has some value, but lumber isn't worth *that* much, and there's a lot of it in Western Washington."

"Yeah," I agreed, as stumped as he.

"The parcels back here rarely go on the market," Lorenzo said. "Most of those not owned by the Savagers are in family trusts that have held them for decades. Those mundane humans use them for much the same purposes as we do—hunting and recreation—and are never keen to give them up."

"Jasmine's mom will get to the bottom of things," I said.

"Yes." Lorenzo nodded. "Even if someone does want to

acquire a large contiguous piece of land for some reason, they will find that *werewolves* are not easy to drive off their properties."

"No, I haven't even been able to drive this one out of my parking lot." I tilted a thumb toward Duncan.

"You've not tried as hard as you could have, my lady." Duncan bowed to me. "Despite numerous threats of towing, a truck has yet to show up for my van."

"I've been busy. I'll yet have it towed. I saw your hose out, mooching water from my spigot again."

He grinned at me.

Lorenzo looked back and forth between us and nodded again, as if our banter meant something. Or confirmed something? As long as he didn't mind Duncan being here.

Trusting that the pack could handle the problem of the real estate agents, I pointed to the door. "Is Mom awake?"

"She is dozing off and on, but she does want to speak with you, so please wake her if she's sleeping."

"Okay."

"Do you want me to come in with you?" Duncan asked quietly. "Or stay out here?"

I hesitated, not sure what *Mom* would want—or if she would manage to offend him with talk of him fathering offspring with me. It might be better to leave Duncan outside, but something told me I would need support.

I clasped his hand, and he nodded with understanding.

After taking a bracing breath, I led the way through the outer room and to the open door of Mom's bedroom. I knocked lightly.

"We're here, Mom."

She lay on her bed, propped against the pillows, her eyes open but with bags under them. Her hair was brushed but hung limply around shoulders that seemed narrower and frailer each time I came up here. The lump returned to my throat.

"Yes, of course. I sensed that one before you turned into the driveway." She pointed her chin at Duncan.

"He does have a blazing and somewhat obnoxious aura," I said.

"Obnoxious," Duncan said. "*Really.*"

"He's full of old-world power," I added.

"Yes, I'm aware." Mom smiled as she noted our linked hands. "I approve of your decision to claim him as your mate."

"We're just holding hands, Mom. There hasn't been any claiming."

Not that it hadn't been on my mind...

Mom looked toward Duncan. "The magic of the moon keeps my daughter fertile beyond the years when a human woman could healthily conceive, but she will not be so young forever."

I flattened my free hand to my face. I'd been afraid this was what she wanted to talk about, or that it would somehow enter into the conversation.

Duncan's mouth opened, but he didn't seem to know what to say.

I squeezed his hand, hoping to convey that he didn't have to say anything—or respond at all.

"This isn't what you wanted to see me about, is it, Mom?" I hoped to sweep the conversation quickly past the fertility topic.

"No, but I long to see you with child—a *full-blooded werewolf* child of his loins—before my passing."

"Yes, you've made that clear, but that's not what Duncan and I want. We're still getting to know each other. And he hasn't yet proven to himself that he'll be a good father. The only kid in his life that he's been working his charisma on wants to kill him."

Mom's brow furrowed. Duncan's did too. Maybe I shouldn't have brought that up.

"Younger werewolves are more driven by instincts and hormones." Mother reached for the drawer in her bedside table.

"They rarely spend a great deal of time *getting to know* each other. You certainly did not with your first mate. I recall catching you naked and howling on the back porch shortly after you met the Cascade Crushers boy."

My cheeks heated, and I avoided looking at Duncan but didn't miss his murmur of, "I knew howling would be involved."

"I am a werewolf," I murmured back.

Mom sighed wistfully and withdrew her medallion from the drawer, then pushed it closed. It glowed softly, and I sensed the matching medallion on Duncan's chest, though it was under his shirt, intensify its own aura.

"This is why I called you up here." Mom waved for me to come closer. "I do not know how much longer I have."

I shook my head bleakly, wanting to deny that the end neared, that nothing could be done, but we both knew the truth.

"You will take this now," Mom said, "so there is no dispute after my passing."

I knew she'd wanted me to have it, but with the moment upon me, my first instinct was to reject the medallion. I had half-siblings with as much right to anything of Mom's as I had. *More* right. They hadn't forsaken their heritage and cut off ties to the pack for years.

"You are the strongest of my offspring." Mom gazed intently at me. "That is why you will take it. It is not about who is most deserving or who did the most for the family over the course of their lives. It is about what is best for the pack. That is the way of the wolf. You have the strength and power to protect the pack, to ensure its continued existence in this era of waning magic and pressure from the outside world, from humanity ever imposing itself on our territory." She looked at Duncan, who'd retreated to the doorway, and then back at me. "I trust you will find a suitable alpha male to help lead the pack."

"You make it sound like the female is in charge of all that," I said.

Everyone knew it was the alpha *male* who led.

Mom managed a smirk and looked out the window. The back of Lorenzo's shoulder was in view as he stood as a silent protector on the porch.

"The male is usually the strongest and a great hunter," Mom said, "but we all know the female cares the most about the welfare of the pack, of ensuring birthrates remain suitable and doing everything possible to survive in the modern era, to retain our heritage. Also, the magic has chosen. Do not forget that. The medallion responds to you." She held it out, inviting me to take it.

All it had ever done was glow a little when I touched it, but I accepted that it didn't do even that for others.

Though I wanted to deny the gift, since it meant Mom believed her end near, I lifted a hand to accept it. Warmth thrummed from the wolf-head medallion as my fingers wrapped around it, and its glow intensified, almost blindingly so. Power flowed from it and into my body, invigorating me, making me long to change into the wolf and go hunt. Or to join the others in chasing away those who trespassed, who threatened the pack.

"I knew it would respond more strongly once that dreadful potion was out of your system," Mom murmured, sounding satisfied. "Put it on."

Yes, the medallion wanted that. I could feel it in the magic infusing me.

Though I couldn't understand why I deserved its interest, it gave me the sense that it had been waiting for me to wear it. To wield its power.

I unclasped the fastener and lifted it toward my neck but paused, sensing that Duncan had moved behind me.

"Allow me," he said in a husky voice that surprised me.

The glow had faded enough that I could see his face when I looked back, his eyes intense as they met mine. Intense and hungry. His own medallion glowed enough to bathe his features in its warm light, to reveal his parted lips, lips on the verge of kissing me. Or... devouring me? His aura crackled in the air around him, the magic brushing my skin, sending a hot tingle through me though he hadn't yet touched me. Heat flushed my body, making my core tighten in anticipation of—

Of what? We were in my mother's bedroom.

"Are you drawn because of the medallion?" I whispered, thinking if I pointed that out he would realize it was influencing him and be less affected.

"I am drawn for many reasons." Duncan took the ends of the chain, brushing the back of my neck as he fastened them.

Another hot tingle swept through me. His fingers lingered, and he stroked my neck, brushing his nails along my skin and up to rub my scalp.

Such desire scorched my nerves that it was all I could do not to turn around and throw myself upon him. My entire body hummed with heat and with need.

But I hadn't forgotten where we were, and I looked toward my mother. She was watching intently. Wanting us to mate? To give her the werewolf offspring she craved?

Yes, I knew with certainty that she wanted that. Maybe she'd even known the medallion would increase my allure to Duncan, or whatever it was doing. This wasn't the first time I'd held it, even worn it in his presence, but it was the first time I'd done so while he was wearing its match.

Since the artifacts had historically belonged to the male and female alphas of the pack, it shouldn't have surprised me that their power might seek to mingle, to bind their wearers together. But I didn't want to have sex with Duncan because magical necklaces were coercing us into it. He couldn't want that either. He had to be tired of being *coerced* by magical devices.

"We need to go," I whispered harshly and slipped away from his fingers.

I swept out of the room, almost running. I didn't intend to give in to my mother's manipulation or that of the medallions either.

Duncan caught me before I reached the front door, his arm wrapping around my waist and halting me. Powerful and irresistible, he pulled me back against him, his muscled chest against my back.

"Luna," he growled, lust radiating off him.

My body responded in kind. Instead of trying to pull away, it pushed back into him, images flooding my mind of Duncan tearing off my clothes and taking me against the log wall of the cabin. I envisioned screaming and howling with intense pleasure as he plunged into me.

One of his hands cupped my breast, thumb brushing my nipple through my shirt, and such scorching desire flooded me that I groaned. Damn the magic, I couldn't resist this. Couldn't resist *him*.

I could feel the outline of his medallion against my back and knew it wanted this, just as the one I wore did. I could feel the outline of *him*, as well, big and hard, and a tremble of need went through me. He kissed the back of my neck, then trailed his lips to my throat, nipping as he inhaled my scent, aroused by it, by me.

"I'll have you," he said, his grip tightening.

Molded to him, I opened my mouth to fervently agree. Then the door opened, daylight flooding in.

Lorenzo blinked as he encountered us scant inches away. Abruptly, as the cool winter air swept in around him, I grew aware of Jasmine and Emilio and a half dozen others outside.

Duncan growled, half lust, half irritation at the interruption. He didn't release me, as if he would take me and not care in the least if my whole family watched.

Though I was aroused and ready for him, I caught his hands. For a moment, he resisted my attempt to move them away from my body. He was stronger than I and could take me if he wanted.

Maybe that should have scared me. But he only resisted for a moment before drawing in a shaky breath, releasing me, and stepping back.

"*Lorenzo*," came my mother's voice from behind me, as if she were chastising him for interrupting.

Hell, maybe she was. This is what she wanted, after all. For Duncan to lead the pack and give me a child.

I was thankful that Lorenzo had opened the door. As badly as I wanted to be with Duncan, I didn't want it to be because of magical coercion or my mother's manipulation. Once his lust chilled, he would come to himself and wouldn't want that either. The last thing I desired was for him to regret involving himself with me—and my pack.

"I heard noises and wanted to make sure you were all right, Umbra." Lorenzo inclined his head toward her, then stepped back outside.

He closed the door, but not before I glimpsed numerous sets of curious eyes turned in our direction.

What kind of *noises* had we been making? I didn't even know.

"Luna," Mom said, gripping the doorway frame for support. "You two must wear the medallions and return to the magical cave in the gully. I had a dream, perhaps even a vision, that you would find answers there about how to protect our people."

More likely, she thought the stronger magic there would make it so that Duncan and I couldn't resist each other, and all that she wanted would come to pass. When I glanced at him, I found his heated gaze still on me. I looked away, trying not to think about how much I would like to slip away somewhere private and continue what we'd started.

Instead, I turned to Mom. "Radomir is dead. I don't think our people are in that much danger now."

She didn't look surprised. She must have heard the story from

Jasmine—my niece had become a confidante, and I'd told her all about that night.

"He is not—was not—the only threat to our people," Mom said.

Did she mean Abrams? Or something more? The stuff with the real estate agents?

"Go to the cave." She pointed through the back window of the cabin. "You'll find answers there. I am certain."

"Okay, Mom. We will."

4

JASMINE INTERCEPTED ME AS DUNCAN AND I HEADED TO THE VAN, and I let her draw me aside.

Walking stiffly, shoulders tense, Duncan looked like he needed a release, not to stay and chat with my family. Since I felt similarly, I couldn't blame him, but Jasmine raised her phone, the text-message screen open, and I suspected she had more on her mind than commenting on the position that Duncan and I—and his hands—had been in when Lorenzo opened the door. With luck, nobody else had gotten a good view of that...

"The reception is so awful up here," Jasmine said, "but a message made it through from home. Mom has had Dad researching what's up with all the land stuff, and he thought to look up the buyer of a property that previously sold in the area. It was last summer."

Duncan disappeared into the van, and I figured I'd better give him a few minutes.

"Did he find anything interesting?" I asked. "The buyer wasn't Radomir or his company, was it?"

"I don't think so, no." Jasmine held up a name on the screen.

"Golden Wildlands Development?" I read.

The name wasn't familiar.

"Yeah. Dad checked out the parcel in the county records, and it's recently been rezoned to rural business."

"What does that mean they can do? Set up a zipline outfit or something?"

"I guess they could do that, but I have a feeling this is all tied together, don't you? Someone got that property and wants more back here. *All* of this." Jasmine waved a hand to indicate the forest around us, including the direction of the cave and gully in her gesture.

"Maybe your dad can learn some more."

"Yeah. I'm sure he can. We'll figure it out. Nobody is stealing the family's land."

"You ensured that when you bit the tires on that truck, didn't you?"

Her cheeks flushed, but she looked more exhilarated than embarrassed. "Those guys will think twice about returning after that, but they're just the agents. They probably don't know much about what the potential buyers are *really* up to."

"But you weren't going to let them go without nipping at their heels?"

"*I* didn't start that." Jasmine waved at her chest. "But people have to be warned away from werewolf territory. For their own good."

"How many of their tires were flat by the time they made it to the pavement?" I glanced at the van, wondering if I'd given Duncan enough time to collect himself.

"Most of them." Jasmine grinned. "They were running on the rims by the time they left the woods."

"And missing a tailpipe."

"Naturally."

"Do you mention your hobby of vehicle destruction on your résumé?"

"I do not. Besides, you don't put *hobbies* on your résumé unless you're fifteen and have no work experience."

"Bolin mentioned his violin and spelling-bee skills on his."

"I'm sure his *parents* got him his first job. Wait, is working for you his first job?"

"I think so. Before that, he was focused on his academics."

"How precious. I'm going to tease him about that. I've been working at least summer jobs since I was thirteen." Jasmine wrinkled her nose. "I wish I'd saved more though. Then I wouldn't still be living at home."

"I guess I won't hit you up to be a backer."

"Backer for what?"

"Duncan suggested that *I* buy Sylvan Serenity."

She wrinkled her nose again and looked toward the Roadtrek. "No offense, Aunt Luna, but you probably shouldn't take investing advice from someone who lives in a van."

"I told him it wouldn't be possible. My net worth, sadly, isn't much greater than yours." And I was more than twenty years older. Trying not to grimace, I reminded myself that I'd pulled myself out of the debt that Chad had left me with and was making progress on saving for the down payment on a property I could conceivably buy one day.

"I guess you could technically put together a syndication and get a bunch of backers," Jasmine said. "Since you'd still be running the complex, I assume, it could pencil out. Do you think the Sylvans would negotiate the price down for you? You're mentoring their son, after all."

"I'm not sure I've taught Bolin anything. He hasn't even been willing to hold the wax ring for me while I install a toilet."

"He's coddled." She smiled fondly. "I've told him."

"I'm sure he appreciates your honesty."

"I think he appreciates my boobs."

"They can be useful assets in discussions with men. But no, I'm sure the Sylvans wouldn't cut me a deal. They're shrewd business-people. Even if they did, what would it be? Asking twenty-nine million instead of thirty?"

"That could make more of a difference than you'd think. Do you want me to math the place out for you? Figure out market rents, the carrying costs, and where it would pencil out? Is that the actual listing price?"

"No, no." I waved my hand in dismissal. "I have no idea what they listed it for. It doesn't matter. I don't have a real estate port-folio of my own nor experience putting together deals and buying properties. As I firmly told Duncan, there's no way *I* could talk people into investing with me."

"I agree it wouldn't be easy, but you have been running almost all aspects of the place for the last twenty years. And you'd be surprised how many people don't have the needed experience but talk people into giving them money on the basis of being smooth talkers."

"I'm not a smooth talker either, unfortunately. I get frustrated and show my fangs."

"That could be more convincing than you might think."

"Or it would prompt everyone to flee the room."

Jasmine opened her mouth, but the door to Mom's cabin opened again.

"You'd best not delay, Luna." She stood in the doorway, Lorenzo at her side to support her.

I wanted to sigh in exasperation, but I also didn't want to argue with a dying woman.

"We won't," I assured her and headed for the passenger door of the van.

"The cave." Mom pointed behind the cabin, a reminder that there was a path, not a road. We would have to visit it on foot.

"We'll head there soon," I said.

Mom hesitated, but Lorenzo murmured something to her, and she let him guide her back into the cabin. A twinge of sadness swept through me. I didn't want to accept that her end was near, but it was inevitable at this point.

Before opening the passenger-side door to the van, I removed the medallion from around my neck. I didn't want to test Duncan's libido—*both* of our libidos—again.

He wasn't in the driver's seat, and I peered warily into the back. He'd gone into the tiny bathroom and closed the door. I put the medallion in his cup holder and waited for him to come out, trying not to think about going back there to see if he needed a hand. *That* I could do without the threat of impregnation and Mom getting exactly what she wanted—against both of our wishes. But after talking with Jasmine, and with several of the pack loitering in the area, I was no longer in the mood for carnal activities.

Fortunately, Duncan soon came out. He'd also removed his medallion; I glimpsed it hanging from the spigot of the tiny sink.

When our eyes met, his face twisted in an expression somewhere between embarrassment and chagrin.

"I must apologize for my behavior, my lady." Duncan managed an impressively smooth bow, considering the tight aisle space with cabinets looming to one side and the bed hemming him in from the other.

"There's nothing for you to apologize for. I shouldn't have taken you into the cabin where my mother could bring up mating and offspring again."

He managed a faint smile and joined me in the cab, easing into the driver's seat. "She has a singular focus, doesn't she?"

"I think it's one of the last things she's hoping to see before she passes, but I resent that she's trying to pressure you."

"*Both* of us, certainly."

"Well, yeah, but I'm family. Mothers pressuring their children is par for the course. You're new."

Duncan gazed thoughtfully at me. "I'm certain that you're disinclined to obey her wishes, out of an understandable desire to be independent, but if she were not requesting more grandchildren from you, would you consider it? Having another child?"

Before, Duncan had always shied away from the idea of children, leaving as quickly as possible when Mom brought it up, but his gaze was more speculative now. His near-death experience with the curse had changed something for him. Since then, more than once, he'd admitted contemplating fatherhood.

"I hadn't originally, no. Because of my age, if nothing else. But Mom keeps assuring me that my werewolf magic means I get more years of fertility than an average human woman."

"Your vitality and glow of power assure me that you're still in your prime." Duncan glanced at my chest.

I almost laughed, my conversation with Jasmine coming to mind.

"I do feel a little more *vital* these days, but I would have to make that decision soon if I was going to make it. It's not like were-wolves *live* any longer than the average person." Sadness returned as I gazed toward Mom's cabin, reminded far more than I wished of our mortality. "Raising kids is a lot of work for a long time. It could kill me."

"It can't be any more trying than cousins trying to end your life, bad guys robbing your apartment, motorcycle thugs attacking you on a weekly basis, and tenants demanding repairs and making complaints at all hours of the day."

"That latter can be vexing."

"*Just* the latter?"

My phone buzzed, distracting me from responding. A text from Bolin had slipped past the poor reception.

Someone here desires to see you.

Someone? I texted back, slumping in the seat, worried Chad had shown up. *Do they have a name or other identifying characteristics?*

Bolin didn't respond. He was either busy dealing with *someone*, or the mediocre reception ensured the signal was heading up to the nearest satellite via carrier pigeon.

"I'd better go deal with that." I showed Duncan the message.

"Before visiting the cave?" He tilted his thumb in that direction.

"Mom just wants us to visit with those medallions so the magic makes us get vigorously horizontal."

"You think *that's* the vision she mentioned?"

"You must be used to women having dreams about you." I waved at the wheel. "If Chad is at the apartment, I need to..." What? Tell him to beat it? That was more or less what I had in mind. Perhaps while kneeing him in the balls. "Show him how good I'm getting with that sword," I finished.

Eyebrows rising, Duncan turned the key in the ignition. "That could be entertaining."

"Are you going to watch me prong him?"

"I enjoy seeing you wield my gift." His half-drooped eyelids assured me that was an innuendo.

"Chad will be furious."

"As people so often are when pronged by swords."

5

When we turned into the parking lot, I eyed the cars, but I had no idea what Chad was driving these days. A rental vehicle, most likely. As far as I knew, he'd been out of the country for most, if not all, of the last couple of years.

Bolin stood on the walkway, talking to a familiar man. Minato, one of the owners of the local convenience store. After one of what had sounded like many robberies, he and his wife had beseeched me to use my werewolf powers to stop crime there and in the rest of the neighborhood.

His presence might mean the motorcycle thugs had reappeared after the last battle that Duncan and I had engaged in with them. In our wolf forms, we'd killed a couple of them. I'd thought —hoped—that would keep the rest from wanting to pick fights in this section of town.

"Is that who Bolin meant?" I wondered as Duncan parked. "It's not Chad who showed up but Minato?"

"Are you disappointed?"

I didn't want to see Chad ever again, but... "I was kind of looking forward to a pronging."

Minato noticed us before we got out of the van and waved to a car parked near the front of the lot. The passenger-side window rolled down, and his wife, Mayumi, held out a manila envelope.

"A new assignment?" Duncan wondered.

"Oh, let's hope not. There's enough to deal with right now already."

After parking, we headed over to join Bolin while Minato collected the envelope from his wife.

"Is this who you texted me about?" I asked Bolin.

"Actually, no." Bolin looked at his phone in surprise. Maybe that carrier pigeon was still in flight. "Sorry, I got distracted with work stuff. The person who came looking for you was Izzy, Ivan MacGregor's sister. You, uhm, met her at the networking event."

"We turned into wolves and battled each other in his closet."

"Hence, *meeting*."

"I had no idea the definition of that word conveyed all that we did."

"The word has a *lot* of meanings. I should think *coming together for a common purpose, coping with,* or *entering into conference, argument, or personal dealings with* would all describe your encounter."

"There was definitely coping."

"Did you know there's an archaic adjectival form of the word *meet* that means *very proper* or *precisely adapted to a particular situation*?"

"I don't even know what adjectival means."

Bolin gaped at me like I was a savage ignoramus, but Minato returned before he could educate me further.

"If you turned into a werewolf," Duncan murmured, "one might consider that *precisely adapted* or *very proper* for the situation of facing off against another werewolf."

"I suppose so. I wonder what Izzy wanted."

Not to attack me again, I hoped, though it was a possibility.

Even though I'd found Ivan's missing magical bracelet in Abrams's now-destroyed lab, and I'd mailed it to him, Izzy had been by Sylvan Serenity to leave me a message, wolf-style. Long ago, I'd killed her cousin, Raoul. Even though I'd loved him and it had been an accident caused by savage werewolf instincts combined with teenage hormones, she hadn't been inclined to listen to my explanation or forgive me.

"Ms. Valens?" Minato held up the envelope. "We brought this for you."

Though worried about other matters, I managed a smile for him. "Duncan thought that might be an assignment."

Minato blinked. "It's a collection of funds from those thankful for your intervention at Harold's movie theater. And we know you helped, as well, Mr. Calderwood. The collection is for both of you."

"Oh. You don't have to pay me—us—for that." I held out my hand. "We're just trying to clean up the crime in the neighborhood. I live here too, after all."

"She'll take it," Duncan said brightly and plucked the envelope from Minato's grip.

"Yes, excellent." He nodded and stepped back, hands at his sides, as if to say he wouldn't take it back.

I frowned. I didn't want to accept money from my neighbors for helping out, especially not after my deceased cousin had been exploiting them, charging them like a mafia boss for so-called protection for who knew how long.

"We're most pleased," Minato said, "that we haven't since seen the brutes who were pestering our store and the establishments of other paranormal business owners in town. We believe you may have scared them away."

"That would be nice. If you do see them again, let them know I'm still around and still..." I showed off my canines.

"Quite, quite." Minato bowed to me and joined his wife in their car.

"Thank you," she called before rolling the window up.

"There's a rule in life. If people want to give you gifts, you should graciously accept them." Duncan handed the envelope to me. "Maybe there's enough to help you with the down payment for this apartment complex."

"Oh, I'm sure." I opened the envelope and peered in. "This might be enough for a down payment on a new cluster mailbox."

Since I'd recently had to replace the ones in the parking lot, I knew how much those cost. Everything was a fortune anymore.

"Not bad for a night's work." Duncan winked.

"You like to look on the bright side, don't you?"

"The world is a more welcoming place if you do."

I lifted the envelope, moved to use the money to do something nice with him. After all, he'd helped me that night—as he'd helped me on *many* nights since coming into my life.

"It is enough for a fancy dinner somewhere like the Space Needle," I said, "if you want to go on that date you mentioned."

"Is that the revolving restaurant downtown?"

"Yeah, I hear it's got a great view. You should be able to see a lot of the Cascade and Olympic Mountains as well as Puget Sound."

"Should be able to? You've lived in the area your whole life, and you've never been?"

"It's out of my price range."

"But not tonight." Duncan waved to the envelope. "And, after a scenic dinner in pleasant company, I imagine you'd be in the mood for a romantic encounter. *Without* intervention or compulsion from magical medallions."

"I might be. Will you be bringing your bed on wheels?"

"I always bring that."

"And will you be distracted by needing to magnet fish in nearby Puget Sound?"

Duncan hesitated. "Nearby, you say?"

"Very much so."

My phone rang, and Chad's name popped up. I growled at it. I'd *known* he would intrude on the day.

"Are you going to answer?" Duncan asked after several rings— and several seconds of me glowering at the screen.

"Absolutely not. *He* doesn't put me in the mood for romantic encounters."

"Having met him, I can agree to having similar feelings."

I almost pointed out that Duncan's impression of Chad hadn't kept him from being willing to work for him, but I didn't want to bring up the past. As I'd been thinking, Duncan had become a good friend—*more* than a good friend—and I trusted him.

An alert popped up. Chad had left a voicemail message.

"I'll regret this," I muttered but hit play. It would be better to know what he wanted than to be blindsided. After he'd reached out so many times, I knew he wanted *something* and wasn't calling simply to say he was in the area. "As if."

"Evening, Luna," Chad said on the recording. "I hear you've been traumatizing our sons by getting feral and furry."

I growled.

Duncan raised his eyebrows.

"Just *one* son," I muttered, and *traumatized* was a strong word. Austin may have found his Christmas vacation a little disturbing, but he'd been cool and collected during the kidnapping. He could handle finding out his mother was a werewolf.

"I'm a little disappointed that you never got furry for *me*," Chad continued, "but I've given up on that. I do need to talk to you though. I'm in town with Cam."

Yes, Austin had mentioned Cameron would be in the area too. And, shoot, I *did* want to see my other son. It had been almost two years since he'd left for parts unknown, angry that he hadn't been able to attend any of the universities he'd gotten into because his college fund had been drained. I hadn't helped the matter when I'd told him not to go into debt to go to school. In the throes of paying off my own debt at the time, I'd informed him that it would ruin his life. That might have been melodramatic, but I'd never been able to rescind that advice—that lecture.

"We'd like to see you," Chad added after whispering an aside to someone. Had he been *with* Cameron when he'd called? "Are you available for dinner tonight? Or lunch tomorrow? It won't take long. Cam has a few questions, and I... Well, I'm curious about how you're getting along too." He lowered his voice into what was probably supposed to be a sultry tone, but the word *sleazy* came to my mind, and added, "I've missed being with you, my sexy wolf."

I cringed, reminded of when he'd called me that, of how, after learning about my secret, he'd often urged me to stop taking that potion. He'd wanted to see me turn into a wolf. For all I knew, he might have known about my heritage from the beginning. It could have been what had drawn him to me all those years ago. All I'd known back then was that, after Raoul's death, I hadn't wanted to be involved with a werewolf. I'd wanted a normal human husband and a normal human life. It had only been recently that I'd learned to appreciate my heritage.

"Does he think you'll jump into his arms after all the pestering he's done?" Duncan asked. "Including the pestering he hired me to do?"

I well remembered the conversations I'd overheard between him and Chad, back when Chad had still believed Duncan might retrieve the case for him. He'd spoken crudely of me, and even though I remembered that Chad *could* turn on charm when he wished, I knew his true colors now.

"I doubt it." I erased the voicemail and didn't call back, though I was torn. I didn't want to see *Chad*, but if my son was in town, I would like to see him. If nothing else, I wanted to apologize for that lecture two years ago. The missing college fund wasn't my fault, something I *hoped* he knew, but if he still wanted to go to school now, maybe I could find a way to help him. Somehow.

I glanced at the envelope, but sadly, college tuition was even more expensive than a cluster mailbox.

"Do you think he's still after the case?" Duncan asked.

"I suppose that's possible. Unlike the medallion, I don't have any claim to it, but... I've always had a feeling it would be wrong to give it to him." I remembered the vision I'd had, suggesting that the case had *wanted* to be brought up here, that it had magically engineered Chad finding it, somehow knowing that was a way for it to be taken to the Pacific Northwest.

"He doesn't deserve it," Duncan said firmly.

"Maybe I should take it up to Mom's cave before he can steal it." I could even *leave* it in that cave. He wouldn't likely find it up there, and only the family knew about the place. "If she really had a vision that I'd learn something by doing so..."

"You think her vision involved more than us getting randy?"

"It might have."

"Maybe it wasn't about us at all."

"She did say it was about protecting our people."

"Why don't we go for our date this evening, and then, tomorrow, I'll take you back up there?"

"Okay. Remind me to stop at the ATM. I need to get some gas money for all the driving you're doing."

"You're not *paying* me to take you on a date."

"No, but you took me to Mom's, and you're offering to do so again." Realizing I held an envelope full of money, I pulled out a twenty-dollar bill and offered it to him. Since Minato had given the money to us both, it didn't seem right to pay him out of it, but it *was* here. Using some of the reward for gas seemed legitimate.

Duncan glowered at the bill without reaching for it. "If we fall madly in love, get married, and have children, will you still be giving me gas money? Five years from now?"

"Married couples here usually combine their incomes, so I wouldn't feel compelled to, no. Unless it keeps vexing you, and then I might pelt you with twenties on a regular basis."

"You're a dreadful woman."

"Yup." I kissed him on the cheek and tucked the bill into his pocket.

6

"AH," DUNCAN RUMBLED WITH PLEASURE AS HE CAST HIS MAGNET over the railing at the end of Pier 57. Laughs and cheers drifted down to us from the Ferris wheel sharing the area. With the cloudy evening almost warm, at least by January standards, numerous people were out. "Now *this* is romantic."

"More so than the tasty dinner and the view of the city?"

"All that was fine, but I'm delighted that you wanted to take a walk afterward and knew of this wondrous locale." Duncan pulled up his magnet, having already found numerous sets of keys.

I wouldn't call them *wondrous*, but it didn't take much to tickle him. Especially if it had rust on it.

"I figured with this being a tourist hot spot," I said, "all sorts of things would have fallen over the edge."

"Oh, and vastly interesting things too." As Duncan pulled a sludge-covered row of staples off his magnet, my phone rang.

Maybe I should have silenced it for our date, but I'd called Cameron earlier, hoping I could speak to him without Chad around. It had gone to voicemail, making me wonder if he was *really* here in Seattle, or if my ex-husband had said that only to manipulate me. Chad had to know I didn't want to see *him*.

"It's Jasmine." I debated whether to answer while we were on our date, but Duncan was peering in fascination at two rusty tin boxes that had come up, fused together by grime. Part of Mickey Mouse was visible on top of one, and the other looked like a Nabisco saltines tin even older than I was. They probably were *both* older than I was. But was tin magnetic? Maybe something inside was. Deciding Duncan wouldn't notice if I took the call or not, I answered before it went to voicemail. "Hi, Jasmine. What's up?"

"The price of hot-springs-filled *resort* land," she said in a triumphant tone.

"Uhm, fill me in?"

"Dad's been busily researching again. Remember that developer he found? Who bought the parcel down the road from your mom's property?"

"Yes."

"And the new rural-business zoning?"

"Yes."

"Dad found out the owner has put out a release that he's starting up a resort on the property. He's looking for backers. In addition to all the usual spa kinds of services—mud wraps, massages, fine dining—it's going to have tours of mining areas and the opportunity for guests to pan for gold, and there's going to be a natural hot springs with private pools, a bathing-suit optional area, a salt cave, and all kinds of therapeutic and hedonistic services."

"Mud wraps and massages in rural Monroe?" I scratched my jaw. It was far from a hoity-toity area.

"Technically, the property is in an unincorporated part of Snohomish County."

"Well, that changes everything. The hordes will descend upon it to be pampered in such an exotic locale."

"Here's the thing, Luna. As far as the pack knows, and I've asked a bunch of elders, the mine shafts and hot springs are on your *mom's* property."

"There are hot springs back there?"

"There are three or four mud holes by the stream where steamy water burbles up through the silt."

"Rich people do line up to enjoy mud holes."

Jasmine laughed. "I think you can excavate a bit if you want to put in a pool or whatever. Developers can do a lot. And people like knowing that natural hot springs are there with all of their healing benefits."

"I had no idea that mud holes had healing benefits."

"A warm one is nice. Minerals that rejuvenate the skin, you know. Anyway, my point is that this is probably the guy."

"The guy trying to get Mom to sell?"

Was that what he was doing? I wasn't sure what those real estate agents had been up to back there.

"We think he wants all the properties in that area, and he wants to get them cheaply."

"Why the properties up that road? It's not even paved. Who's going to drive through potholes to get to a resort? Besides, there have to be hot springs everywhere."

Duncan got the lid open on the Mickey Mouse tin. The *treasures* inside were old nuts, bolts, and washers from someone's spare-parts collection. He eyed a couple of laundry tokens with speculation. Maybe such things were collectable.

"I'm sure he would pay to have it paved as part of the development, and there aren't hot springs *everywhere*. They're not that common. And a lot of the stuff around there is on federal or state land, so you can't develop it. It's pretty rare to find parcels as big as the ones the family holds, especially relatively close to town."

"Well, warn Mom and Lorenzo, I guess. And the elders. They

can keep an eye out for developers with nefarious intent." I couldn't imagine what *I* could do.

"I already did. I figured you'd want to know too."

"I do. Thanks for keeping me in the loop."

I hung up and regarded Duncan.

He didn't look disappointed by what he'd found. If anything, he gave me a relaxed and pleased smile before asking, "Are the hot springs romantic?"

"You mean the mud holes?" I had a distinct image in mind after Jasmine's description, and *romantic* wasn't the descriptor that went with it. "Probably not more so than a pier with Mickey Mouse tchotchkes nestled underwater among the barnacles and algae."

"This spot *is* perfect." Duncan wrapped an arm around me and nodded toward the rusty and grimy treasures lining the railing, the finds he'd already pulled off the bottom.

Some of the people getting on and off the Ferris wheel had looked curiously at the collection—and at him—but nobody had asked what he was doing. Most of the visitors were probably tourists.

Another call came in. Bolin, this time. He wasn't at the apartment complex this late in the evening, was he?

"What's up, Bolin?" I answered.

"Your, uhm, ex-husband is here."

Damn it, was Chad skulking around? Planning to search my apartment for the artifact?

"At Sylvan Serenity? Why are *you* there this late?" Maybe I should have asked what Chad was doing, but I already had a good idea. I might need to head back and confront him, but my mind rebelled at the idea.

"Jasmine and I met here and took my car to a laser show," Bolin said. "Riding in hers is harrowing."

"Did she like your plush leather heated seats?"

"She accidentally turned on the seats' cooling feature and complained that her tail was cold." Bolin hesitated. "She doesn't have a tail, does she? You know, as a human. I haven't noticed that you... not that I've looked in that area. I mean, I have. A respectable and polite amount only. But..."

"She's mentioned having phantom tail twitches, but no, we don't have any weird werewolf parts when we're human. Just slightly sharper canine teeth."

"Weird," Duncan said with a sniff.

"Okay, good. I used a little magic to deter your ex-husband's initial attempt to gain access. Then Rue placed a potion wafting blue smoke in front of the door of your apartment, and it's so far deterred him from attempting to enter or get too close."

I would have to thank Rue for that. I wondered how she'd known who Chad was—or at least recognized him as someone up to no good. Maybe he'd had his nose pressed to my window when she'd chanced past.

"Do you want me to tell him that you..."

"Moved out and live in Hawaii now? Yes."

"I was trying to deter him from forcing his way into your apartment, so I said you would be back soon. He said he'd wait, and he's leaning against a tree outside the leasing office with his arms crossed over his chest."

"Oh." I sighed. "I guess I'm on my way home then."

Oh, how I did not want to see him.

"I'm afraid I need to end our date early," I told Duncan, disappointed that we hadn't yet kissed.

"It's all right." He reeled in his magnet and gathered his finds, not looking disappointed in the least with how the night was going. "These tins are magnificent. They have to be from the mid-twentieth century. *Antiques*."

"Their magnificence is what's foremost on my mind right now too."

Duncan chuckled. "I'm sure it's not. Let me take you home. When we get there, do you want me to come over and growl at your ex?"

"Yes, and maim him horribly, please." I shook my head. "Why is he even *here*?"

"I guess this is your opportunity to find out."

I bared my fangs.

7

DREAD FILLED ME AS WE TURNED INTO THE PARKING LOT BACK HOME. Duncan, who kept fondly patting the rusty tins he'd found, didn't seem nearly as concerned. Of course not. Chad had only been a brief acquaintance for him, not someone who'd been a part of his life for twenty years and whose name evoked memories of pain, frustration, and betrayal.

As we parked, a howl greeted us. A young howl.

"Your assassin is here." I looked toward the greenbelt.

"I hear that."

"He stays up late. Doesn't Abrams impose a curfew?"

"Assassins usually ply their trade after dark, so this isn't unexpected."

"Kids need to go to bed early so they can be perky and alert for early-morning cartoons. It's a parenting rule."

"Interesting. I have much to learn about such things." Duncan pointed toward the woods, as if to imply he would go practice parenting again but said, "I'll come with you to see your ex-husband before checking on Lykos."

The howl came again. It sounded more lonely and full of longing than threatening.

"You can go see what he wants first." I poked in my purse and pulled out a half-consumed bag of dark-chocolate-covered almonds. "Here, share these with him. You can bond over them."

Duncan eyed the bag. "He might be luring me out to a poisoned bear trap that I'll step in, immediately incapacitating me, and giving him an opportunity to slay me without much risk to himself."

I stared at him. That was oddly specific.

"Last time, Lykos suggested that as a possible means of fulfilling his mission for Abrams."

"He probably shouldn't have informed you about it ahead of time if that's what he's planning."

"Exactly what I told him. He waved and said he was already thinking up other better plans, so it didn't matter if I knew about that one." Duncan accepted the bag of chocolate-covered almonds, then picked up the Mickey Mouse tin. He'd dumped the nuts and bolts into the other canister and wiped out the Disney one. "I'm going to offer him this, as well. Children enjoy cartoon characters, right?"

"Absolutely. Maybe he can store his assassination tools in there."

"Everyone appreciates good tool storage." Duncan opened the door. "I'll check on him briefly, then come lend moral support to you with your problem."

"Don't forget about the maiming."

"I'm always available for that if needed." He saluted me with the tin, hopped out, and trotted toward the woods.

"Watch where you step," I called after him, though I was already looking around for Chad.

This late at night, there hadn't been much traffic on the drive back, but forty-five minutes had still passed since I'd spoken with Bolin. After taking a long breath that wasn't as bracing as I wished, I slid out of the van and headed toward the leasing office.

"There you are," came a familiar voice, if gruffer and crankier sounding than when last we'd spoken. Chad must not have come because he'd been pining for me all this time and wanted to reconnect. That was a relief.

"Here I am."

Shoulder muscles tense, I tried to loosen my arms as he stepped out from between Bolin's G-Wagon and a tenant's car that I recognized. Chad glanced at the protective bubble around the Mercedes SUV before looking at me. Whatever rental car he'd driven up here didn't stand out to me in the lot.

With short brown hair that he hadn't allowed to go gray, a mustache above full lips and a clean-shaven jaw, and an aquiline nose, Chad hadn't changed much since the last time I'd seen him. He might have put on a few pounds, but he remained strikingly handsome, with blue-gray eyes that I'd once likened to storm clouds. Back in the day, I'd thought that exotic and appealing.

"What brings you to Seattle?" I asked after a long, silent moment, eyeing his loafers, khakis, and brown leather jacket.

He was checking me out as much as I was him, his gaze lingering on my curves. Once, I would have found that flattering, but, now, I was tempted to punch him and tell him to look at my face.

He squinted slightly. Trying to determine if I was noticeably different now that I wasn't taking the sublimation potion? To someone with magical blood, I was, but I didn't know if a mundane human would be able to *sense my aura*, as we were-wolves called it.

"Besides wanting to get into my apartment when I'm not there?" I added, raising frank eyebrows so he would know I knew he'd been skulking about. "If you're still looking for that case, don't bother. I gave it to a druid family."

Yes, it was a lie, but after all the lies he'd told me over the course of our marriage, I didn't feel bad about prevarication.

"You what?" His eyebrows flew up as he met my gaze.

"After doing some research, I learned that druids long ago made it, so I figured it belonged to their kind."

"And there are so many druids in the Seattle area," he snapped, looking around, as if he might catch me in a lie and spot the case in the crotch of a tree.

No, it was in my heat duct...

"Of course there are druids here. It's got a similar climate to their old-world origins, and it's full of trees and nature. Druids *love* nature." I kept from glancing at the bubble around Bolin's SUV to protect it from bird droppings. I didn't want to do anything that would lead Chad to learn that Bolin was a druid and might know something about the location of the case.

"It has a wolf on it," Chad said. "It has to do with *werewolves*."

"Actually, the artifact inside the case was designed to protect *against* werewolves. Didn't you ever have the inscription translated?"

"Yes, of course." Chad hesitated. "It said it has to do with poisons, venoms, and werewolf bites."

"Not *has to do with* but *protects* people from them."

He worked his jaw back and forth, a gesture I'd almost forgotten that he did when he was stewing over something. It made him look like a cow chewing cud. I wondered if whoever had done the translating for him had come up with a different interpretation than Bolin's father. I was more inclined to trust my druid allies' translation, especially since I'd now seen the artifact in action.

"You wouldn't have given something so valuable away," Chad said.

"It's not that valuable. You only paid a few bucks for it from a street vendor."

He opened his mouth for a quick retort but didn't issue it. "How... do you know where I got it and what I paid?"

I'd both overheard him discussing it when he'd spoken to Duncan and seen the purchase in a vision. I decided to smile cryptically rather than sharing the information. Let him think I had supernatural powers. Technically, I did.

"That ass Calderwood told you." Chad looked toward the Roadtrek we'd arrived in. "Is he here? Is that his van? Are you *screwing* him?"

"Wow, it only took you thirty seconds to get crude and into my business. You used to at least pretend to be a suave gentleman."

And I'd fallen for it, for a time. That galled me.

"I'm not here to prove anything to you."

"Why *are* you here?" I asked. "Why is that case so important to you?"

"It's not." Chad shrugged. "I had a buyer lined up, but I haven't been able to get in touch with him lately." He shrugged again. "I came to Seattle about something else. Business. I got called in by someone who wanted my expertise."

I couldn't keep from scoffing. "What expertise do you have?"

He smiled, looking me up and down again. "I know a lot about werewolves."

"Whatever you believe you know, it's less than you think. Trust me."

His eyes narrowed, and he stepped closer. "I'd know more if you hadn't been so determined to hide that half of yourself during our whole marriage."

That step closer made me want to skitter back, but I refused to be intimidated by him. I did, however, lament that I'd left the sword in the apartment. Chad would look quite fine with the tips of his ears lopped off. Maybe some other appendages too.

"I wanted to be a normal human being for the sake of our children." And my haunted past. The memory of Raoul's face still lingered whenever I thought of that time.

"I always figured you'd get over that, feel the call of the moon, need to throw your head back and howl."

"I know you wanted that."

"You almost did, sometimes, you know. In bed." He smirked at me. "You were wild and exciting, but you never quite went the whole way."

My cheeks heated. This was *not* what I'd come to discuss with him. I hadn't wanted to *discuss* anything at all.

"Because of that potion, right?" Chad continued. "You're not taking it anymore. I can tell."

So, he *could* tell. Even without paranormal blood. Huh.

"It's been an eventful winter," was all I said. "If you're not here about the case, why *are* you here?"

"Like I said. Wolf business." Chad looked toward my apartment.

He had to be lying. Otherwise, he wouldn't keep sending longing gazes in the direction he believed his case was located.

"What kind of *wolf* business? I know nobody in my pack has reached out to you. Most of them don't even know you exist."

He curled his lip. "They might soon."

I frowned at him. "What does that mean?"

"Nothing you need to worry about here in the city." He looked smug.

Why?

My fingers twitched. Would it be wrong to throttle him while asking questions? He glanced once more toward my apartment.

"If Radomir is your buyer, he's dead now," I said.

Chad's gaze swung back to me, his mouth drooping open. Huh, I'd guessed right. Maybe it shouldn't have surprised me. Who else in the area would have been purchasing werewolf artifacts?

"How would you know that?"

I wanted to say, *I killed him,* but Chad could be recording the conversation. Even if Duncan and I had been defending ourselves from Abrams and Radomir and all their thugs, it wasn't as if I could claim we'd run Radomir off the road—off that *cliff*—purely in self-defense.

"I know a lot related to the werewolf artifacts in the area," I said.

"Even if what you say is true, there are other buyers around." Chad laughed shortly. "If what you say about the translation is true, the people I'm working with now might even buy it."

Hell, *was* he legitimately up here on some kind of business? What *business* would have to do with werewolves? Most people didn't even know our kind existed.

Chad took another step closer. "Why don't you go get it, and we'll sell it together? Even though *I'm* the one who found it, I admit that my means for retrieving it weren't that ideal."

"No shit."

"Make things easier on me now, and I'll cut you in. Half of what I make. I remember what you earn working your ass off here, that little pittance. I know you could use the money."

My fingers curled into fists, the temptation to punch him rearing up again. The suggestion that I had a problem with money angered me more than anything else he'd said. *He* was the only reason I'd ended up in debt in the first place, and *he* was why the kids hadn't had money for college when they'd been ready. All along, I'd been putting some aside, saving it for them, and he'd stolen it before I'd ever spoken the word *divorce.*

"If you're going to throw money around," I said, "Cameron and Austin are the ones who could use it for school."

Well, Austin had found another route now via the Air Force, but maybe Cameron would still like to go.

Chad glanced toward the parking lot, then focused on me

again. "There'd be plenty for that. If you just get the case and bring it here. Don't be selfish about it."

"I told you that I gave it to its rightful owners."

"I don't believe you. You've never been a good liar."

My knuckles tightened, my face red, and the first tingle of magic swept through my veins. I swallowed, irritated that he was getting a rise out of me. The *last* thing I wanted to do was change into a wolf in front of him. Less because I cared if I lost myself to the moon magic and my wild instincts and more because I didn't want to give him the satisfaction of seeing it.

"You turned into a wolf in front of Austin," Chad whispered, as if he knew my thoughts. He could probably see the rage in my eyes, maybe even sense, in his mundane human way, that I was close to changing. "You never did for me."

"I never needed to save *you* from kidnappers." I wondered how much of the story Austin had shared.

Chad smiled tightly, not looking surprised—or concerned at all that Austin had been threatened. "It would have been handy for the debt collectors."

"Which we wouldn't have been harassed by if you hadn't been keeping women on the side and been so infrequent with the money you brought in. If not for the so-called *pittance* I made here, we wouldn't have gotten by at all."

He watched my face as I glared at him, then inhaled, as if our confrontation was invigorating him. Did he have no idea how badly I wanted to punch him? That if he goaded me and I turned into the wolf, I might do much *worse* than punch him?

"You're still sexy when you're angry. You always were, but it's more magnetic now." He lifted a hand, as if to reach for my chest.

If he touched me...

"I always wanted this," he said, his voice husky. Was the bastard *aroused*? "Wanted the wolf," he added.

"I know what you wanted, and you're not getting it. Leave now before I do something..." That I would regret? That was the saying, but I wouldn't regret it. I would enjoy lashing out at him. Never in all the years we'd been married had I tried to hit him, but with my magic no longer sublimated, the pull to unleash my temper and my *power* was stronger than ever. "...that'll get me arrested," I finished.

Chad laughed. "You wouldn't do that. You may be part animal, but you're a good girl. You always obeyed the law. I just want to hear you howl." He lifted a hand and touched my breast.

I punched him in the nose so hard that he flew backward. He cried out as he landed on his ass and rolled away.

"Shit, Luna!" he barked, jerking his hands to his face. "You broke my nose!"

I growled, tempted to spring upon him and break a lot more.

But I sensed Duncan running across the lawn toward us. I tried to still my anger, not wanting to lose my equanimity completely, to be an animal in front of him.

Still swearing, and oblivious to Duncan's approach, Chad staggered to his feet. He gripped his nose with one hand, blood running freely down his face, and reached into his jacket with the other.

In all the years I'd known him, he hadn't carried a weapon, so I hadn't expected him to have one. But his fingers wrapped around the hilt of a revolver, and he drew it. He pointed it in the air rather than at me, but his eyes were locked on mine.

Not seeming to notice Duncan running toward us, he said, "Go get the case, Luna, or I'll—"

What he would have done, I didn't find out. Duncan smashed into him like a cannonball. He roared, more like an animal than a man. With a start, I realized he *was* an animal.

As Duncan had run, he'd turned into the bipedfuris. He not only took Chad to the ground, but he then snarled, sprang to his feet, grabbed Chad by the shoulder and the crotch, and hurled him over the first row of cars. Chad bounced off the top of the SUV's protective bubble, the gun flying from his grip to land halfway across the parking lot, and he came down with a thud on the pavement in the lane between cars.

I rushed toward Duncan, though my instincts made me want to stay back—if he was as wild and possessed by his magic as I sometimes was, he might not recognize me as an ally. But he was about to spring after Chad, maybe finish him off. As much as I detested my ex-husband, I couldn't allow Duncan to murder the father of my children.

I grabbed his arm, sleek salt-and-pepper fur covering the taut powerful muscles there. "Stop, Duncan. Thanks for coming, but you can't kill him."

A groan came from the parking lot, and I feared more than Chad's nose was broken.

Snarling again, Duncan crouched, barely seeming to notice me.

Grip tightening, I whispered, "Duncan, please. Stop. I'm fine. I appreciate you coming to help, but I can take care of myself, okay? You know a little handgun doesn't faze me." I doubted Chad would have pointed it at me, not that Duncan had known that. Chad had brought the weapon in case he needed to threaten me—or maybe he'd even wondered if he might need to defend himself against me if I turned wolf? He hadn't come to kill me. I didn't believe that.

The bipedfuris didn't spring away from me and toward Chad, but he seethed, radiating fury and power. In this form, Duncan stood two feet taller than me, his torso and muscled limbs larger and stronger. When his brown eyes swung toward me, they were wild and savage. Fear shot through me. It was like when I lost my rational mind to the wolf magic and couldn't tell friend from foe, could only follow wild, magic-driven instincts to lash out. To kill. Did Duncan even recognize me?

Though it felt like reaching toward a hissing rattlesnake, I lifted my free hand to his torso.

"It's okay," I said in my most soothing tone and stroked his furred chest.

Duncan's muscles quivered with tension, but he didn't leap away. He didn't exactly *relax* either, but I kept stroking him and murmuring that things were fine, that he didn't need to do anything else. I was safe.

Another groan came from the lane between the automobiles, and Chad peeked between the SUV and a car. Blood smeared his jaw and cheek, and he gripped one of his arms. He stared at Duncan and then at me, shock mixing with the pain in his eyes.

Had he known Duncan was a werewolf? Maybe not. Even if he had, he wouldn't have known that Duncan could turn into a bipedfuris.

Another growl emanated from Duncan's chest as his eyes locked onto Chad. Chad who was standing there, gaping like an idiot. What, was he fascinated by the appearance of a werewolf? Or too dumb to realize how much danger he was in?

"Get out of here," I whispered harshly to Chad.

Duncan crouched, his tail twitching, his clawed fingers curling. The longing to rip Chad to pieces, something he absolutely had the power to do, hung in the air around him.

"He'll kill you," I added.

Maybe that realization finally sank into Chad's thick skull because he nodded jerkily and backed away, moving out of view behind Bolin's SUV. A curse that was more pain than vitriol came from him, followed by the thump of a car door.

Duncan's tail twitched again. He didn't appear as utterly savage now, but he *did* look like he longed for a release, maybe to go on a hunt. But the direction of his eyes—pointed toward the sound of that car rather than toward the woods or the distant mountains—

promised he wanted to hunt Chad, not an animal to enjoy for dinner.

The engine started, and I let out a sigh of relief as the car drove toward the exit. An unassuming brown Toyota, it had to be a rental vehicle. The passenger-side window was down, and someone unexpected gaped in our direction as Chad departed.

Cameron.

8

STUNNED AT THE REALIZATION THAT MY SON HAD BEEN WITH CHAD and must have seen and heard everything, I stopped stroking Duncan's furred chest. He grunted in protest.

"Sorry." I returned to my attempts to soothe him, but my whirling thoughts distracted me.

If I'd realized Cameron had been watching, I wouldn't have punched Chad. Well, maybe I would have. He'd deserved it. But I had no idea how Cameron had reacted to that, especially if he hadn't been close enough to hear the conversation. If he'd only been able to see what was happening, would he think his father had been trying to get close to me—he and his groping hand had definitely done that—and I'd spurned him for no reason? *Punched* him for no reason?

I hoped it hadn't looked like that. It had always bothered me that Cameron had essentially stopped speaking with me, other than sending half-hearted gif replies to texts that I made sure weren't too frequent. I'd wanted him to have his independence and not feel I was badgering him, but I missed having a relationship with him. I'd always hoped, if I gave him time and space, that he would come around.

A stirring of magic beside me pulled my attention back to Duncan. He grasped my hand, careful not to brush me with his claws, and gazed down at me.

With Chad gone, the savageness had left his eyes, and I stepped back, sensing that he would change. He kept my hand in his though. Wanting me close?

His outline blurred, fur disappearing, and his body shifted from that of the bipedfuris to the man. The naked man.

"I do appreciate it when you fondle my chest, my lady."

"Oh, I know. Thanks for charging over to help. Even if I didn't expect your help to be quite so furry."

"You didn't? When you keep company with werewolves, you should expect fur rather often."

"I suppose that's true, but I thought you were busy foisting an eighty-year-old rusty tin off on a kid."

"Really, my lady. The way you speak of that excellent find as if it were junk instead of a grand treasure."

"I can see where my attitude would confuse you." I squeezed his hand and slid my fingers out of his grip, though he didn't seem to want to let me go. "Why don't you slip into your van and find some clothes?" I looked toward the lawn, wondering if he'd pulled off anything before the change had taken him. Only his phone gleamed, the screen reflecting the glow of one of the landscaping lights. He must not have felt he had time to remove anything else. "It's late but not so late that tenants won't be coming and going."

"And it would harm your professional reputation here if you were seen fondling the chest of a naked man?"

"It would just be hard to explain. And someone might call the police."

"Why? Nudity isn't a crime here, surely."

"There *are* laws against it. In public, at least."

"Oh, yes. I forgot our previous discussions on this topic and how repressed Americans are."

"We are indeed." I waved toward his van. "Look, if you go put on clothes, I'll join you, and we can finish our date." After my encounter with Chad, I was amped up and couldn't imagine snuggling into my bed for sleep anytime soon. "You wanted to go to a drive-in movie, right? We can prop one of our phones on your dash and watch something together. I've got some microwave popcorn in my apartment that I can heat up and bring out."

"I would enjoy continuing our date." Duncan bowed to me, picked up his phone, then ambled toward his van, taking his time and making sure I had a good view of his butt as he went.

I snorted and might possibly have enjoyed that view for a while before heading to my apartment. On the way, I veered toward the leasing office to see if Bolin was inside. His SUV was in the lot, so he ought to be on the grounds, right? I was surprised he hadn't gone home yet. If he'd stayed to protect my unit from being robbed by Chad, I appreciated that.

Other than the glow shining through the window from a computer monitor, the lights were off in the leasing office. Maybe Bolin was standing guard right in front of my unit.

I grabbed the knob to make sure he'd locked up. But the door opened, and I sensed someone within. Two someones.

Curious, I peeked inside. A startled gasp and thump came from the small sofa where tenants sometimes sat while waiting for me to get off the phone. Bolin had fallen onto the floor. Only then did I realize that was Jasmine I sensed with him. She sat on the sofa, her shirt untucked and rucked up. She'd been reclining against the armrest but hurried to straighten herself and scrape her fingers through her hair.

"Luna," Bolin blurted from the floor. "I, uhm."

"FYI," I said, "you should lock the door before engaging in a necking session."

"Yes, of course." Cheeks flushed from embarrassment or arousal or both, Bolin glanced at Jasmine several times. He seemed worried to hold her gaze.

She looked less flustered than he did. I gave them both a thumbs-up, then closed the door. When Bolin had been describing his date with Jasmine, it hadn't led me to believe I might find them engaged in an intimate moment. Maybe he'd performed some studly druid magic that had impressed Jasmine.

I reached my apartment and was contemplating a flask of smoking blue liquid that was in front of the door when a text came in. Jasmine had sent a photo of Bolin on the very walkway on which I now stood, arms spread as he faced off against Chad. It had been taken before the potion had been placed. The photo showed Bolin with a stern face, looking older and more powerful than his years, and a vine growing out of the sidewalk and toward Chad's ankle. A second photo taken a few seconds later showed Chad turning to run away as the vine, much larger now, swatted him in the butt.

"He's had a rough night," I murmured but did not feel sorry for my ex-husband.

Not an omega, came Jasmine's accompanying text.

I snorted, remembering our conversation and when she'd realized that Bolin had the potential to be the powerful—or maybe just exciting—mate she'd wanted.

Nope, I replied agreeably.

Sexy, huh? came Jasmine's follow-up text.

Maybe Bolin confronting Chad had turned on her libido after the chilling incident with the butt coolers.

You like a man who can summon vines out of the ether, huh? I texted back, wondering if she would show the phone to Bolin.

Apparently, I do! Wolves are into nature, you know.

I do know that.

The nature *I* preferred was of the lupine variety and waited in his van for me. Key in hand, I reached for my doorknob, but the blue smoke wafting from the vial increased, curling up like a long finger toward my wrist. I pulled my arm back, and it billowed, forming a cloud around the doorknob.

"Hm."

Though it was late, I called Rue.

She sounded groggy when she answered. "Yes?"

"Thanks for helping keep burglars out of my apartment, Rue, but how do I get in?"

"That was your ex-husband, was it not?"

"Yeah, but he had burglary in mind."

"So we deduced. Hence the placement of my Potion of Protection."

"It's doing a good job of ominously wafting smoke."

"I'm glad you appreciate it. Such potions are not simple to make. I left an invoice in your mailbox."

"For... an item I didn't order?"

"Bolin assured me that you would desire it to be placed in front of your door."

"*Bolin* wanted someone else to watch my apartment so he could make out with my niece."

"I did sense that possibility. They are a cute couple, are they not? The wolf and the druid. A natural pairing."

"Yes, I understand that. How do I move the potion so I can go in? My own pairing is waiting to happen as soon as I grab some microwave popcorn."

"I did sense the bipedfuris on the premises. I hope he slew your thieving ex-husband."

"Just... hurled him over some cars to break his arm. I didn't think I should allow a slaying. It's against the law, and there's *always* someone around here with a phone camera, ready to take photos."

"I'm well aware of that."

"How do I move this potion and get into my apartment without being attacked by misty vapors?"

"I brewed the potion in such a manner that it would allow the proper owner to enter the premises. You need not fear the vapors. You may even wish to leave the potion on guard there. It'll remain viable for a week."

"So I can just step around it?" Not entirely believing the potion would leave me alone, I reached for the knob again.

Once more, the finger formed. I resisted the urge to yank my hand back, instead turning the key in the lock. The tendril of vapor reached me but merely brushed my wrist. Touching me as a way to identify me and decide I could be allowed access? Or...

"Your potion is getting fresh with me." I decided the brush was more of a caress.

Rue cackled.

"I punched my ex for that."

"Just go past. You'll be fine." Rue yawned and hung up.

I stepped over the flask and into the apartment. Fortunately, the handsy vapors didn't follow me inside. Just in case, I shut the door firmly.

While the microwave snack popped, I peered around the living room and bedrooms, making sure Chad hadn't found a way in. The apartment was as I'd left it, and I sensed the case under the floor near my bed. That was a relief. It reminded me of my mother's request that we take the medallions to the cave.

"Tomorrow," I murmured, removing the popcorn from the microwave, the buttery scent filling the air.

Tonight, I wanted to relax with Duncan and let him know that I appreciated him leaping to my defense. Usually, he didn't turn into the bipedfuris for that, but maybe seeing Chad being a dick had made his beast come out of its own accord. The idea that such a thing would move Duncan to that action pleased me more than it should have. I shouldn't want anyone to lose his equanimity or become violent on my behalf, and yet... it touched me that he cared, that he wanted to protect me.

In addition to the popcorn, I grabbed paper towels and a newly acquired bar of dark chocolate with bacon bits to share with Duncan. I also remembered that I'd picked up a few items from Goodwill for him the last time I'd visited. We'd both lost clothing the night of our battle at Abrams's laboratory.

On an impulse, I grabbed the sword too. If Chad showed up again, I would have it close at hand, perhaps forestalling the need for anyone to get furry.

"Ah, my lady has brought gifts," Duncan said, pushing the passenger-side door open for me when I reached his van.

I leaned the sword inside and placed the stack of shirts and trousers on the seat for him. Even though he'd put on clothes, he would need more soon if he kept engaging in unplanned shiftings. His small home on wheels couldn't hold *that* many jeans and shirts in its tiny cupboards.

Duncan didn't comment on the sword, only picking up the stack of garments to examine.

"More experienced clothing?"

"You wouldn't want to pay top dollar for *inexperienced* clothing that will end up vanishing into the ether."

"Something that's been happening a lot since I met you."

"Do I test your self-control?"

"Oh, *vastly*." After moving the clothes, Duncan waved me to the passenger seat, though he also gestured an invitation to his lap. "If you're uncomfortable or cold by yourself over there, I've got room for you here."

"I'll bet you do." I smirked at him as I rested a hand on the back of the passenger seat, intending to say I had no interest in sitting in his lap, but was that true? The more time we spent together, the more I appreciated his companionship, his loyalty, his willingness to help and defend me, and... how desirable and sexy he was.

The memory of him grabbing me in my mother's cabin came to mind, his powerful arms wrapped around me, his hands going expertly to the right places to instantly stoke my arousal. By the moon, that had been hot. *He* was hot.

"I think you'd enjoy watching a movie in my lap," Duncan murmured.

My cheeks flushed with heat. Not embarrassment but desire. When he took my hand from the passenger seat and shifted it to his shoulder, my whole *body* heated with desire. I slid into his lap, his body taut through his clothing, and raised my eyebrows.

"I'm surprised I didn't find you in the bathroom again," I murmured.

"Seeing you punch that loser did get me excited." Duncan slid his arm around my waist and stroked me through my shirt.

"Was that before or after you turned into the bipedfuris?" I hadn't looked down when he'd been in that form to check.

"Well, your ex-husband was presuming to touch you when I first started across the lawn, so I lost my mind a bit there. Excitement isn't quite the word for the savage desire to kill him that I felt. It was more in the aftermath, while you've been gone, that I've had time to fully appreciate the punch."

"I see." I shifted a bit in his lap. "And feel."

He grinned wickedly at me, keeping his gaze on me as he delved into the bag of popcorn and tossed a couple of pieces into his mouth.

"Everything okay with your assassin?" I realized I hadn't asked for an update on the kid.

The main reason I did now was that I wanted to make sure Lykos wasn't out there in the woods, watching us through the windshield. It was late enough that not many tenants were passing through the parking lot, but that kid didn't seem to have a curfew.

"When I didn't walk into the trap he'd set, he asked me a few questions, took the tin and some chocolates, and left."

I blinked. "He really did lay a trap?"

"Very similar to the one we'd discussed. He didn't seem surprised when I didn't step into it, nor did the failure to ensnare me noticeably concern him. But he did take a photo of the trap. To show Abrams that he'd attempted to capture and slay me, perhaps."

"That kid may need therapy."

"I'm certain of it. Being raised by a mad scientist will give you a few issues to work through." Duncan's lips twisted wryly.

"I can imagine," I said with sympathy and rested a hand on his shoulder, brushing the strong tendon in his neck with my thumb.

His eyelids drooped as he shifted under me, snuggling me closer against him. The heat radiating from his hard body seeped into me as I inhaled, his masculine scent mingling with the popcorn aroma in the air. It was intoxicating. *He* was intoxicating.

"What movie shall we watch?" I murmured, though it hadn't escaped my notice that he didn't have anything paused on the phone. The screen wasn't even on.

"I've got exactly what I want to watch right here." He squeezed me, then freed a hand to offer me the popcorn bag.

"I'm not very exciting."

"You know *that's* not true. I just told you how much I enjoyed seeing that punch. Maybe I'll replay it over and over in my mind as we exquisitely explore each other's bodies."

He slid one hand under my shirt and up to stroke my breast, sending a streak of hot desire through me. There was no uncertainty in his eyes or hesitancy in his touch that suggested he worried that I might not want his hand there, that I would punch someone else tonight. By now, he knew I was into him, that I longed for his touch. Why had we waited so long to get to this moment?

I bent to kiss him, sliding my tongue along his lips, tasting the lingering salt and butter from the popcorn. He returned the kiss, his mouth hard and hungry, and groaned as his arm tightened around me. His free hand slid up to peel off my bra strap, giving him unfettered access to the sensitive skin of my breast. I might have groaned too, shifting my chest toward him so he could more easily touch me. I gripped his shoulders, wondering why I'd insisted that he put on clothes, and reveled in his stroking fingers. Already, I was thinking of requesting—or demanding—that he take me to bed.

This time, we weren't wearing our medallions. We longed for each other—*lusted* for each other—without the presence of their magic. I pushed my fingers up into Duncan's hair, using my nails to massage his scalp. His roving hands slid my shirt off my torso, leaving it and my bra on the floor next to us.

Giggles outside made us both pause.

Duncan's eyes opened, and he looked out the windshield. "Hm."

I kept my focus on him, hoping that whoever it was would get quickly into their car without wandering in this direction. Perhaps, we should move into the rear of the van where equipment and tinted windows would block the view of the bed from passersby...

More giggles sounded, and I turned enough to follow Duncan's gaze out the windshield.

Not ten feet away, the two twenty-something tenants with ghostometers and other paranormal monitoring equipment were setting up on the sidewalk. Cameras on tripods pointed toward the woods, the grounds around the closest apartment buildings, and at the parking lot. A weird funnel attached by a cable to equipment in a suitcase aimed right at Duncan's van.

The girls were looking at something on one of their phones and might not have spotted us making out in the driver's seat, but I wasn't sure about that. It could be that the camera feed of us was showing on their phone. With a zoom lens activated? The thought made my cheeks heat in embarrassment and indignation, and I grabbed my clothes off the floor, hurrying to put them back on.

"Should I go over there and assure them that there are no ghosts in my van?" Duncan asked.

"I don't even know if they're looking for *ghosts*." I recalled that one of the women had witnessed a fight in the parking lot where I'd turned into a wolf. She'd sent a photo to the police.

Duncan raised his eyebrows and touched his chest.

"We may well be the target of their investigation." I didn't know if they'd figured out yet that their property manager was the wolf they'd caught on camera. "It's too bad they have good credit, pay their rent promptly every month, and don't break any of the rules of the complex."

"Meaning you don't have an excuse to evict them?"

"Sadly, no." I probably couldn't justify going on a rampage and breaking all of their equipment either.

"We could adjourn to your apartment and a more private setting."

"The bed in there *is* larger."

"Just not surrounded by SCUBA gear and treasure-hunting equipment."

"You say that like that's a downside."

"I do get excited by being among my favorite things."

"I think I can get you excited even in the barren and inhospitable habitat that is my bedroom."

"I suspect that's quite true." Duncan winked at me, tossed a couple more pieces of popcorn in his mouth, and reached for the door handle.

Before I could slide off his lap or he could open it, an engine roared.

I grimaced, afraid the motorcycle thugs were back. Hadn't they learned at the movie theater to leave werewolves alone? Duncan and me specifically?

But the thirty-year-old dented Corvette that sped into the lot, possibly lacking a muffler, wasn't familiar. It drove down the lane closest to the women and halted hard in front of their equipment. Their giggles stopped as they lowered the phone, glancing at each other and backing up.

Two big men got out of the car. Neither was from the gang of thugs who'd pestered the property before, but they carried tire irons and reminded me of them. There was just one difference. They had paranormal blood.

A guy with a ponytail who had muscles that bulged at the seams of his shirt emanated power. The other man lacked hair entirely, his bald head gleaming under a parking-lot light. And it wasn't the only thing gleaming. When he lifted his hand, a glowing yellow light danced between his fingers. Was he a wizard?

Together, the pair advanced on the women with menace.

9

"LOOKS LIKE THE PROBLEM OF THE LADIES SNOOPING ON OUR AFFAIRS might resolve itself," Duncan noted as the two ghost-hunters skittered back, one woman almost tripping where the sidewalk transitioned from cement to grass.

"If we do nothing, maybe," I said.

"*Should* we do something? A moment ago, you were speaking with longing about evicting them."

"I said I *couldn't* evict them. They're good tenants."

"Who are eager to out any werewolves or other paranormal beings in the area," Duncan said, though he didn't appear surprised when I plucked up my sword.

The men—the *wizards*—stopped by the tripods and other equipment, alternately eyeing it and the ladies.

"*This* is what they used to ruin our business," the bald man with the glowing hand said. Snarling, he grabbed a camera off its tripod, electricity flaring around his grip and crackling in the air.

"Don't touch that!" One of the women halted her retreat. "It was expensive."

A pop came from the camera, smoke wafting from it, and the

guy hurled it into the grass. His long-haired buddy raised his tire iron toward the suitcase of equipment.

"No!" Now, both women surged forward in objection and sprang at the men.

The bald guy grabbed one of them before she could claw at his face. She screamed when his grip tightened around her wrist, white light flashing and magical electricity surging up her arm.

"Hell." Sword in hand, I climbed out of the van and strode toward the group.

The ponytail guy dodged the second woman and smashed his tire iron into the suitcase, annihilating equipment. Furious, she sprang onto his back and tried to snatch the tool from his grip. But he was bigger and stronger by far, and spun, hurling her off him and into the parking lot. She lost her footing as she landed hard on the pavement.

Anger twisting his face, the guy stalked toward her and raised the tire iron, as if he meant to smash *her* next.

"Knock it off," I yelled, raising the blade.

The wizards glanced at me. At first, they looked like they would ignore me, continuing to take out their ire on the women, but they glanced again, then followed up with longer looks that took in me and the sword. Since they had magical blood, they should have been able to sense that both the blade and I were dangerous.

"Knock it off," I repeated, making my voice cold. "This is private property, and you're trespassing, among other crimes."

"These snooping little bitches ruined our business." The one raising the tire iron over the woman's head thrust it toward her chest. "They made up bullshit photos and put them all over social media, and you wouldn't believe how many people *follow* their stupid sites. We haven't gotten any business since the word got out."

At his feet, the woman shook her head but didn't otherwise

deny the accusation. Given my experience with these two, I wouldn't be surprised if they had done something to harm the reputation of the men's business, but I doubted it justified this level of violence. The woman lay crumpled on the ground on her side, an arm up, fear contorting her features. He looked like he meant to kill her.

"Put that down," I said. "You're not beating anyone up—or worse—on the property I manage." I glanced toward the street where the police, at Officer Dubois's request, often parked a patrol car. It wasn't there tonight.

I lifted my chin. That was fine. There wouldn't be witnesses if I turned wolf to scare these guys off—or bite them in the balls.

The bald man on the sidewalk had released the other woman but had his glowing hand up to keep her back. With a defiant snarl at me, he kicked over another of the tripods.

I surged forward. He whirled, lifting a tire iron toward me, but I knocked it aside, as if I were parrying a sword. Just like in Lesson Number 5. Thank you, Yuto.

After deflecting the tire iron, I lunged in and rested the sword tip against his throat.

"Shit." He dropped the tire iron, and his glowing hand extinguished, his magic fading.

Less cowed, the ponytail guy grabbed the woman and hauled her to her feet. "These two owe us thousands of dollars in lost business."

"Take it to court." I turned my glare on him while keeping the blade at the other guy's throat.

"Oh, sure. We're going to the mundane *courts* about our summoning business. We'll explain to the judge about how we call up the dead so people can pay their last respects and make sure their spirits are at rest."

"Your business is *haunted*," one woman said. "And the building it's in is a harbinger of evil."

"It's in a strip mall across from the golf course. There's no *evil* there."

"There are dead souls all over it."

"Because people pay us to *call* them."

"Just go away," I told the men. "Nobody attacks my tenants in their own home."

The man with my sword on his throat spread his arms and didn't look like he would cause more trouble, but the ponytail guy released his captive and tightened his grip on his tire iron while eyeing the remaining paranormal equipment. She stumbled and dropped to one knee again, but he ignored her. And me.

He had to sense my power, but maybe he thought I was bluffing. That I wouldn't stop him from enacting further mayhem?

I growled, feeling the cool air of the night and the magic of the nearly-full moon rising behind the trees.

Ponytail Guy squinted at me, then sprang toward the equipment with the tire iron. Abandoning the bald man, I surged forward to intercept him. He swung the tire iron at one of the cameras, but I batted it aside with the sword.

The air around him buzzed, magic crackling against my skin. It was intense, like it might cause an explosion. I punched him in the face, and the buzz halted.

Behind me, a growl sounded. Without looking, I sensed Duncan back there.

"Oh, shit," the other wizard said.

The one I'd punched also swore. I pointed the sword at him, promising I would do more than flatten his nose if he didn't leave. He glanced from me to the sidewalk behind me. Duncan had shifted into a wolf and stood there, lips rippling as he growled and showed off his fangs.

The men sent glares at the women but backed away, hurrying to their car.

"Stay away from our business," one barked as they drove away.

One of the women surged forward, cursing and grabbing the damaged equipment as she threw wary glances at Duncan.

I offered a hand to help her friend up off the ground. Eyes round, the woman grasped it, looking at me and the sword but also at Duncan. He'd opted for the wolf rather than the bipedfuris, but he was intimidating in either form.

"Thank you for the help," she said to me.

"I *knew* there was a wolf," the other whispered to her. "A *were*wolf."

"Did you see him change?"

"No."

"He's just a wolf," I said firmly. "He helps me keep an eye on the grounds."

Neither looked like they believed that, but they didn't speak their objections out loud.

"He's magnificent," the one gathering their broken equipment whispered.

Duncan raised his chin, looking pleased by the statement.

"You have popcorn grease on your tail," I told him.

His tongue lolled out in the wolf version of a laugh.

"Will you two do me a favor?" I put the sword aside and helped the women pack away their equipment. "And do your ghost monitoring elsewhere? This place is..."

"Reeking with chaotic energy and paranormal signatures?" one suggested.

"My home. And his territory." I pointed at Duncan. Actually, it was *my* territory, but if they hadn't yet figured out I was a werewolf, I wouldn't give that away. "We're not looking to have it featured on social media. We try to keep it a safe place."

"But it's already *on* social media. All kinds of cool stuff has happened here."

Cool stuff? Like thugs burglarizing apartments and being killed in fights in the parking lot?

Her friend gripped her arm and gave a warning head shake as she glanced at Duncan.

"We get it," she said. "We won't ghost hunt here." A mournful look at the equipment suggested that enough of it had been damaged that they would struggle to do so anyway.

I couldn't be sad about that. It was possible I hadn't reacted quite as quickly to defend the bashing of the equipment as I might have if something more important had been under fire.

"Thank you for helping us," she added. "For *protecting* us." She looked at her roommate. "I knew it wouldn't be a mistake moving in here."

They gathered their gear and headed back to their unit.

Still in wolf form, Duncan sat at my side and gazed into the woods. Unable to help myself, I licked my finger and tried to rub the glistening smear of grease off his fur.

He gave me a flat look, then pointed his snout toward the woods again. Was he trying to tell me that Lykos was out there? No, I realized as I sensed the presence of a werewolf. It wasn't the kid but Izzy.

In wolf form? Or her human form? Probably the former. It was hard to imagine the wealthy real estate maven skulking in the woods as a woman.

Duncan's head swiveled back toward the street. A noisy engine idled out there. The Corvette? Maybe we hadn't successfully scared those guys away, and they were plotting their next move.

Arms full of their mangled gear, the women headed to their apartment.

"Lock your door," I called after them.

They glanced warily back and quickened their pace.

Duncan looked toward the woods again. He growled in that direction. Though he hadn't met Izzy, and I hadn't explained much about her or her former pack, the Cascade Crushers, he might have caught her scent on the premises before. A few days back, Izzy had rather pointedly marked a rhododendron in front of my apartment. Presumably in her wolf form, but one couldn't be sure.

Duncan growled toward the street.

"Threats in all directions, huh?" I eyed the sword, wondering if I should have lopped off one of the wizards' ears. But, as brutish as they'd been, I wasn't sure they didn't have a legitimate grievance with my tenants.

Duncan's pointed ears flickered. He was listening to me, but he didn't take his eyes from the street.

"Why don't you make sure those guys head home?" I pointed in the direction of the idling car. "I've fought Izzy before. If she does more than mark the bushes, I can handle her."

Besides, I doubted it would take Duncan long to convince the wizards to leave fully. Ripping the fender off an old car would be a simple matter for a powerful wolf.

Duncan swished his tail and brushed his flank against my hip as he padded away.

"I don't know if that was a bump of agreement or a promise that we'll return to our date in the van soon," I called softly after him.

He looked over his shoulder, tongue lolling out.

"Okay, I look forward to it."

Tail up, he trotted toward the street.

My senses suggested Izzy hadn't moved. Maybe, like Duncan's little clone brother, she would start with spying on me to assess my strengths and weaknesses before she made an attempt on my life.

"As if she didn't get to assess everything when we were rolling around on the floor of that closet," I muttered.

Sword in hand, I headed across the damp grass toward the woods. I would have preferred to go back to my apartment, hide behind Rue's protection potion, and ignore Izzy, but a larger part of me wanted to confront her and end the threat she represented.

At the edge of the lawn, on the trail leading into the woods, I stopped, catching the glint of a pair of eyes at wolf height.

"Do you want to discuss it?" I called. "I sent back Ivan's bracelet. You know that, right?"

A growl emanated from the direction of the eyes. Izzy didn't care about her half-brother's werewolf artifact. She cared that I'd long ago killed Raoul, the werewolf I'd loved who had also been, as I'd only recently learned, her cousin.

"Your brother mentioned reward money," I said though I didn't expect anything and didn't want to see Ivan again. He hadn't been a jerk, but he *had* hit on me. I'd avoided dropping off the bracelet in person since I hadn't wanted to encourage more of that. "I don't suppose you're carrying a little envelope in your jaws."

Izzy growled again.

"I also accept Venmo and Zelle," I offered.

The eyes moved. Izzy padded toward me.

My nerves tingled with the call of the wolf, the temptation to draw upon my magic to change. The sword, its alloy imbued with silver, would have the ability to wound her, but in the dark, at the far edge of the influence of the landscaping lights, I would be more comfortable fighting as a wolf. But, as a wolf, there was the danger that I would lose my rational mind to the savage magic that always lurked, prepared to come to the surface. When that happened, as it had with Raoul all those years ago, I could kill without meaning to. Rewards would be the last thing on Ivan's mind if I slew his sister, and I didn't need any more enemies.

Unaware of my thoughts, Izzy padded closer, her dark fur growing visible as she stepped out of the undergrowth and onto the trail.

The headlights of a car entering the parking lot made me glance in that direction. It wasn't the Corvette—I no longer heard its engine and suspected the drivers had spotted Duncan—but a large brown delivery van. Given the late hour, that was strange, and I was immediately suspicious. Was it bringing another package for Duncan? Something poisoned sent by an enemy?

With another growl, Izzy stopped less than ten feet from me. Her hackles were up, and she looked like she would attack, but she was also eyeing the sword.

"Our last battle didn't go well for you," I said. "If you want to kill me, you should have brought backup."

In the parking lot, the uniformed driver hopped out of the cab of his vehicle. I would have only glanced at him, not wanting to turn away from an enemy, but he carried something that looked more like a weapon than a parcel for delivery. It reminded me of a Civil War Gatling gun.

"What the—"

The driver leaped onto the hood of a car, lifted the big weapon, then started shooting. Instead of cracks that would have signaled bullets firing, a rapid series of *thwump, thwump, thwump* sounded as oblong objects shot out. They glinted, reflecting the outdoor lights as if they were made from glass. They flew all over the grounds, some landing in the parking lot and shattering, and others coming down in the lawn.

"You'd better get out of here." Using the sword, I made a shooing motion toward Izzy, then ran across the grass toward the parking lot.

Taking my own advice would have been wise, but this guy was a threat to me, my territory, and my tenants. My intent, as I ran toward him, was to confront him with the sword and words, but when he saw me and pointed his weapon straight toward me, lupine magic flooded into me.

As I ran, I tore off clothing and tossed aside the sword and my phone, not wanting to lose either in the change.

"Duncan!" I yelled. With the call, I meant to warn him and

hoped he would come help, but it came out as more of a snarl than his name. Also, I no longer sensed him, so I doubted he heard it.

The driver fired his weapon again. One of those glass objects—was it filled with liquid?—sailed straight toward me.

I dove to the side, rolling as I hit the grass. With magic and adrenaline flooding my veins, the wolf came over me, and, when I sprang up, I landed on four paws.

The object he'd fired flew past me and struck a lamppost, shattering. Yes, there was indeed a dark liquid inside. An acrid scent wafted from it as it dribbled down the side of the post.

Broken vials all over the grounds were wafting the scent. It didn't smell like the odor those metal bugs had emitted in the last lair I'd battled in as a wolf, but it reminded me of that. That scent had to represent danger.

The driver was still firing from the hood of a vehicle. I ran toward him, certain all who resided in my territory were in danger, but my instincts warned of a new threat. A dark wolf bowled into me from the side, sending me rolling in the grass again. Izzy.

She'd waited until I was distracted to take advantage. Indignation and fury made me lash out, forgetting the shooter and biting into the wolf attempting to bite and pin *me*. Twisting, I snapped my jaws rapidly, trying to catch her by the throat. My fangs sank into her shoulder, and I managed to shift out from under her, my muscles strong, and my weight greater than hers, at least in this form.

The scent of her blood filled my nostrils, but that acrid odor was there as well, growing ever stronger. Even as the wolf tried to jerk away, biting for me while I ground my jaws and pulverized her shoulder, I grew aware of a haze creeping over the grounds. All those shattered vials were emitting vapors that gathered in a low cloud.

As we thrashed about, I managed to maneuver atop the enemy

wolf. It helped that her movements weren't as fast as I remembered from our previous encounter. More than that, they were sluggish. Only when I lunged for her and my head felt heavy did I realize that my movements were slow too.

The vapor. It *was* similar to what those bugs had emitted. Heavy numbness crept into my limbs, and when the enemy wolf snapped toward my throat, I barely evaded her. But it was as if we both moved underwater, strangely slowed. Even the world around us seemed slow, everything hazy.

A screech came from the parking lot. The parcel van leaving? No, it was still there, though its driver had climbed back into the seat. More human vehicles were entering, a couple of black vans that I had not seen before.

Seemingly oblivious to all the threats, the enemy wolf attacked me again. When her snapping jaws came toward my face, I deflected her snout with mine, gouging her with my own fangs. She stumbled and lurched sideways to catch her balance. No doubt her limbs were as numb as mine. I could have taken advantage, perhaps finishing her off, but I realized what she didn't: we were in trouble from an outside threat. We had to get away from that haze.

I tried to bark a warning at her, though maybe I shouldn't have cared if a proven enemy died, then turned and ran toward my den. With my movements painfully slow, I reached the first building. My den lay deeper in the complex, so I hurried around the corner but not before looking back. Humans in black clothing and wearing strange coverings over their faces were running onto the lawn. The haze made it hard to tell who they were or if I'd seen them before. I expected them to run after me, but they spotted the other wolf and went to her instead.

She'd fallen upon the grass, injured and maybe unconscious after breathing too much of the vapor. When they surrounded her, she didn't stir.

I paused, debating what I could do. Even though she'd declared herself an enemy, she was a werewolf, the same as I. And those humans would do... *What* would they do to her? What did they want?

With my brain as numb as my limbs, I couldn't imagine. Were they enemies of mine or of Duncan's? I had no idea but doubted they had come for Izzy. Did they know they were surrounding the wrong wolf?

They knelt, picked her up, and returned to the parking lot. I almost howled a protest, but if they believed they had me, it would be unwise to alert them otherwise. For all I knew, they would kill Izzy once they had her in their vehicle.

I turned, intending to continue into my den, but a flask of liquid in front of the door made me pause. Tendrils of blue vapor wafted from it. Something else placed by an enemy?

Confused, I backed away. Limbs heavy, I navigated toward another place in the complex that was familiar. The office where, when in my human form, I worked. Would it be locked? No. Using my jaws, I turned the knob to open the door.

Two humans lay on the floor inside, their presence startling me. But I recognized them as allies who'd fought with me before. The druid and my niece.

But like the enemy wolf, they lay unmoving. The haze had infiltrated the workplace, and they'd lost consciousness. Or worse.

I lay on the floor, my muscles too weak to support me any longer, and rested my head between my paws, fearing I was about to succumb to the same malady. Sleep. Or death.

10

As I lay on the floor, too weak to check on my niece or my druid ally, the wolf magic faded. Nothing changed as I shifted back into my human form, except that my thinking grew sharper, more human and rational. The air in the leasing office remained cloudy and foul-scented, almost as much as outside.

I needed to escape the grounds, to breathe in untainted air, to get the toxin out of my system. But I struggled to even push myself into a sitting position and cross the office to check on Bolin and Jasmine. By the blessing of the moon, they had better not be dead.

Car doors slammed in the parking lot, and I remembered what I'd seen as a wolf. Men in gas masks carrying Izzy away.

"Gas mask," I rasped, then almost laughed and crawled to the desk and opened the bottom drawer.

Half-serious, half-jokingly, I'd bought an old military-grade gas mask to wear while cleaning some of the more noxious vacated apartments. Even though cat urine and the other unsavory odors tenants left weren't truly toxic, I kept the mask in working order. It even had a newer activated-carbon filter.

It was probably too late, but I dragged it over my head and

tightened the straps. That took all my energy, and I flopped onto my back. Tears leaked from my irritated eyes. Too bad I didn't also have an air purifier in the office. Whatever vapors had flowed from those vials had to be potent to have spread so far in the open air and to have infiltrated rooms through closed doors and windows.

No, not potent. *Magical.*

Had some colleague of Rue's given my enemies potions? No, I realized numbly. Abrams could make potions himself. That was the whole business that he and Radomir had started.

Staring up at the ceiling and inhaling the air filtered by the mask, I wondered if those men had found Duncan. Was he the wolf who they'd come for? Who *Abrams* had come for? I had irritated a lot of people of late, including Izzy and all those motorcycle thugs, but I couldn't imagine any of them attacking me with magical concoctions. This had to have been orchestrated by Abrams.

My mind slowly cleared as I breathed the filtered air. When I flexed my fingers, they were still numb but not as much as before. Even so, it took me a long moment to roll to my hands and knees so I could crawl over to check on Bolin and Jasmine. My stomach knotted with the worry that they would be dead. If Abrams killed my friends—killed *anyone* in my territory—I would find him and tear his throat out.

Bolin and Jasmine were both alive, but their heartbeats were sluggish, so my worry didn't dissipate.

When I managed to rise to my feet, naked except for the mask, I opened the door warily. Outside, the complex lay utterly still, nobody coming or going in the parking lot. The vans that had rolled in were gone. I didn't sense Izzy, and I feared they'd taken her away. Or maybe, when they'd realized she wasn't me, they might have killed her.

At least the haze seemed a little lighter, a faint breeze whispering through and stirring it. The rumble of late-night freeway traffic came from the other side of the woods, promising the rest of the city was unaffected. The haze had probably settled only over Sylvan Serenity.

"Of course. I—" I broke off, sensing someone's approach. "Duncan?" I called.

Relief swept through me when he answered.

"I'm here," he called, his voice thick and raspy. "I'm glad you're alive."

He walked between two trees and into view, though he paused when he spotted me.

After spending time as a wolf, he was as naked as I. *More* naked since I wore the mask, though the Medallion of Memory and Power did hang around his neck, the artifact emanating magic as it glowed faintly. Had it helped him remain conscious when he'd inhaled the vapors?

Blood ran down his arm, suggested he'd also had a run-in with the invaders.

"That's an interesting new fashion choice that you're making." Duncan nodded to my mask. "Was it also acquired from your Goodwill store? And experienced?"

"The army-surplus store, but I believe it *was* experienced, yes."

"The air is loathsome out here, so I don't blame you for wearing it. I think this is the only reason I haven't passed out." He ticked the wolf head on the medallion. "I could feel its magic protecting me."

"Guess I should be wearing my mom's."

"Absolutely. And isn't it... Well, it seemed like she was giving it to you to be yours. To keep and wear."

I hesitated. I *had* gotten that vibe from Mom, but wearing it before she was gone... didn't seem right. Didn't it still belong to her? Until the end?

Not wanting to explain my feelings, I only said, "I think she mostly wants me to wear it up to the cave so it can magically coerce us to have sex."

"If you dress like that and take me to a cave, I won't be able to help myself, whether there's outside influence or not." Duncan waved at my naked form.

"Oh, is the mask turning you on?"

"All of you turns me on." His gaze shifted past me—Bolin had stirred slightly—and his expression grew more sober. "Did everyone else get knocked out?"

"Maybe. Being inside didn't seem to help people. And... they got Izzy."

"Got her?"

"Picked her up, put her in their van, and drove off."

Duncan scratched his jaw. "That's unexpected. As far as I could tell, they were after *me*. They spotted me in the street and tried to snag me, but I wasn't that close when their hired delivery driver was shooting those vials all over the place, so I was able to get away."

"Do you have any idea who they were?"

His shoulders slumped. "I can't know for sure, but since they were using magical alchemical substances..."

"Abrams?"

Duncan nodded. "I assume so. Unless Rue has decided to ply our enemies with knock-out potions."

"I certainly hope not. I gave her *two* ten-percent discounts, and I didn't charge her for the first two months of rent."

"You're a most kind property manager. She should feel beholden to you." Duncan gazed toward the woods.

Another werewolf had arrived. Lykos.

In his furry form, he padded along the edge of the property, his dark silhouette just visible in the night and the lingering haze. He looked over at us but didn't approach, instead turning deeper into the woods.

Had he come to spy? Or... to take advantage and kill Duncan if he'd been knocked out? What if Lykos, who'd been trying to set traps for Duncan, had been the mastermind behind this?

I looked frankly at him. "You're going to have to confront Abrams, you know."

"I do know that, yes."

"Before his little assassin gets old enough and smart enough to get the best of you."

Duncan sighed and didn't deny it.

11

A PRE-DAWN TEXT FROM LORENZO RELAYED A QUESTION FROM MY mother.

Have you visited the cave yet?

No, I hadn't, and, after the strange night before, including Izzy's kidnapping, it wasn't at the top of my to-do list. Nonetheless, I texted back that I would talk Duncan into driving back up there with me. Even though I suspected Mom's motives for wanting us both in that cave while wearing the medallions... one couldn't deny the wishes of a dying woman.

Around breakfast time, I showed up at Duncan's van with to-go cups of espresso, a basket of biscuits slathered with butter and peanut butter, hot bacon wrapped in paper towels, and egg sandwiches I'd made using toasted English muffins. As I'd seen before, he had an appetite that rivaled that of a growing teenage boy. Thanks to my heritage, I wasn't the lightest of eaters either.

"You're a wonderful woman, Luna." Not surprisingly, Duncan went first for the bacon—werewolves *did* have carnivorous streaks after all.

"I am wonderful, but this is also a bribe."

He surveyed the spread I'd laid out on the tiny table in his camper van. "One that doesn't involve any chocolate?"

I pulled out a bar of dark chocolate with bits of reishi mushrooms and coconut flakes.

"Ah, that's the kind of bribe I expect. But... mushrooms?" Duncan raised his eyebrows.

"I bought a stack of these for my mom. Just in case." I pointed to a few words on the label that toted the health benefits of cacao and reishi mushrooms and suggested cancer-fighting properties. "They're sufficiently rich and sweet and don't taste medicinal. Or, er, fungal. I taste-tested them."

"How many squares? A sufficient amount to know for certain?"

"Three bars. Maybe four. It's been a hectic week."

"I won't deny that." Duncan looked out the windshield toward the lawn, though all sign of the strange vapors had disappeared.

Later, I would take my hand broom and pan outside to sweep up shards of broken glass from the vials. Most of them hadn't landed near the walkways, so I wasn't too worried about tenants stepping on them. I wanted to get my mother's request out of the way first.

"What's the bribe for?" Duncan asked around a bite of a sandwich. "Oh, there's *more* bacon draped over the eggs. Fabulous." His eyes rolled back in his head.

Even though I'd never considered myself a talented chef, I had a few staples in my arsenal that were, in my opinion, delicious. It was always nice to see someone else enjoy my food.

"I'd like you to come up to the cave with me. And with this." I lifted the chain around my neck to draw the medallion out from under my shirt. "And with *that*." I pointed to the matching male medallion that he wore.

"Ah. Because you spent the night aching with need and want to seduce me there?"

"Because my *mom* wants me to seduce you there." I grimaced.

"Don't worry. I'm not planning on that. But I... did pack condoms, just in case."

Duncan arched his eyebrows.

"I'm not on birth control anymore," I explained, though I didn't know if that was his silent inquiry. "After my ex-husband left, and with me, uhm, not that interested in seeking out companionship, I went off it."

"Makes sense. You didn't know a new virile stud would come into your life."

"Yeah, and then there's you too." I smirked at him.

"Ha ha. Unless you've a thing for Abrams, I'm not aware of any other virile studs in your life."

"He is sexy in his medical scrubs."

"And a mere seventy years old."

"With all those potions he knows how to make, he could have all kinds of enhancements that belie his age."

"I suppose that's true. I'd rather not know about such details. Regardless, I'll certainly accompany you to the cave. I haven't yet figured out how to deal with the Abrams problem—mostly because I don't know where he is. After the chaos last night, I attempted to track Lykos back to him, but he must have guessed I would do that. Lykos walked through water several times to hide his trail, and I lost him out on Ballinger Way. He might have gotten on a bus."

"The preferred method of transportation for eight-year-old werewolves."

"He's informed me that he's almost nine and is a force to be reckoned with."

"Thus making him more of a public transportation fan?"

"Well, I don't know if Abrams has a vehicle. We destroyed Radomir's SUV, and he was presumably the moneyed half of that partnership." Duncan finished his sandwich, licked his fingers a few times, and eyed the remaining bacon.

"Go ahead. I had a few pieces before coming out."

Besides, if he'd been chasing the kid all over town last night, he would be hungry.

"You're a delightful woman." Duncan popped a piece in his mouth, then also took one of the biscuits. "Still warm. Excellent. Even werewolves enjoy peanut butter."

"Who doesn't?" I opened the chocolate bar and laid a couple of pieces on the table for his dessert.

"Nothing like washing a meal down with cancer-fighting properties." He placed a square onto his tongue to melt.

"It's always a good idea. Like brushing your teeth."

"No doubt." Despite his teasing, Duncan took the rest of the chocolate bar with him to the driver's seat. "I've half-expected one of those black vans to return and toss the female werewolf out onto the lawn."

"Izzy," I corrected.

"Yes. By now, Abrams must know that his henchmen got the wrong wolf."

"I hope he's not planning to run science experiments on her." I frowned as Duncan drove us out of the parking lot. "Even if I don't like her, she doesn't deserve that."

"What we read in Abrams's journal suggested he had moved on from believing werewolf blood would be useful for him, and he was focusing on the magical artifacts." Duncan looked at me. "Are you bringing the case as well?"

"I have it." I patted my purse where it lay nestled in a towel inside. "I did question whether I should or not. What do you think?"

"Depends on if you believe it's safer with you or under the floor in your apartment."

"It might be safer there, but I was thinking more about how the medallions, and every other magical artifact in the area, get extra excited when the lid is open. We might learn more if that happens, but I'm also not sure I *want* the medallions to be more excited and potent than usual when we're in the cave." I looked somberly at him. "As much as I'd enjoy getting horizontal with you, I'd rather it not be because their magic is coercing us to do so."

"If the medallions had gotten their way in your mother's cabin, I believe we would have ended up *vertical*. My thoughts, or urges, I suppose, believed the log wall looked like a fine place to..." He glanced at me, turning his palm apologetically upward. And were his cheeks a touch pink?

"Had the medallions gotten their way, I wouldn't have minded." I doubted I would have minded the wall—or anywhere else—with Duncan, magic regardless, but... "I'd just like things to be our idea if they're going to go in that direction. In *any* direction."

"I agree that free will is appealing. Especially given recent circumstances when I haven't always had it." Duncan waved toward his forehead, though the medallion, after it decided he was worthy of wearing it, had healed him of that lifelong scar.

"Yes. And I don't want my pack's medallions, or my *mother's* plans, taking that from you. From either of us."

"But we're going to the cave anyway." Duncan smirked at me, not looking like he minded that much.

"To fulfill my mother's... request." I didn't make that *dying request,* but the term came to mind, a fresh lump forming in my throat. "Besides, it's possible her vision was about more than us having sex. She mentioned something that could help our people. Our people who are currently being schemed against by resort developers."

"Not as fearsome of foes as potion-enhanced thugs with silver bullets." As he finished off the chocolate bar, Duncan navigated onto the freeway and picked up speed.

"No, but who knows what complicated and obscure legal methods they might know about to try to take the family land. I'm sure Mom and the pack would prefer that all humans forget that their territory exists."

"For the sake of your family, I'll hope that bringing the two medallions together in that cave *can* suggest some solutions." Duncan gazed pensively at me before brake lights on a car ahead made him focus on traffic. "If the medallions only have a singular focus, I hope... Well, I give you permission ahead of time to do whatever you need to do in order to wrap my package."

For a confused moment, I thought of the delivery-truck driver from the night before. No, not *that* kind of package.

"I'm a little concerned," he continued, "that the magical compulsion will make... Erm, let's just say that package wrapping wasn't on my mind when we were almost, ah, overcome with ardor in your mother's cabin."

"Gotcha. Yeah, it wasn't on my mind either."

"It's hard to be a responsible adult when magic wants to turn you into a sex fiend."

"I haven't noticed that werewolf magic is ever that concerned about responsibility." I lifted my purse, tapping the side by the case again. "As long as there are no nefarious types about, we'll leave this in the van when we visit the cave. We could even leave it with my mother. She didn't mention that she thought *it* should visit with us. The medallions were her only concern."

"Yes, the true heirlooms that belong to your pack."

I wondered if we would ever find out where the case, and the mushroom-shaped artifact inside, belonged. More than once, it had crossed my mind to give them to Bolin since the artifacts had been made by druids, and he and his father were the only druidic types I knew.

"For the record, if something were to happen..." Duncan glanced at me. "I wouldn't want anything to occur against *your* wishes, but as I've made your fine acquaintance and re-contemplated fatherhood of late, I've found the notion of a child less unappealing."

For some reason, my cheeks warmed. Maybe because he'd briefly looked at my chest when he'd remarked on my fine acquaintance. Or maybe just because we were discussing things that could only result once we had—*finally* had—a physical relationship.

"That's a little surprising," I said, "given that the kid you're trying to practice fatherhood on is plotting your demise."

"Yes, but he accepted the Mickey Mouse canister while doing so."

"You're winning him over."

"I'd like to think so. Anyway—" Duncan waved a vague hand, "—I certainly wouldn't want to push you into something you're not interested in, but just know that if you were ever to *become* interested... Well, I suppose it's premature to discuss such things. We haven't even... not that I don't *want* to..." He waved his hand again, his eyes focused on the road.

"Duncan, are you flustered?"

"Certainly not. I'm far too mature and self-assured to feel such an emotion."

I gazed over at him.

He pinched his thumb and forefinger together in the air. "Perhaps, due to the influence of the medallion, I'm the tiniest bit... disconcerted."

"My mom complicates it all too." If not for her, the thought of having more children wouldn't be occupying any nooks of my mind.

"She does seem to be a complicated—or maybe complicating —woman."

"She's from another era," I said. "And devoted to the safety and continuation of the pack. Never mind that she has full-blooded werewolf grandchildren already, thanks to my half-siblings. They just weren't born of *your* loins."

"Terribly distressing for them, I'm certain."

"Mom is into your old-world blood."

"Don't remind me. When I took off my clothes to change into the bipedfuris in her room, she studied me a lot like Abrams always did."

"Like a scientist, huh?"

"I much prefer the way *you* study me."

"Like a randy housewife ogling a pool boy?"

"Well, like a randy property manager longing for a night of wild abandon after dealing with the demands of needy tenants."

"That's less of a simile and more right on point."

"I figured." Duncan smiled at me before taking the exit for Monroe.

"Why don't we do our best to tamp down our randy thoughts today?" I suggested, glancing at his medallion. "And then, after we deal with Abrams and have another date, sans influential magical artifacts, we can let ourselves fully enjoy each other's company?" We could have done that the night before if not for ghost hunters in the parking lot and Abrams's kidnapping attempt.

No, not an attempt. He'd *succeeded* in kidnapping a wolf. Just not the right wolf. I also felt obligated to find Izzy before letting myself have another date.

"Must we deal with him first?" Duncan asked. "He's a pest. It could take days or *weeks* before I'm able to find him and convince him to leave us alone."

"If you have a reward waiting for you, then there will be more incentive for you to finish that task quickly."

"A reward, you say? More mushroom chocolate?"

When he glanced over, I unbuttoned a couple of buttons and let my finger trace the outline of my breast.

"Oh yes, that would be a most appealing reward," he murmured.

"Even better than a rusty Mickey Mouse tin?"

"Oh my. I might trade *both* tins for it. For you." Duncan managed to give me a sultry look while navigating around the first of the potholes on the way up to Mom's cabin.

"Goodness. You know how to make a woman feel sexy and desirable."

He started to reply, but something up the road drew his attention. I followed his gaze, wondering if the pack might be chasing off more real estate agents. Still a ways from Mom's driveway, we were approaching the frog pond. Surprisingly, numerous trucks and SUVs were parked in a queue in front of it, taking up half of the narrow road.

Duncan was forced to slow down.

I scratched my jaw as I peered through the windows and looked at the sides of the vehicles for signs. One Toyota looked familiar, but I couldn't place it. Maybe a similar one belonged to one of my tenants. It was a common make of car.

Of all the vehicles, only one had writing on the door, and it wasn't the vehicle of the real estate agent that the pack had chased off. The sign read *Sierra Surveying*.

"We're not near the property with the for-sale sign." I pointed farther up the road, remembering that was around a bend and on the opposite side from the frog pond and Mom's cabin.

They had to be surveying another parcel, but why would so many people be here for that?

"I don't sense anyone magical about or see anyone in the cars." Duncan stopped even with a green truck, the foremost vehicle in the queue.

"Maybe someone has listed another property for sale—without informing the owner—and these people are here to check it out." I thought of the company Jasmine's dad had dug up, the outfit planning to put a resort in nearby. They had to be responsible for this. Who else would be trying to buy up land here?

"Do you want to park and try to find the owners of these cars?" Duncan tapped his nose. "This many ought to be easy to track down, even without changing into a wolf."

I started to shake my head, figuring we could tell Mom and Lorenzo, and they could send the pack to scare off these guys. But my gaze went back to that Toyota. With a start, I realized why it looked familiar. The night before, Chad had driven it out of the parking lot at Sylvan Serenity.

It was probably a coincidence. There were tons of brown Toyotas. And why the heck would Chad be up here? He didn't even know where my family lived.

Still...

"Yeah," I answered. "Park, please."

As soon as Duncan did, I hopped out and walked to the Toyota. I hadn't paid any attention to the license plate the night before, so I couldn't say if they matched, but...

"I think this is a rental car," I stated.

Duncan had paused to peer into the driver-side window of the surveyor's car, but he joined me. The Toyota must not have made an impression on him because he didn't remark on the coincidence. Of course, he'd been the bipedfuris, and cars didn't stand out as important to wolves.

His nostrils twitched, however, and his head came up. He growled, managing to sound feral and deadly even in his human form, and his eyes slitted with displeasure. "I smell your exhusband's scent."

I nodded. "Let's track these people down and see what they're up to."

Duncan growled again.

12

BEFORE WE HEADED INTO THE WOODS TO SEARCH FOR CHAD AND THE mob of people surveying the land and who knew what else, I grabbed my purse. In case one or more of the drivers returned before we found the rest, I didn't want anyone poking into the van and finding the magical case. Maybe I should have left it in my apartment, but Abrams might have had people poking around there.

"So much poking," I muttered.

Duncan looked at me. He hadn't changed into a wolf or biped-furis, but he led the way, striding into the trees with confidence. Since his senses were keener than mine, he probably *could* follow a trail by scent even in his human form.

"Just musing that it's hard to know where to stash the case for safekeeping," I said.

"Ah. It'll be safe with us."

"You're not afraid of a pack of real estate developers?"

"Not in the least."

My stomach, on the other hand, writhed with nerves, though that had to do with Chad's presence in the area, not real estate developers. For someone whom I'd never wanted to see again, he was popping up a lot this week.

Another thought occurred to me. "Can you tell if my son is with them?"

"I've only met one of your sons. Austin. He's not here."

"No, I know. You probably didn't notice last night, but as Chad was driving off, I saw Cameron in the passenger seat of the car." I waved back toward the Toyota, but we'd traveled far enough through the densely packed trees that the vehicles were no longer visible. "He's twenty with straight brown hair down to his jaw and an athletic build. Leans toward snark, if you can imagine that from one of my kids."

"Strangely, I can. Is he more supportive of his father than of you?"

Was he asking if Cameron would be a problem if they were together?

"I'm not sure. He hasn't talked to me much since he moved out, but I don't know how close he is with Chad." I dearly wanted for Cameron not to be close to his father *at all*, but their showing up here together... didn't bode well for that. A dense tangle of emotions centered around distress joined my nerves in upsetting me.

"A son should always speak with his mother," Duncan said. "That's a rule, isn't it?"

I smiled sadly. "It should be."

I thought of my own mother, who, because of the subject she kept bringing up, I'd been hesitant to be around. I needed to visit her again too. Who knew how much time she had left?

"Not enough," I murmured.

Duncan, nose in the air and leading the way between ferns, over moss-blanketed logs, and around the pond, didn't look back at the words. I crept after him, my shoes squishing in water-filled muddy footprints on the ground. Even without a wolf's keen senses, following these men wouldn't have been difficult.

I was surprised how far from the road we traveled before we heard voices. Still in the lead, Duncan slowed down and stopped behind a thick cedar, resting his hand on its rough bark. We'd come up a rise that overlooked a gully.

The same one that ran some distance behind my mother's cabin and led to the magical cave? Yes, a familiar stream gurgled roughly down the middle of the depression, ferns dense on either side of the waterway.

Was it possible these men knew about the cave? Was *it* the reason they wanted the land? Maybe their motivations had nothing to do with resorts and hot springs. But, unless some of them had the blood of paranormal beings, would they sense anything special about that cave?

Duncan raised a finger, directing my gaze to a draw perpendicular to the stream. It had to be close to a mile from the cave, but the voices came from back in that direction. Most were male, but at least one woman spoke intermittently. From our perch, I couldn't make out any of their words. I didn't think I heard Chad among the speakers but couldn't be certain.

After holding a finger to his lips, Duncan indicated that he would move closer. Curious about everything, I crept after him.

We chose our route carefully, not wanting to step on branches or trip and make noise. Once we crossed the stream and advanced into the draw, the gurgling of the waterway faded, making it easier to hear the speakers.

"...not that impressive," a woman was saying.

"What did you expect?" a man asked. "The Hollywood version of an Old West mine shaft?"

"Well, sort of."

A third speaker said, "We can spruce these up. Add some wooden supports and make them look more like what people would expect. And we can bring in old rusty sluicing equipment from our resort in Alaska. We can give people the opportunity to pan for gold out here in the stream."

"Come and get a massage, facial, and seaweed wrap, and then pan for gold?" the woman asked.

"Sure. Package deal. People eat that stuff up. And don't forget the hot springs. You saw the tests on the water, right? It has all sorts of minerals that are good for the body. There were even traces of gold in some of the samples. Who wouldn't want to soak in *gold*?"

"Does that have health benefits?"

"Our brochures will promise it does."

Duncan looked at me. I shrugged. Maybe these people *were* here because of the mines and hot springs, and it had nothing to do with the magical cave.

"The legends of werewolves in the area should add to its appeal too," a new speaker said.

I froze. That was Chad.

"We're not going to put that in the brochure, but we'll have some seemingly unaffiliated social-media accounts mention it. People eat *that* stuff up too. If you find any old werewolf relics, like you said you could, we can put them in glass cases in the lodge."

"Decorations for a resort," Chad said. "The ideal use for price-less magical artifacts."

The guy he was speaking to snorted. "If you can prove there's anything out here that's *magical*, we can talk about what uses it might have. I'm just building the resort. Assuming we can get the werewolf infestation out of the area."

"Two weeks ago, you didn't believe werewolves existed," the woman said.

"That was before Tommy got chased out of the area by a pack of them wrenching pieces off his truck."

"So he claims."

"I *saw* the tooth marks in the frame. And the missing fender. He had some footage he took with his phone out the back window as he was ripping out of there. Biggest fucking wolves you've ever seen."

"The biggest wolves are less interested in fucking than you'd think," Chad said.

My cheeks heated at the suggestion that he meant me.

"Just figure out how to get the land from them. I don't care if there are werewolves in the area—like I said, that should add mystique and draw in clientele who wouldn't come for seaweed wraps and gold panning—but we need to legally own the land before we can break ground."

"Isn't the parcel you got enough?" Chad asked. "There are hot springs and mines right here."

"I think we're on the woman's land at this point."

The woman's? Mom's? It had to be.

"We've picked up a couple of smaller parcels," another speaker said, "but this stream and all the way up that gully are hers. Another chunk belongs to what looks like a sibling. That whole family has been squatting out here for generations."

"It's not squatting when they're the rightful owners."

"*Normal* families sell land when civilization grows out to it and the property increases a ton in value."

The woman laughed shortly. "You're not offering what the value is."

"No, this wouldn't pencil out if we had to pay a fortune for each acre. We need a deal." Voice grim and determined, the male speaker added, "And we're going to get a deal."

The hell they were. I clenched my jaw.

"Someone might need to scare these blokes into changing their plans," Duncan murmured.

"Are you offering to go furry and toss a few of them around?" Maybe I shouldn't have found the idea appealing. Other than scheming, the developers hadn't, as far as I knew, done anything terribly evil. Not like Radomir, who'd repeatedly sent men with rifles loaded with silver bullets after my mom and the family.

"I'd be happy to go furry. I—" A twig snapped, and Duncan looked in the direction of the speakers.

Movement stirred branches, and we eased off the trail the group had trampled on their way to the mine shaft. Foliage rustled, and people muttered, heading in this direction. We moved farther off the trail, ducking behind evergreen trees and bushes.

No fewer than ten men and a couple of women passed by, some pausing to take photos with their phones. The gurgling stream meandering through trees and around mossy boulders *was* picturesque, but I gritted my teeth at the thought of it ending up on a brochure for a resort built by sketchy means.

Chad wasn't with the group. Had he stayed behind to look for werewolf *relics*? I doubted he wanted to soak in a muddy hole, no matter how appealing the mineral content of the water.

Duncan pointed after the group and arched his eyebrows. Asking if he should do something to scare them?

I bit my lip, debating. I also wondered if Cameron was with Chad. By now, Cameron had heard all about my werewolf heritage, but the idea of changing and doing something savage in front of him made me wince. It had been one thing when I'd been saving Austin from kidnappers. But this would be... bullying, essentially. Arguably for a good cause, and *Duncan* was volunteering to handle it, but still. I wanted to be noble and a good mom for my son, damn it.

"Let me talk to Chad first," I whispered, assuming he was still back there.

"Do you want me to come with you?"

"And throw him over a car again?"

"It would take quite a throw to do that from here, but I'm game to try."

"That's all right. I can handle him if he gets violent." I grimaced. "Or handsy."

Duncan's eyes closed to slits. "I fully acknowledge that you can handle him, but if he does either of those things, I won't be able to keep myself from intervening."

Since my own savage instincts could take over my rational mind when the werewolf magic came upon me, I neither doubted him nor would I blame him if that happened. I understood all too well. But I also didn't want to put Chad in a position where Duncan might kill him. He was a sleaze, and I didn't want him in my life, but I didn't hate him enough to want him dead. And I definitely didn't want him to be killed in front of our son. Nor did I want Cameron to be in any danger. The thought that he might be, if Duncan lost himself and turned savage, sent an icy chill down my spine.

"Maybe you should keep an eye on those guys then." I pointed in the direction the rest of the group was disappearing. "They might be less excited about their resort plans if their fenders were all ripped off."

Duncan hesitated but then nodded. "All right."

He stepped back enough to bow toward me, then headed across the stream and leaped lightly over it without making a sound.

A part of me wanted to call him back, second-guessing my decision to confront Chad on my own, but for all the reasons I'd just been thinking about I didn't. Instead, I crept in the direction his voice had come from.

The first person to come into view was Cameron, not Chad. With a fur-lined parka on, he sat perched on a boulder and tapping at his phone. As I well knew, there wasn't much reception out here, but maybe he was playing a game that didn't require it. I peered about, expecting Chad nearby, but didn't see him. I did see a hole in the rocky side of the draw, branches dangling down and half obscuring it.

The old mine shaft that had interested the group?

There were also a couple of pools of water between boulders, steam wafting from them. They didn't look as muddy and unappealing as Jasmine had implied, but they wouldn't have made me promptly think *resort* if I'd stumbled across them while on a hike. It hardly seemed worth dealing with werewolves over, but I supposed that was why the developers were trying to buy up all the land, in the hope that the werewolves would move away without a confrontation.

I considered stopping to speak with Cameron, but he'd been in Seattle for however long and hadn't reached out to me. I also worried about what he thought after seeing me deck Chad the night before. And he'd seen Duncan hurl Chad over a car. He might not want anything to do with me ever again.

Trying not to feel like a coward, I skirted Cameron. Leaving him to his game, I continued up the draw. Chad wouldn't have wandered that far, would he? Unless... Could he know about the cave and have gone in that direction?

No, a rustling sounded up ahead. I crept closer until I spotted Chad's back between the trees. My senses picked up on something magical. Chad was hunched over whatever it was.

I moved forward and to the side, debating whether to call out or not. I wanted to confront him about scheming with the real estate developers, but I didn't know what I would say. Was he even doing anything illegal? Besides trespassing?

The arm holding the magical device was in a sling, making me feel guilty that he'd been hurt the night before. At least, if he was using it somewhat, the bone shouldn't be broken. He might only have sprained his wrist.

Soft beeping came from Chad's device. I blinked. It reminded me of Duncan's magic detector, and when I stepped to the side enough so that I could see it, it *looked* a lot like it too, a box-shaped device with a couple of divining-rod-like antennae sticking out of it. They quivered slightly to accompany the beeping.

"Huh." Chad bent forward and plucked up a mushroom. "You *can't* be what it's excited about."

To my human eyes, the mushroom didn't glow, but it might have if I'd been in my wolf form. Unusual purple speckles on its blue cap reminded me of one of the specimens at Radomir's mushroom farm.

"I'm looking for *werewolf* artifacts," Chad told the machine and tossed the mushroom into the bushes.

"Why do you obsessively seek them out?" I asked, stepping forward. "I've never understood that."

13

CHAD DROPPED THE MAGIC DETECTOR AS HE SPUN TOWARD ME, utter shock on his face.

That surprised me. Had he not realized the werewolves up here were my family and considered that he might run into me?

"What are you doing here, Luna?" Chad glanced around, as if seeking the rest of his group and hoping for backup in dealing with me. Or was it more that he worried that Duncan might be in the area?

Good guess...

"My family owns this territory," I said, though I had no idea who this parcel belonged to. It had sounded like it might be part of Mom's property. If so, she had a lot more land than I'd realized. "The question, I believe, is what are *you* doing here?"

"Like I told you, I'm working with a real estate developer who called me in because of concerns about *werewolves*." Chad raised his eyebrows, then looked in the direction of my mother's cabin, though we were a mile away from it and couldn't see anything but trees.

"The werewolves own this land. Your developer doesn't have any right to be here."

"He said he's wrapping up a deal to get it."

"Uh-huh. He's a bigger schemer than you are. He's *not* getting this land."

In the mud at Chad's feet, the magic detector started beeping. It shifted of its own accord, and its antennae pointed at me. No, at my *purse*.

"What do you have in there?" Chad asked.

"Nothing that belongs to you."

His eyes narrowed with suspicion. "Are you sure it's not the wolf case that I legitimately bought and stored in our apartment and that you have presumed to keep? Even though it's not yours?"

I didn't want to admit that the exact scenario he'd described had happened and that he was right. The case wasn't mine. But it *wanted* to be here, or so it had shared with me in a vision. Of course, that might have been a delusion... a hallucination.

"It's probably beeping at this." To avoid answering his accusation, I pulled the wolf-head medallion out from under my shirt. "It's a family heirloom that belonged—*belongs*—to my mother."

She wasn't gone yet, and I refused to talk about her in past tense.

As if to validate the statement, the magic detector beeped happily, and its antennae wavered between pointing at the medallion and at my purse.

Chad's gaze locked on the medallion. "What can it do?"

Good question.

"When I've touched it, it's glowed brightly."

The male version had not only healed Duncan but removed a powerful curse, but I didn't mention that.

"It must do more than *that*," Chad said. "Leave it to you to not bother studying it."

I bristled. "It's my mother's, not mine. I didn't know it existed until recently."

A far-off yell sounded, barely reaching my ears. Right after, glass shattered, the sharp sound carrying more clearly. Duncan had to be responsible, doing as I'd asked and scaring the developers.

"My magic detector thinks it's powerful." Chad, his hearing not as keen as that of a werewolf, might not have caught the commotion in the distance. He picked up the device and looked at whatever reading it displayed on the screen. "And it thinks you have something else."

Eyeing my purse again, Chad took a step toward me.

My skin prickled, adrenaline and magic flowing through my veins, my instincts promising the wolf was available if I needed to defend myself.

"Don't come any closer." As I held up a warning hand to stop Chad, I took a deep breath to tamp down the magic. I had to keep my cool. I didn't want to change and risk losing it and hurting him —or worse. Especially not with Cameron nearby.

I glanced over my shoulder, worried my son might have heard us and come closer. I didn't see him, but if I changed and fought with Chad, Cameron was close enough to hear that.

Chad stopped, but he also glared in indignation. "You stole that case from me. And you divorced me. You don't have any right to tell me what to do."

"You *cheated* on me. Many times over the years. And you stole the kids' college fund. You *deserved* to be divorced."

Chad's fingers clenched around the magic detector. "That has nothing to do with you stealing that case from me."

"The case you hid from me. Like everything else about your conniving life."

Heat flushed my face—my entire body. If I wasn't careful, I would lose the battle to keep the wolf—and my temper—from taking over. But more than twenty years of history with him—painful history—made it hard. And the fact that he was up here, working with the people who wanted to drive my family off their land? I longed to punch him all over again.

"Like you never hid any secrets." Chad looked past my shoulder and opened his mouth, as if he was on the verge of calling out to someone.

Cameron? Did he think our son would help him against me?

"Don't tell me you're afraid to deal with me on your own," I hurried to say, not wanting Cameron brought into this, not wanting him to witness any of it.

"I'm *injured*. Your feral boyfriend threw me over a car."

"You're lucky he didn't kill you. You'd better leave Seattle before something worse than a sprained wrist happens to you."

"Screw you, Luna. You don't get to tell me what to do anymore." Chad glanced at my purse again, then also at the medallion. Avarice and calculation gleamed in his eyes. "Ryder, Baxter!" he called. "I found some wolf relics for your boss."

I blinked in surprise. I'd expected him to call Cameron, not other allies.

Branches snapped on a hill to one side of the draw, and two men with rifles charged into view. I cursed. Had they been there the whole time? They didn't have paranormal blood, or I would have sensed them. I didn't detect magical bullets in their rifles, but that didn't mean their weapons couldn't hurt me.

Chad startled me by throwing the magic detector at me. I ducked, and it bounced off my shoulder. He sprang toward me, lunging for my purse.

I recovered quickly enough to club him in the head with it, then sprang back. He stumbled but snatched again for the purse. I spun on my heel and kicked, planting the sole of my shoe in his stomach. With a pained grunt, he pitched forward, but the fight wasn't over. The other two men charged down the slope and into the draw.

The wolf magic roared into me. I wouldn't be able to keep from changing, not with this new threat barreling down on me.

"Get her purse," Chad rasped as he gripped his abdomen. "And the necklace."

"It's a medallion, asshole." I flung down my jacket, phone, and purse, and kicked off my shoes, but there wasn't time to remove the rest of my clothing.

My skin flexed, muscles and bones morphing, as the change took over. Fur grew from my flesh, and I dropped to all fours, the medallion remaining with me through the transition. It hung around my neck, glowing against my black fur as it emanated power.

The one who'd once been my mate—Chad—stared as, for the first time since we'd met, I changed in front of him.

"Shit!" The men who'd been sprinting toward me halted, their arms flailing as they gaped at me.

One recovered and pointed his rifle toward me. At the same time, Chad lunged for the bag I carried as a human. Though such items had little significance to a wolf, I recalled and sensed that a powerful artifact lay within, something important to my people. I sprang toward my ex-mate, both to keep him from reaching the bag and to escape the rifleman's aim.

My enemy fired, but I'd moved in time, and the bullet did not strike me. I bowled into Chad, knocking him back, and he landed on his ass in the mud.

I bit into his thigh, drawing blood. I might have done more to ensure he couldn't steal my belongings or endanger me further, but both rifles had shifted to point toward me. The men might have hesitated to shoot a woman, but now that they believed me a wild animal... Their eyes promised they would have no trouble firing.

I rushed into the ferns, hoping the fronds would hide me. But I wasn't a small wolf, and the foliage moved with my passing.

The men fired into the foliage. One bullet grazed my flank as the other flew over my head.

Fear and pain prompted savagery, the rising of my wild instincts, and the magic threatened to steal all rational thought. Forgetting where I was and who these people were, I rushed through the ferns until I drew near the riflemen, then sprang at them.

One might have had time to fire again, but his eyes widened with fear, and he stumbled back, heel clipping a root. The rifle flew upward as I smashed into his chest. He released the weapon, and it clanked onto a rock several yards away. I bit and tore, ripping into my enemy's arms and torso to ensure he couldn't attack me further.

To the side, the other man clubbed me with the butt of his rifle. My hard muscles armored my body, and the blow didn't hurt badly, especially not with magic and adrenaline flooding my veins. I turned, leaving the first man, and lunged at him. My foe jerked his arms up to protect his head and neck, almost but not quite dropping the rifle.

I bit into his side, my fangs slicing through clothing to tear away a chunk of flesh. The man screamed, the noise so loud that it hurt my ears, and he tried to club me again. I bit deeply into his leg.

When he jerked his arms down, trying to knock me away, I clamped my jaws around his rifle and flung it into the woods.

"Stop right there, Luna," came Chad's voice from ten feet away, surprisingly calm.

When I turned, I saw the reason. He'd picked up one of the fallen rifles and was pointing it at me.

I crouched, debating whether to spring at him and try to knock it aside before he could fire, or to leap into the bushes, hoping to dodge when he did.

"Do I...?" an uncertain voice asked.

It was one of my offspring, his brown hair dangling around his jaw. He crouched a step away from Chad, staring at me with round eyes.

I froze, not wanting him to be harmed and also remembering that I hadn't wanted him to see this, to witness me turning into a wolf and fighting his father. *Hurting* his father.

Chad leaned on his good leg, not putting much weight on the one affected by my bite wound. His torn trousers were dark and damp with blood.

"Get the purse," Chad ordered without looking at Cameron.

Human words didn't entirely make sense to me when I was in wolf form, but I got the gist.

My offspring licked his lips, crept forward with his gaze on me, and reached for the bag.

Frustrated, I growled, but I couldn't attack my offspring. He picked up the bag and backed away. Chad kept the rifle pointed at me. Groans came from the two men I'd attacked, but they were crawling away. They wouldn't fight further. Chad was the only one I needed to worry about. Would he fire? Even though I'd known him well once, it was hard for me to tell.

"Take it back to the car, and stay there," Chad ordered Cameron.

"But what about—"

"Do it," Chad snarled. "She's feral as fuck. She could attack you at any second."

Lies. I wouldn't harm my own offspring. All I was doing was protecting my belongings from a thief. From the bastard who stood in front of me, aiming that rifle between my eyes.

Cameron licked his lips again and glanced uncertainly at me, but he did as his father ordered, backing toward the stream with my bag.

Again, I debated if I could reach Chad before he could fire at me. The presence of my offspring had kept me from trying, but if I dodged to the side as I ran toward him... I was fast and powerful, and the magic of the medallion coursed into me, making me feel invulnerable. I was more concerned that I would kill him if I attacked.

"I always wanted to see you change," Chad said. "I admit I thought we'd have sex afterward, not that I would shoot you, but you've been standing in my way for too long. And I think if I lowered this gun, you'd kill me."

I growled at him.

He glanced over his shoulder. Because he was waiting for our offspring to be gone? So that he could shoot me without a witness? And later tell Cameron that it had been self-defense?

The hell with that.

I rushed toward Chad, zigzagging to present a more difficult target. My power combined with the magic of the medallion made me fast, a blur to his human eyes. He had time to get one shot off, but it slammed into the ground where I'd been an instant before. Unharmed, I bowled into him, my momentum and weight taking him to the ground. As he hit with a grunt of pain, I snatched the rifle from his grip and flung it into the woods.

Fangs parting, I lowered my jaw to his throat, letting my warm breath hit his skin. He pushed his hands against my chest but found that he lacked the power to push me away.

My eyes meeting his, I stared into his soul, letting him know that I could kill him. And in that moment, I wondered if I should. He'd meant to kill me. He'd declared himself an enemy. If I let him go, would he keep coming after me?

The scent of urine reached my nostrils. He'd wet himself.

I stepped away, deciding to release him. Maybe it was naive, but I thought him too afraid to come after me again.

As soon as he was free, Chad rolled to hands and knees, gasping and groaning in pain from his injuries. Only with the help of a log did he manage to push himself to his feet and stumble in the direction that Cameron had gone.

I sat back on my haunches, aware that my offspring had escaped with my bag—with the wolf case. Soon, Chad would have it. Perhaps... to be done with him, it would be worth letting it go.

As Chad clawed his way across the stream and out of the gully, I grew aware of another presence in the area. The bipedfuris crouched on a stump at the top of the draw, gazing down at me.

How long had he been there? Distracted by the heat of the battle, I hadn't noticed his powerful presence.

When our eyes met, I knew he had witnessed me defeating my enemies. I lifted my snout, pleased that he'd seen it and that he'd waited nearby without interfering. He'd believed me capable of dealing with the situation.

He lifted a clawed hand, a strap wrapped around it. My bag. I sensed the artifact within.

A hint of uncertainty touched me, and I cocked my head. Was my offspring all right?

The bipedfuris roared, flexing his powerful muscles, then lifted his face toward the sky and howled.

That hadn't answered my question.

Realizing we would need to return to our human forms for a discussion, I swished my tail, snatched up my jacket and shoes, and headed for the stream. The bipedfuris hopped down from the stump and also strode in that direction.

14

MY INTENTION WAS TO FOLLOW MY OFFSPRING'S TRAIL AND ENSURE for myself that he was okay, but halfway back to the road, my magic faded. Too bad I hadn't salvaged more of my clothing. Branches scraped me, and damp pine needles slapped at my skin. At least the bullet that had grazed me earlier hadn't left a deep wound, and my regenerative magic would heal it soon.

Duncan also lost his magic, the bipedfuris form leaving him so that he walked beside me as a human. Before changing, he'd probably neatly stacked his clothes somewhere, but, for now, he carried only my purse, a sight that made me smile.

"Thanks for collecting that," I said.

"You're most welcome, my lady." Pausing in our walk, Duncan bowed low to offer it to me, like a knight of old extending a sword in both hands as he swore fealty.

The gesture touched me, and I paused, not only to accept it but to take a moment to appreciate him. I might also have appreciated his powerful frame, his bare muscled shoulders and arms, and the way the dappled sun highlighted his soft salt-and-pepper hair.

"I admit it didn't require a great feat," Duncan added. "Your son was startled by my appearance and dropped it."

"I'm relieved you didn't have to fight him for it. That's a battle that wouldn't have gone in his favor."

"No. This day did not require any great battles on my part, alas." Duncan waved toward the road, which we'd almost reached. "Going on a challenging hunt would have been more enjoyable, but I did find some small satisfaction in wantonly damaging the vehicles of those who seek to displace your pack."

We resumed walking and crested a small rise, the pond coming into view. The road also came into view, and I stopped and gaped.

The vehicles were more than *damaged*. Only Chad's rental and a couple of the trucks and SUVs were gone. The rest... It looked like a tornado had descended upon the rest.

Several were tipped on their sides or even pushed off the road. Doors, fenders, and roofs had been ripped off and scattered among shattered glass. Numerous tires had not only been deflated but torn entirely from their mounts. A detached door hung halfway up in a tree on the opposite side of the road.

I looked at Duncan, a little incredulous. The last time we'd battled, he'd been weakened from the curse. Clearly, he had recovered his tremendous bipedfuris strength.

"You did ask me to scare them," he pointed out.

Worried I didn't approve of this wreckage?

No, he'd done exactly what I'd requested. And then he'd hurried back to the gully to see if I needed any help.

"You're amazing." I dropped my purse and hugged him.

"Ah." Duncan wrapped his arms around me. "I do enjoy hearing those words, but *you're* the amazing one." He lowered his lips to my throat, nuzzling me. His touch awakened my nerves, rousing heat and tingling sensations that had nothing to do with the magic of being a werewolf. "I love watching you fight," he added.

"I'm sad I missed seeing you tear up all those cars."

"I'll happily destroy more of your enemies' vehicles later, if you wish."

His hand slid down my bare back, nails lightly grazing my skin. My body tightened in response as delicious sensations coursed through me.

"You'll get me excited with such promises," I whispered, lifting my face to look at him as I molded my chest to his, his skin radiating warmth.

"I do enjoy getting you excited." Duncan shifted against me, his hard body promising that *he* was getting excited too. He gazed intently into my eyes. "I want you, Luna. I have for so long."

"I want you too." I slid my hands over his shoulders and down his back, exploring his firm planes as I parted my lips, offering them for a kiss.

His gaze snagged on them, but he paused in stroking me to hold up a finger.

"You don't want to get intimate in the forest?" I guessed, glancing toward his van.

It was almost laughable how normal it looked, parked among the carnage. The *tornado* had missed it.

"Oh, I'm quite fond of forest intimacy, but..." His gaze lowered to my chest. One of his hands left my back to curve around my body, fingers raising goosebumps as they trailed over my sensitive flesh. He stroked my breast, and I leaned into him, relishing his touch. His fingers lingered, as if they'd been distracted from their mission, and he bent to touch his lips to my bare skin. My leaning turned into a thrust toward him as my fingers dug into his shoulders. "*Very* fond of intimacy," he murmured, tasting me, then drawing his lips to my nipple for a suck that sent desire flooding to my core. "But..."

"But?" I gasped a protest, my eyes toward the branches over-head as I gripped and kneaded his muscles, my body pressing itself into him of its own accord.

Instead of answering, his mouth remained on me, lips and tongue teasing as he evoked the most wondrous and arousing sensations. The stubble from his beard shadow brushed my skin, adding to the sensations of pleasure coursing through me. His fingers shifted to the medallion hanging heavy between my breasts. It was glowing, bathing his face in its magical illu-mination.

He lifted the chain over my head, then dropped it onto the purse at our feet. Before I could question him, he did the same with the medallion around his neck, and I realized what he wanted. To have me, and for me to have him, without any question of whether some ancient magic was manipulating us.

Yes. I approved.

Arms tightening around him, I found his mouth and kissed him. Hard.

I'd wanted this for far longer than I'd let myself admit. Before either of us had known about the medallions, and before he'd crossed paths with my mother, I'd been drawn to him. The first day he'd ambled through the woods by Sylvan Serenity, that cocky smile on his face as he'd winked and swung his metal detector about, I'd been attracted to him.

But for so long, he'd been a question mark. Could I trust him? Would he hurt me? After being hurt before, I hadn't wanted to let myself fall in love again, hadn't even wanted to enjoy a man's company lest it end badly.

But as Duncan kissed me back, his hands sliding from my breasts to my hips to caress me in the most intimate of spots, I opened myself fully to him. I had no doubts about his intentions. I trusted him and felt no apprehension, only excitement and arousal as he rubbed me evocatively and our kisses grew hungrier, needier.

Words left, breaths shortening as we shifted and stroked, eager to touch and be touched everywhere, nerves delighted by the attention. With our chests pressed together, we could feel each other's hearts pounding, just as we felt the proof of each other's great desire.

When Duncan drew me down to a mossy patch of ground free of mud, I went eagerly with him. A human woman might have preferred the bed in his van, but the forest floor appealed to the wolf in me, the scents of ferns and moss and decomposing wood magnificent in my nose. And there was his scent as well, masculine and exotic, from a far-off place, a time that I'd never known.

Duncan groaned with desire as he inhaled *my* scent as well, his hands continuing to stroke me as his mouth left my lips to taste the rest of my body. His avid gaze held mine as he took my breast again, making me arch and pant. My body ached with need even as my soul appreciated the way he looked at me, as if I were the greatest of exotic beauties, not a mom muddling through life, a woman who'd denied her destiny for far too long.

I groped through the moss to grab my purse and fish out the condoms, excited that we would, after so many interruptions, finally be together. He didn't pause in his ministrations, but he turned to let me sheathe his sword, even pushing eagerly toward me, craving my touch.

My fingers lingered, rubbing and stroking, marveling at his magnificence. Until he distracted me with his arousing nips and licks, his assiduous attention to giving me pleasure.

When his tongue trailed from my breasts to the quivering muscles of my abdomen and lower, I not only groaned but *growled* like the wolf. He parted my lower lips, his tongue sliding into my heated core, and I couldn't maintain any measure of control, of decorum. Like a wild animal, I bucked and writhed on the cool, damp moss as his warm mouth worked me expertly, making me cry out as I thrashed.

"By the moon, you're hot, Luna," Duncan rasped, gripping my hips, sweat gleaming on his skin as he continued stroking me with his tongue.

I growled an inarticulate response and arched toward him, needing him to take me over an edge I'd never reached before.

His eyes full of lust, he nipped and licked, creating more intense desire than I'd ever known. More intense *pleasure* as his touch quickened, power radiating from him, electric as it wrapped around my body, my every nerve singing.

I gripped his shoulders, rising as far as I could toward him. Sensing exactly what I wanted, he wrapped his lips around my throbbing need and sucked until an explosion of pleasure blasted me over the edge. Magic crackled inside of me and in the air around us, extending my pleasure and making the moment last. Finally, I slumped to the ground, reveling in pure blissful satisfaction.

Between my legs, Duncan watched my response, looking pleased, but that avid desire continued to burn in his eyes as he breathed heavily. Hard and full, he still craved a release, and he prowled up my body.

Before I could praise him for his expert lovemaking, his mouth took mine, and a hungry growl of his own rumbled in his chest. I wrapped my arms around him as his fingers slid down to stroke me once more, wanting to rekindle my fire so he could this time quench it with his great need.

Though I wouldn't have guessed I could match his desire again so soon, I wanted him to enjoy this as much as I did, and I opened myself for his touch—for all of him. His intensity and skill roused me far faster than I would have imagined. As we kissed, magic and power flowed from him, igniting my desire all over again. Soon, my muscles quivered with need, and I found myself reaching for him, wanting to hold him, to guide him into me.

His entire body tightened at my light touch, coiling at the invitation. As we kissed hard, Duncan almost frenetic, he pushed past my hand and toward the welcoming core of my body. Once more, I arched toward him, greedily craving another climax but also to give him all that he wanted. He deserved that.

With a snarl of pure pleasure, he plunged into me, filling me with his great animal energy. Sensations even more exquisite than before made me ecstatic as I eagerly matched his every thrust. With his muscled arms to the sides, fingers splayed in the moss, he plunged deeper and deeper, his possessive growls claiming me as much as his body did.

I sensed that he'd wanted this even longer than I had. It felt like he wanted me like no one he'd ever been with before, and that filled me with such love for him, the emotion mingling with my animalistic need as we arched and thrust faster and faster, all awareness of everything except each other gone.

"Duncan!" I cried his name as we came together. No, I *howled* it, letting the forest know that he was mine as another explosion of ecstasy rocked my body.

He also threw his head back and howled as he found his release. I clung to him, basking in the cascades of relief and pleasure that came after the climax, eventually leaving me trembling in the moss, exhausted but more satisfied than I'd ever been.

Duncan lowered himself, the tension finally gone from his body. He wrapped his arms around me, shifted onto his back, and pulled me onto his chest, cradling me and stroking my hair as we recovered.

I reveled in the aftermath and in him. Never had I thought I'd experience such amazing pleasure again. Or at all. Even my first love, when teenage hormones had made everything intense, hadn't been as incredible as this. So strong were my emotions that I had to blink away tears.

"I love you, Duncan," I whispered.

He nuzzled my ear. "I love you too, Luna."

15

SNUGGLED ON TOP OF THE MOSSY BLANKET BY THE POND, WITH FROGS croaking on the far side, Duncan and I might have spent the rest of the day and into the night cuddled on our sides, my back pressed into his chest and his arms around me. The medallions, which lay on the ground a few feet away, weren't glowing and hadn't tried to foist any visions or compulsions on us, and the case also lay quiescent in my purse. Nobody had returned to the area for the destroyed cars, though I'd half expected a tow truck or two to roll up the road while Duncan and I were thrashing naked by the pond. Somehow, we'd never made the trek to his van and the bed in back.

My phone ringing from... somewhere made me lift my head. I'd lost all track of time, and impending rain made it hard to tell if it was twilight or simply getting cloudier. I might have been cold if I hadn't had warm arms wrapped around me. We'd also generated a lot of body heat during our activities. I smiled at the memory.

"You're not thinking of answering that, are you?" Duncan asked.

"Well... it might be Lorenzo. We were *supposed* to be on the way to visit." The cave, technically, but I'd planned to stop by to see Mom too.

I was surprised the phone was ringing. Whenever I'd tried to call from my mother's cabin, the signal hadn't been strong enough.

"A gentleman would retrieve the phone for me," I added.

"A *gentleman* has been busy satisfying your every physical need and ensuring you remain warm."

"Is that what your hand is doing on my boob?"

"Most certainly. You've tender and sensitive flesh there. You wouldn't want it to catch a chill."

"It's funny how often your hand finds its way to that spot."

"It would be pleased to explore other spots if you wish." Duncan kissed the back of my neck while his hand trailed lower, his fingers creating tingles of pleasure. "I knew being with you would be amazing—*hot*—but if I'd known *how* hot, I would have been more persistent and dedicated with my flirting."

"Your glowing forehead was more the problem than your flirting. And then you were dying. That was a bit of a buzzkill."

"So the flirting was good?"

"You're good."

"Yes." He smiled lazily, hands expertly stroking me.

I knew I should be responsible and get up and find my phone, but a tremble went through me, and I rolled over and flung a leg across Duncan. His lips were right there, waiting for mine, and we met in a kiss as his fingers did what he'd promised, exploring other spots and making me forget all about responsibilities. Our passionate eagerness overflowed, as if we'd both waited far too long and now, finally having this time together, couldn't stop hungrily touching and rubbing, insatiable despite the intense satisfaction we'd found with our earlier joining.

Full darkness had fallen by the time we parted, hunger playing more of a role in the decision than a desire to check voicemail. Duncan climbed over the log, my night vision good enough to see his bare butt, and hunted around for my phone. I sat up, intending to help, though I did enjoy watching him. Even on his hands and knees, he managed to look agile and powerful—and appealing.

He retrieved my belongings, including the medallions, and stacked everything on the log in front of me.

"Thank you, Duncan. I think I said it before, but you're wonderful."

"Whether for ravaging enemy vehicles or retrieving a phone, a man can't hear that often enough."

"I should have invited you to my bedroom weeks ago."

"I've been telling you *that* since we met."

"Since we met? You were just trying to swipe the case then."

"That doesn't mean I didn't want an invitation to your bedroom. You might not have noticed, since I'm such a subtle fellow, but I've been rather into you since I saw you carrying that loo across the parking lot."

"I had no idea that was so arousing."

"A man likes a strong lady."

"Hence why women carrying toilets feature so often in pornos."

"I'm sure I wouldn't know *anything* about what's featured in those."

"Naturally not. You being so wholesome."

"Indeed." He leaned across the log and kissed me.

A car drove past, someone with the aura of a werewolf driving, and we drew apart. Was that Emilio's brother I sensed?

Whoever it was looked toward the pond, probably also sensing us. I grabbed my stuff and knelt back behind a shrub.

Fortunately, the driver didn't slow down. If anything, he sped up, in a hurry about something. I had a feeling Mom was about to learn that we were in the area.

The phone rang again, reminding me that I'd wanted to check it, not spend the whole day and night by the frog pond with

Duncan. It was a local number but not a contact I had programmed in, and I might have ignored it, but it was the same person who'd called before, and three new voicemail messages suggested that some of those calls hadn't gotten through.

"Hello?" I answered.

The hint of a man speaking came through, but the call ended. There was indeed only one bar of reception, so it wasn't surprising. I tried playing the voicemails.

"Luna Valens? It's Ivan MacGregor. Are you there?"

I frowned at the phone and glanced at Duncan, hoping Ivan hadn't called to ask for a date. I hadn't mentioned to Duncan that he'd been interested.

"I'm looking for my sister, Izzy," Ivan continued, and guilt swept over me. *Of course* that was what he'd called about, not dates. How had I forgotten that? "I showed her that you were kind enough to send back my bracelet—you'll have to let me know what reward I can arrange for that—but she wasn't... Well, I understand you two have some history. She's still holding a grudge over that, and even though I, as the stern and authoritative older brother, forbade her from pestering you, her daughter said she'd mentioned going to your apartment complex. That was yesterday, and she's not back yet. Normally, her comings and goings wouldn't be any of my business, but it's strange that she would leave Olivia here without making arrangements if she was going to spend the night somewhere. And she hasn't answered her phone today. I called the Sylvans to see if they knew anything about her disappearance, but they said they haven't been over there lately. Anyway, you might not have seen Izzy, but if you could let me know, I'd appreciate it."

The second voicemail message had come in hours later and was a shorter update saying he was still looking for Izzy and checking with everyone again.

"Hell." I rubbed my face. "I should have called him as soon as she was kidnapped." I'd forgotten about the daughter. Even if Izzy hated me, making me disinclined to worry that much about her, I didn't have anything against the girl or Ivan.

"You were almost passed out from those vapors yourself at the time," Duncan said.

"Tell me about it." I grabbed my jacket and shoes. "I think the cave visit is going to have to wait, but I want to ask Mom and whoever is at the cabin tonight if they've heard about anyone kidnapping werewolves. I'm sure that had to do with Abrams and you and me, but... I don't know. Maybe my kin have heard something." I looked at Duncan. "You haven't gotten any updates, right? Nobody has told you where Abrams is and if he might have Izzy?"

"Sorry, no." Duncan spread his arms, then pointed to his van. "Let me drive you to the cabin and offer you some clothes."

"You think I should show up in more than a jacket, my purse, and shoes?" With those items in my arms, I headed for the road.

"Werewolves ought to understand if you're missing a few garments, but I do have plenty to share. You were even kind enough to bring me extras recently. Clearly, you foresaw this day coming."

"Lately, this day comes almost every day." I gestured to encompass our nudity.

Duncan grinned. "This day was particularly unique in a historical sense, but I do hope that many of the events repeat themselves in the future. *Regularly*."

"I did enjoy some of the events."

We reached his van and climbed inside.

"I should think that *most* of the events appealed. You took a sizable bite out of your ex-husband's hip."

"I was just trying to keep him from shooting me. I didn't *enjoy* that."

Duncan slipped into the back and opened a cabinet to pull out clothes. "*I* might have enjoyed it. He was deserving of a few bites."

When he handed the stack of clothes to me, his face grew more serious. "Had he succeeded in shooting you, I would have killed him."

"Had he succeeded in shooting me, I wouldn't have minded." I smiled, even if that wasn't quite true.

Face still sober, Duncan said, "I almost lost it. It was right as I was arriving, and I was on the verge of springing down there, but you were charging him by then. Ducking his bullets and taking him to the ground." His expression lightened. "At that point, I knew I could sit back, take some popcorn out, and watch the show."

I snorted as I unfolded a shirt to put on. "You didn't have any popcorn. I know that for a fact. There wasn't any grease on your tail."

"True. I wanted to keep my tail in pristine condition for our inevitable and exhilarating sexual encounter." He tugged on his own clothes as he headed to the driver's seat. "Our *many* exhilarating sexual encounters."

"Don't tell my mom about them, or she'll be smug."

"You don't think she might get the gist of what happened when you walk into her cabin in my clothes?"

"Maybe I'll tell her that I fell in the frog pond after we scared away the developers."

"I might also struggle to keep the contented satisfaction off my face."

I considered his features as he turned the key in the ignition. "I'll bet that's a similar expression to the one you wore after tearing up those vehicles."

"That was also quite satisfying."

"As wanton destruction so often is."

"Quite."

Before Duncan pulled out into the road, a truck drove past us, going fast over the ruts and potholes. I sensed another werewolf inside, one that reminded me of Jasmine. Her mother? I hadn't seen Renata for a long time but remembered her.

"There might be a hunt starting at Mom's tonight," I said.

Or was it something else? Both of those werewolf-driven cars had been going fast, their drivers full of urgency.

My stomach knotted at the thought that Mom might have gotten sicker. Or... what if she'd already passed? While Duncan and I had been... frolicking in the woods.

I rubbed my face as he drove up the road and told myself that was the last thing I needed to feel guilty about when it came to Mom. She *wanted* frolicking. Admittedly, she wanted the kind of frolicking that led to children, and we'd used my condom stash, so that wouldn't happen. Not tonight anyway. And in the future? I wanted to deal with my enemies and get my life straightened out before putting more consideration into children. I didn't want to have a grade-school-aged werewolf assassin lurking in the woods outside the nursery window.

The van turned down the long gravel driveway leading to the cabin, and I pulled my thoughts to the present, glancing at my phone to check the time. I realized I hadn't played all three voice messages and thumbed the last open. I'd figured it had been another one from Ivan, but it was Bolin's number. I played it as we pulled in behind four trucks and cars parked in front of Mom's porch.

"Luna, pick up if you're there," said Bolin's message. After a pause, he added, "Okay, call me back when you can. It's about Jasmine. More delivery-van drivers hurling vials full of knock-out gas showed up. More guys than last time. Jasmine was in the parking lot when they arrived, and they got her. I charged out and threw some of my *own* potions, but the wind shifted, and I didn't get out of the way fast enough." His voice grew tight and rapid as he added, "It's not my fault. They were attacking her. I had to get to her!" He groaned. "When I came to, the drivers and their vans were all gone, and Jasmine was gone too. Her car is still here, so I know she didn't drive off. I'm trying to get into the footage from the security cameras to check, but I think they took her, the same as Ivan's sister. Why would they want *Jasmine* though? She's nice and pretty and— She shouldn't have any *enemies*, Luna. Why?"

I slumped back in the seat, staring at the phone. That was the end of the recording.

Duncan had turned off the van and looked gravely over at me.

"I don't understand this either," I said to him. "When they took Izzy, I assumed they thought she was me. Though I don't even know why Abrams would want me, except to chain in a dungeon so he could torture me and take revenge for his lost business partner."

"It's *me* he wants dead," Duncan said. "Though, knowing him, he very well might want revenge. More for his destroyed laboratory and lost potions than his dead partner."

"Either way, Jasmine and Izzy didn't have anything to do with that." I pointed to my chest and then Duncan's. We'd equally been responsible.

"No."

I tried calling Bolin but couldn't get enough reception to dial. I sent him a text to let him know we would be back soon to help. Though what *help* we could offer, I didn't know. Unless Abrams sent a ransom note, we didn't know where to find him.

Duncan looked out the window as someone walked up. Emilio. He skirted the driver's seat and approached my side of the van.

"Sorry," I said, rolling down the window. "I didn't bring any salami this time."

"That's egregious, if not an outright criminal act, but it's not why we're all here. Did you hear? Jasmine is missing."

I winced. "I did just hear that, yes."

"Your mom and Lorenzo think it's the same dumbasses who

are trying to buy up the lands out here." Emilio waved toward the woods to either side of Mom's property.

I started to shake my head, Abrams's face large in my mind, but did we know he'd been responsible for the kidnappings? The use of alchemical concoctions seemed to suggest it, but it wasn't as if other people couldn't have purchased such things. Rue had a whole business selling potions, and there were other alchemists in the Seattle area.

A part of me hoped someone besides Abrams had been responsible. Then it wouldn't be my fault that my niece was missing. Though with Chad now wrapped up with the real estate developers, I didn't know if that was entirely true. Somehow, I kept ending up at the center of everything.

"Lucky me," I murmured.

Emilio pointed toward the cabin's front door. "We came to have a family powwow and figure things out, but your mom wants to speak with you first."

Lorenzo stood outside the door, outlined by the porch light, and beckoned when I looked toward him.

"Do you think this is about frolicking?" I asked Duncan quietly, fastening the medallion around my neck and waving for him to do the same with the other one. We'd taken them off so they wouldn't influence our choice to have sex, but I believed Mom would want to see us wearing them.

"I suppose it might be, but it looks like your family has more profound things on their minds tonight."

Normally, I would be relieved something had Mom distracted from the topic of frolicking—and especially offspring—but not at Jasmine's expense. I hoped she was okay.

"Let's find out." I took a deep breath and led the way to the door.

16

LORENZO NODDED AT DUNCAN AND ME WHEN WE STEPPED INTO MY mother's cabin, but he didn't follow us inside. She sat in a chair in the living room, wrapped in a blanket and holding a mug of tea. Every time I saw her, her cheeks were more hollow, and I wondered if she was eating at all.

In case her taste buds would like a treat, I lay a bar of dark chocolate on the table near her elbow.

"Chocolate enhanced with reishi mushrooms?" She made a face. "Are you falling for *all* of the health-nut propaganda?"

"Only two-thirds of it."

"Can't you bring me something delicious without any supposed nutritional value or cancer-fighting properties?"

I delved into my jacket pocket and withdrew a half-eaten truffled caramel and dark-chocolate bar.

"That looks more promising." Mom pushed the mushroom bar aside and pulled the other close to her chair, then eyed me, or, more likely, my borrowed clothing. Her nostrils twitched a couple of times as she sniffed, and then she looked at Duncan. He appeared perfectly normal—after all, he'd taken his clothes off before shifting—but whatever Mom saw—or smelled—caused her to nod in satisfaction. "You've finally mated."

I barely managed to keep from rolling my eyes. "Yeah, I was overcome with ardor and aching desire for Duncan."

"I assumed he would prompt such feelings in you eventually."

Duncan arched his eyebrows but didn't offer any hint of disagreement. He even gave me a slight smile.

Mom sipped from her tea. "He's handsome and powerful."

I sighed at the suggestion that a guy's *power* was what would attract me but didn't want to quibble with her, so I offered, "He ripped a bunch of cars to pieces for me and left their dented fenders in ditches and bushes alongside the road."

"I heard there was some carnage on the way up here," Mom said. "We assumed the vehicles belonged to the real estate developers, and many of your relatives were disappointed that they'd already been destroyed."

"The early bird gets the worm. Or the fender."

"Indeed." Mom pointed to our medallions, which we again wore around our necks. "What did you learn in the cave? From the vision I had... Well, it seemed that instruction might be given to the chosen individuals about how to protect our people."

"Ah." I glanced at Duncan. "We haven't been yet."

Mom's lips pressed together with disapproval.

"Life has been a little chaotic back in town. An enemy... well, we're not sure exactly who was responsible yet... kidnapped a visiting werewolf. I think they meant to get me." I waved toward myself. "And now they have Jasmine too."

Mom nodded. She probably had more news about that than I did. "We suspect it is part of some plot. The real estate developers haven't been pleased that we've fought them when they've tried to force the sale of *our* land."

"Rude of them."

"They're loathsome. I wish I'd seen the destruction of their vehicles. Did you, perchance, ruthlessly slay any of them?" Mom looked hopefully at Duncan.

"They would have deserved it, but I did not. Luna asked me to only scare them."

"At the time, we didn't know they might be involved in the kidnappings." I still didn't know if they were. "I don't suppose you have any idea where, if they *were* involved, they would have taken Jasmine?"

"I know very little about them except that they are conniving parasites." Mom set her mug on the table, took a slow breath, and leaned her head back in the chair.

I sensed her weariness, and it saddened me. Even this conversation was tiring her. Her days of hunting or even changing into the wolf might be past.

"We'll find Jasmine, Mom."

"You must visit the cave," she said without opening her eyes. "You should have already."

I thought about pointing out that we'd had sex *without* being lured into the cave by her and the medallions, but she'd mentioned protecting our kind more than once. Maybe my assumptions were wrong, and this wasn't simply about her desire for me to mate with Duncan and have offspring.

"We can give it a shot," I said.

"Tonight." Her eyes opened, her expression firm as she held my gaze. "I don't know what it will share with you, but I believe you will learn something important. When I had my vision, I had the inkling that if I'd been hale and capable..." She grimaced. "I think it would have told me more. But the moon knows I haven't the strength to combat villains these days. Wear that." She pointed to the female medallion. "The magic will know that you're my successor."

"Okay, Mom." I fought back a yawn at the thought of traipsing off into the woods. It was getting late, and my activities with

Duncan had worn me out, but I wouldn't admit that to her. Besides, if there was a chance the cave would help...

"We'll go now." Duncan nodded.

"Good." Mom pointed toward the back door. "I look forward to hearing what you learn."

A knock sounded at the front door, and Lorenzo leaned in. "Some of us are heading to Shoreline to see if we can pick up tracks at the apartment complex and find where the kidnappers took Jasmine."

I wanted to ask them not to go, since a pack of werewolves roaming the premises might alarm the tenants, but maybe they would find something Bolin hadn't been able to. It wasn't as if he had a wolf's nose, after all. "Just don't let anyone eat my tenants, please."

"Unless they taste like salami, that shouldn't be a problem." Lorenzo stepped aside to let someone else walk in. Rosaria, the wise wolf.

"I'll take care of you while Lorenzo is gone, Umbra," she said.

"I don't need a caretaker. I can still walk and toilet myself."

"I meant to say I'll keep you company during this trying time," Rosaria said.

Mom's lips thinned again.

"She's still a dreadful patient," Rosaria told me, turning to close the door.

Before it shut, I could hear Emilio ask, "Did I hear someone promise there would be salami on the adventure?"

"That boy has a singular focus," Mom murmured, then pointed Duncan and me toward the back door again.

"I guess that means she's not going to offer us any cured meats to sustain us on the long journey to the cave," I told him.

"Take the mushroom bar." Mom's lip curled.

"What about the caramel truffled one?"

"Absolutely not." She removed it from the table and laid it in her lap.

As Duncan and I walked out the back door, the sounds of engines starting up wafted to us from the front. As many of the pack drove off, heading to my home in Shoreline, I felt I should be with them, not only to keep them from creating any chaos at Sylvan Serenity but because, if it turned out Abrams was behind everything, it was a problem that Duncan and I should handle.

Maybe he was thinking the same, because he gazed pensively back toward the driveway as we headed in the other direction.

"I hope they don't find Lykos and object to him... existing," Duncan said.

Ah, I hadn't thought of that. Of course that would be a concern for Duncan. The kid had practically moved into the woods out back. My family would sense that Lykos was powerful, with old-world blood, but they might not realize that he was Duncan's clone brother. What non-sci-fi-reading werewolf would guess that? And if Lykos started talking about laying traps and assassinations... the pack might deem him a threat, someone who should be dealt with.

I stopped walking. "Do you want to go back and warn him to beat it?"

"I—" The medallion around Duncan's neck flared with golden light, bathing his face with it.

Mine responded by brightening as well, the magic it could emanate growing strong, warming my flesh through my clothes.

"I think your mother isn't the only one who wants us to visit that cave," Duncan said.

"Apparently."

"Lykos is good at hiding. I think he'll be all right for a few hours." Duncan nodded with determination, clasped my hand, and we walked side-by-side into the night.

17

THE FIRST TIME WE'D VISITED THE CAVE IN THE GULLY AT THE BACK of Mom's property, she'd given us a map, and we'd stumbled our way to it, navigating past rough terrain, magical mushrooms in nooks, and raccoons and other critters with glowing red eyes. This time, the medallion around my neck drew me straight toward our destination, the magic almost insistent that we maintain a quick pace without pauses or detours.

The artifacts were manipulating us, but what choice did we have? It was what Mom wanted too. Besides, it was just a cave with a magical pool and paintings inside. What was the worst that could happen?

"I could get zapped and knocked on my ass," I muttered as we descended a slope toward the stream that meandered through the gully.

That had happened *last* time, the magic hurling me back and knocking me unconscious. Poor Duncan had been worried and rushed back to get my mom and Rosaria. Would those events repeat?

He must also have been thinking of that night because, when

he looked at me, he didn't ask for clarification. "I'll be ready this time and catch you if there's zapping or knocking."

"Thank you. You're a good werewolf."

"As I've been assuring you for some time."

"Well, I'm convinced now."

"I assumed from your enthusiastic lovemaking." He winked at me, then led the way along the stream.

This time, I noticed a hole in the rocky slope on the opposite side and thought of old mine shafts and the real estate people who'd swarmed all over the nearby land. Would the cave be destroyed if they got their wish and developed the place? No. I wouldn't allow that. As my mom had said before, it had held meaning to our people for a long time, ever since the pack originally left the Old World and settled in this area.

When we reached the entrance, tucked into the steep rocky incline on the far side of the stream, I stepped across the waterway and took a bracing breath before walking inside. Thanks to the glow of the medallion, I didn't need to activate my phone's flashlight app. The illumination shone onto the rocky paw prints painted on the sides and roof of the cave, and it also reflected in the pool in the center.

On the way here, we hadn't seen any animals with glowing eyes, but I trusted they were out there, drawn to drink the magical water. I caught Duncan eyeing it when we stood still to look around. My gaze was drawn to the paw prints, specifically the one I'd touched before. The one that had knocked me unconscious.

A thrum emanated from my medallion, and it gave me the impression that I should head toward it. "Better than drinking the water, I suppose."

Duncan looked at me.

"I'm chatting with my medallion and mentally bracing myself," I said.

He cocked his head. "Does your medallion chat back?"

"No. But it sometimes gives me vibes." Like the come-touch-the-painted-rock vibe.

"Yes, that's what I've received from this one too." Duncan tapped the wolf head on his chest. "And it was also the source of the... intense urge to join with you yesterday."

"Yeah. I got that too." I headed for the paw-print painting, flexing my fingers at my sides.

Duncan had promised he would catch me, and he stayed close.

The paintings glowed warmly, inviting me to touch them. I drew a deep breath, hesitant to reach out.

Duncan rested a supportive hand on my shoulder. Both of our medallions flared brighter, and I sensed... satisfaction, at least from mine. This was what it wanted.

Though the manipulation made me uneasy, I had to trust that the medallions were looking out for the pack. Of course, they might not be as concerned about looking out for *individuals* in the pack, but...

"Here goes," I whispered.

Duncan brushed his fingers along the side of my neck—a gesture of support?—then returned his hand to my shoulder and bent his knees. Bracing himself? Just how hard had the magic thrown me last time? Since it had knocked me out before I'd landed, I didn't know, but he'd mentioned me being in the pool several feet away.

"All right, tell me where I can find Izzy and Jasmine, please," I said to the wall or medallion or maybe both. "Someone's been kidnapping werewolves, and Mom thinks you can help."

I gripped the medallion with one hand and rested the other on the wall. The stone should have been cool, but tingling warmth spread from it to my hand, then flowed up my arm. It infused my entire body. The edges of my eyesight flickered, and a dream swept over me. A vision.

In it, I stood atop a cliff overlooking the forest with the snow-capped Cascade Mountains to one side of me. Below, I could make out the shingle roof of Mom's cabin as well as a couple of small homes owned by Rosaria and other pack members in the area. Between them, the road meandering back toward civilization was visible.

In the vision, the medallion glowed on my chest as I held up the wolf case, the lid open. The mushroom-shaped artifact, glowing even more than my medallion, floated into the air.

It beamed a feeling of dismissal at me. At least it hadn't zapped me. After the dismissal, a sense of resignation came from it, and the artifact descended toward the ground. A foot from the edge of the cliff, the mushroom stem nestled itself into the earth. Once settled, the artifact pulsed waves of energy—or maybe *magic*—outward. They had a purple tint, making them visible as they flowed out, one concentric circle after another stretching over the land for several miles in all directions. Eventually, the magical and visual disturbance ceased, the forest returning to normal.

Or did it? Insects buzzed, squirrels chattered, and birds chirped, as if nothing had happened, but I had a sense that something had changed. The cabins and cottages and trees appeared the same, but the road had grown... fuzzy. It was still there, but something hazed it, making it hard to make out.

Strange.

More light glowed around me, filling the cave and shining on my skin.

You will place the protector, a female voice spoke into my mind. It seemed to come from the medallion, but I sensed the magic of this place enhancing it, giving it power it hadn't demonstrated before. Like *speaking.*

The protector? I asked silently.

Though I was vaguely aware of standing in the cave, Duncan close behind me, I felt detached from my body, and my mouth couldn't have voiced the words. In my mind, the vision continued, and I saw myself on that cliff, still holding the case and standing behind the mushroom artifact as it did who knew what.

It was made to protect humanity from our kind, but we shall use that to our advantage, the voice said.

How so?

Place the protector.

Uh, okay, but I'm not sure where that cliff is, and I have something else I need to do. Family I need to retrieve. Can you tell me where the kidnapped werewolves are? Do you know?

You are the future of the pack.

Glad to hear it, I said, even if I wasn't. *The kidnapped wolves? Do you know?*

You will ensure the protector remains and that the power of the Old World reinvigorates the line and gives the pack the strength to withstand an uncertain future.

Behind me, Duncan eased closer, his hand sliding from my shoulder to my waist and then around it. His chest pressed against my back, and a zing of awareness swept through my body.

Since the wall hadn't tossed me across the cave yet, I doubted he felt he needed to be close to keep me from being knocked unconscious. More likely, the medallions were using their magic to influence him. To influence *both* of us. I caught myself leaning back into him, reveling in the heat of his hard body molding itself to mine.

I don't object to helping the pack, I said, trying to keep my thoughts straight as Duncan's mouth lowered to the side of my neck. My nerves zinged with pleasure as his teeth teased my flesh and he inhaled deeply, as if he'd never breathed in anything as amazing as my scent. *But Jasmine is part of the pack. I need to help her. Do you know where she's being held?*

Maybe neither the magical cave nor the medallion had any way to know what was going on in the suburbs. Whether real estate developers or Abrams were behind the kidnappings, it had little to do with our artifacts.

"Luna," Duncan growled, sounding more animal than man. His arms tightened around me, one hand straying to my waistband. "I need you."

The growly words and his powerful grip made my body thrum with desire, and I caught myself rocking back into him as he pushed into me, his powerful frame trapping me against the wall. When I turned my head to look at his face, hunger burned in his dark eyes, sparking my own passion, a need to have him take me.

Where's she being held? I tried to ask silently one more time even as I gave into my desire and kissed Duncan.

Our lips were demanding, our need rising with such intensity that I forgot where we were and why we had come. Even with the medallions glowing between us, I lost my awareness of being manipulated. When he unfastened my pants and slid his fingers into me, I gasped and bucked, savage wildness leaping into me.

I twisted in his arms, grabbing him as I mashed myself against him, a frenzy of need leaving me panting, magic mingling with passion, manipulation with true love. Such a desire to sate myself with him swept into me that I snarled and cried out. All animal. All werewolf.

We bit and clawed, instincts ruling us instead of our rational minds. Such pleasure rocked into me that I hardly cared. When Duncan tore our clothes away and plunged into me, we howled.

The cave walls hummed and glowed with magic, with power that wrapped around us as we came together again and again. Never had I known such intense pleasure. Never had I wanted more to be with someone. If this was what protecting the pack involved, I would give my everything to have it again and again.

The lupine howls that tore from our throats when we crashed together for a final time, an explosion of magic leaving us shaking, must have been audible outside of the cave and miles into the forest.

Panting with our hearts pounding, we finally sank to the ground, entwined and exhausted. The medallions continued to glow, satisfied, as if they'd shared in our joining, our pleasure. Their light gleamed, reflected in Duncan's eyes.

His hand slid over my womb, fingers splaying. As my rational thoughts returned, I realized we hadn't used contraception this time. Even if I'd had the wherewithal, something told me the medallions and the magic of the cave wouldn't have allowed it. They'd wanted to secure the future of our kind, to leave me with a werewolf child that had our power, the power to protect the pack into the future.

18

ON THE FLOOR OF THE CAVE, I LAY WITH DUNCAN, HIS ARMS pillowing me and protecting me from the cold chill of the rock as he dozed. My eyes were wide open as I stared into the darkness. Their mission complete, the medallions had stopped glowing, and little light remained. Only a couple of the paintings on the wall continued to emanate faint silver illumination.

I stared at the closest paw print and touched it, disappointed that the cave had offered up only what *it* wanted, not what I'd wanted. If finding that cliff and planting the mushroom artifact could help the pack, I would do it, but what of Jasmine and Izzy? I...

A tingle spread into my finger from the cool wall, and a second vision came to me.

This time, I stood in the restaurant at the top of the Space Needle, the same table where I'd dined with Duncan, and looked out upon the city at night. The view, however, wasn't familiar, at least not all of it. There was Puget Sound and Lake Union, but in a clearing amid the streets and buildings, a great garden sprawled, with paths meandering between exotic trees and raised beds and planters. Here and there, fountains rose between patches of blue-, purple-, and pink-flowered foliage. Beyond the borders of the garden, the city of Seattle remained, but I was confused, certain so much verdant space didn't exist in that location in the real world. And those flowers weren't like anything I'd seen before, certainly nothing native to the region.

The vision swept me down one of the garden paths, showing me a hazy darkness with Izzy and Jasmine in the center, tied inside cages in their wolf forms. A wispy-haired figure in medical scrubs stood in the shadows. Abrams.

The wolves tilted their snouts upward to howl mournfully. Abrams advanced upon them with a dagger.

I lurched into a sitting position, the vision shattering like a nightmare. My heart pounded with the certainty that I'd experienced reality, not a dream. Maybe because Jasmine was part of the pack, the magic of the cave had deigned to show me her location.

Beside me, Duncan stirred.

"Wonderful," he murmured.

I pushed hair out of my eyes. It was damp from the exertion of our lovemaking. No, we'd made love before, on the mossy forest floor without the medallions manipulating us. This had been... savage, wild sex with nothing tender about it. I couldn't say I hadn't enjoyed it, but the next time I got horizontal with Duncan, I intended to do it without manipulative magical hardware around our necks.

Thoughts probably still muzzy with sleep, Duncan patted my leg and issued another, "Wonderful."

Maybe he hadn't minded the manipulation.

"I have an idea about where Jasmine and Izzy might be," I said, the vision haunting me. What if those events were happening right now? While Duncan and I lay in this cave, dozens of miles from Seattle?

"Oh? Did the cave tell you?" He lifted his head but then frowned toward the entrance.

Had he heard something? Sensed someone?

Other than the faint gurgle from the stream, I didn't see or hear anything out there in the dark, but Duncan rolled away from me and patted around for his clothes.

"We've got company," he said.

"Vile enemies hellbent on our destruction?" I thought of the real estate developers. Or what if Chad had come back?

"Your mother."

"Oh." I slumped.

I would rather have dealt with enemies.

"And the wise wolf. They seem to travel together."

"Rosaria did say she would keep an eye on my mother."

Duncan and I dressed and stepped outside. Now, I could also sense Mom and Rosaria. They stood on the rise across the gully, mostly hidden by the trees, but a partial moon shone through a gap in the branches, and I could make out Mom, standing on a log or boulder to gaze down toward us.

Thanks to the privacy of the cave, I knew they hadn't *watched* us, but my cheeks heated as I remembered how noisy we'd been. If they'd arrived in time, they would have heard us. Hell, they might have heard us from the cabin.

Over the ferns and the distance, our eyes met. Mom looked... pleased. Her gaze shifted toward my stomach—no, my *womb*. Then she nodded at me and mouthed something.

Goodbye?

I opened my own mouth, debating on yelling that I didn't appreciate her interference, but she turned, letting Rosaria help her down. They disappeared into the woods and soon faded from my senses.

Aware of Duncan beside me, thinking who knew what, I said, "Sorry about that. I didn't mean to... Well, I knew she wanted this, but I wouldn't have gone along with it of my own accord. I *tried* not to."

"It's all right. It's not your fault she wanted you to enjoy the pure delight of having such a fine wolf as myself mate with you."

"Yeah, it was my *delight* that she was concerned about." I lay a hand on my abdomen, wondering if... Had the magic ensured I would become pregnant tonight? Did it have that power? "She manipulated us. And so did those medallions."

Could I trust them or the vision from the cave when it came to Jasmine and Izzy's location? Since the magic was determined to protect the pack, it *should* want Jasmine saved. I hoped it had known and given me their accurate location so we could find them.

"It's all right," Duncan repeated. "We had sex *before* the manipulation started too. I'm hardly disappointed. I've been trying to lure you into my bed for weeks."

"The sex isn't the part I thought you'd object to." I patted my abdomen, though I would wait until I could take a pregnancy test before assuming anything had happened there tonight.

Duncan stepped close and wrapped his arms around me. "You'll be an amazing mother."

He already knew what I suspected. Maybe his medallion had been giving him visions too.

"I already know you are," he added.

"Are you ready to be... an amazing father?"

Any kind of father. He'd been musing about it, but that wasn't the same as deciding to become a parent.

"I'm working on my skills in that area," Duncan said. "If I can keep my clone from killing me, we'll know I'm getting there."

"Winning over an eight-year-old can be a challenge."

Duncan kissed my cheek and stroked my side. "Would you be willing to explore the idea of travel with me? With a child? Your life could be full of adventure."

Full of throwing magnets into water and hauling up rusty junk, maybe. If I was with Duncan, might I enjoy that? For a time?

"I guess if I'm going to need to get a new job anyway," I said, "I can try to find something that allows travel. I'm not sure how I'll fix toilets remotely though."

"Maybe it's time for you to aspire to something grander."

"But I like the toilets," I said.

"You're an odd woman."

"Which is not keeping you from holding my boob."

"No, it's quite magnificent and draws me, despite its odd owner."

"Hilarious."

"You'll laugh every day you're with me."

"I'll be even more inclined to laugh if we rescue my niece and deal with Abrams."

Duncan sighed, released me, and stepped back. "You said the cave gave you insight into that?"

"Surprisingly, yes." I filled him in on both visions.

"Are you familiar enough with the area to locate those gardens?"

"Well. I'm familiar enough with the area to know those gardens aren't *there*."

Duncan scratched his jaw.

"We'll have to drive around and hope to find... I'm not sure what." I shrugged. "Maybe the gardens in the vision were symbolic of something."

"Abrams could have a base downtown near the Space Needle."

"Yeah. Maybe if we go up to the restaurant again, we'll be able to see something. If there's magic involved, the medallions might help us find it."

"I'll take you to look," Duncan said. "I'm always amenable to driving you around."

"Remind me to stop at an ATM and get more gas money."

He smirked but didn't try to tell me I didn't need to pay. By now, he knew I would regardless of what he said.

We headed back to Mom's cabin. A part of me was tempted to bypass it, hop in the van, and depart before she could make any comments about Duncan and me getting randy in the cave, but I felt I should say goodbye. Though I hated to think about it, every time I left now, it was possible it would be the last time I saw her.

When we reached the cabin, the parking area was empty, save for Duncan's van. I didn't sense Mom or Rosaria in the cabin but climbed the steps to look inside anyway.

"Do you think they went to Sylvan Serenity to join the pack there?" I asked.

"I don't know, but the property you manage is going to be overrun by werewolves."

"Almost as bad as werewolf kidnappers."

Inside, the lights were off, save for a small desk lamp. A sheet of paper lay under it, a few lines of handwriting scrawled across it.

A letter from Mom?

We'd just seen her. I was surprised she'd had time to write something, but my gut told me that the note was for me.

My feet led me to the desk. Maybe she'd started it while Duncan and I had been... busy.

I stopped in front of the desk, spotting my name at the top of the letter. A sense of dread rolled ponderously into my gut. I lifted the page and tilted it toward the light to read.

Luna,

I'm relieved you've finally given in to your destiny and joined with the old-world wolf to produce powerful werewolf offspring. It is all that I desired for you, and now I can die at peace, knowing my heritage will be carried on and suitable leaders will watch over the pack. I trust that you and Duncan will be respected by most and can handle those naysayers who may object to your position as pack alphas. This is the way of the wolf.

I've asked Rosaria to help me walk once more in the wilderness and bathe in the moon's magic. I do not wish to die in a bed in a cabin like a human. That is not how wolves are meant to go.

I paused, my throat constricted, to wipe my damp eyes. The realization crept over me that I wouldn't likely see my mother again. I hadn't gotten a chance to say goodbye, other than that head nod we'd shared. Maybe that had been enough of a farewell for her.

As I already told you, the Medallion of Memory and Power is yours, and, as I believe your Duncan will remain with the pack and bound to you, the male version should stay with him. I do have one last request for you that I hope you'll prioritize, especially given the trouble the world keeps bringing to the threshold of our caves and cabins. Retrieve your niece, yes, but also do what the vision suggested to protect our people, and do it soon. I'm not sure how much time we have. The pack must continue.

I would not be displeased, should you have a daughter, if you named her after me. From the stars and moon, I shall attempt to watch over her. And you. Be well, Luna.

~ Mom

I set the page down and wiped the tears from my eyes.

"Are you all right?" Duncan asked quietly.

He remained by the door.

"No."

"Do you need anything?"

"To find that cliff and plant the mushroom, apparently." I handed the letter to him, then looked around the cabin until I found a map of the area, one that showed topography. If the vision had been accurate, that cliff wouldn't be far. The artifact had been doing its magic from the middle of our pack's territory.

"I'm sorry, Luna." Duncan lowered the letter after he finished reading. "I've not had any family over the years, but I'm sure it's hard to lose a parent."

"Yes." I took the map to the desk, having located a likely spot, and drew the case out of my purse. "I need to go for a hike before we return to find Jasmine." The wolf case zapped me. I set it down and scowled at it. "Are you *really* going to be integral in protecting our people?"

My medallion hummed against my chest. Was that supposed to be encouragement? Maybe Duncan's medallion did the same thing because he glanced down and touched it.

"All right," I muttered and grabbed an oven mitt from the kitchen.

With my hand thus insulated, I picked up the case again and headed for the door. "Off we go."

19

DRIZZLE FELL FROM THE CLOUDY NIGHT SKY AS DUNCAN AND I clambered up a treed slope, the undergrowth dense and undisturbed. Dawn approached, but the gloom made it hard to tell. Only my phone confirming the time assured me that we'd been up all night. As we climbed, I yawned often and wiped my eyes, not certain if the moisture came from sorrow, the rain, or simply weariness.

I felt more like I was going to set a gravestone rather than plant an artifact and couldn't shake my somber mood. It didn't help that my niece was still in danger, and who knew what was going on at the apartment complex with the pack.

Glad to have Duncan with me, I bumped the back of my hand against his as we walked. "I appreciate your support."

"I could tell that from your gentle touch with that oven mitt."

"It's how American women show affection."

"Interesting." Duncan nodded toward a portion of the sky visible ahead, a suggestion that we would soon reach the top of the slope. "I don't sense much in the way of magic around. Are we looking for something in particular?"

I considered my memory of the vision. "Just... high ground, I think. Like a spot you'd set up an antenna. Or a cell tower."

Duncan eyed the case. "Or a funky metallic mushroom?"

"I hope so."

Since there were no trails here, it took several more minutes to reach the top. Trees grew densely, but a rock shelf provided a clear viewpoint, and when we walked out onto it, I recognized the vista. In the vision, I'd been able to see Mom's cabin and those of other werewolves. That was harder in reality, but I did pick out the road that led to Mom's home.

"I think this is the place." I held the case out on my oven mitt, wondering if the artifact inside had somehow been filled in on the vision. Would it know what to do? That the lid needed to open, and the mushroom needed to float out? What if it didn't *want* to do what the medallions and the cave wished?

"Do you need me to turn into the bipedfuris?" Duncan asked after a few moments with nothing happening.

"I'm not sure. Visions never come with as detailed of instructions as you'd wish."

Duncan touched his medallion. "I'm having an urge to get furry."

"An urge or a magical compulsion?"

"Well, they're about the same." Duncan stepped back and started removing his clothes. "You may want to look away so you're not so overcome with lust for my naked body that we're distracted."

I yawned. "I'm too tired to be overcome by anything."

"That's a touch disappointing. I'd like to think my body, which I naturally keep in peak physical shape, is enough to invigorate women and fill them with energy and lust."

"Your mind must be an interesting place to inhabit."

"Oh, it's a delight." Duncan bent to remove his shoes.

Wondering if the reception was better up here, I set the case between my feet and pulled out my phone. Maybe I could get a text through to Bolin, and he would send an update.

But he'd already sent a message at some point during the night, one that might have just come in.

There are wolves sniffing all over the place, Luna. Are they here looking for Jasmine? I hope so. They won't talk to me. They're not bothering the tenants, but some people are out here taking photos of them. Do you want me to do anything? Is there anything I can do? I was looking for locating spells in my druid texts, but none were as helpful as I'd hoped. Even though some have potions and tools, like the Orbs of Entanglement, that can be made from ingredients, they're not alchemy tomes.

An idea struck me, one that should have occurred when Izzy had disappeared. I took off the oven mitt so I could use both hands to text back more quickly.

Check with Rue. She can make potions for finding people. She'll need some hair or blood or saliva or something from Jasmine though. And Jasmine will need to be within ten miles for the potion to take us to her, but... that should be doable. I have an idea of the general area where she's being kept.

It occurred to me that Bolin hadn't likely asked Jasmine for blood or hair samples on their dates. I was on the verge of texting that I could swing by her house and ask her parents if I could poke in her bathroom for a hairbrush.

But Bolin texted back first. It had to be a testament to his concern for her that he was awake at dawn. *There's a napkin here that she dabbed her mouth with and a coffee cup she drank from. It's got some of her lipstick on it. There should be some saliva, right?*

Maybe so. Check with Rue.

Okay.

A glow and pulse of magic came from between my feet, startling me. The lid of the case opened.

A growl from behind me let me know that Duncan had

completed his change. Tall, furred, and muscular, the bipedfuris crouched between me and a large pine. He glowered at the case, which reminded me of something he'd said before. The artifact didn't like him—didn't like any werewolves—and sent irritating magic crawling all over him when he was in that form.

I stepped back, not wanting a glowing magical artifact doing who knew what between my legs, and wondered anew why this ancient tool that didn't like our kind would help us. The vision had promised it would, but I still didn't understand.

The glow intensified, and I backed further away. Duncan did too. We ended up half in the trees, torn between squinting toward the case to see what would happen and wanting to look away.

As it had in the vision, the mushroom floated up out of the case. Several strong pulses came from it, the usual glow limned with purple, creating circular waves that spread outward in all directions over the forest. After a few minutes, they faded, and the mushroom slowly descended to the ground.

The cliff appeared to be made from solid rock, but magic surged from the artifact's stem, and snaps sounded and smoke wafted. It was drilling a hole, one that it nestled itself securely into. The light grew less intense, but I continued to sense the artifact emanating magic. Its cap also glowed a soft purple.

The lid on the case *thunked* shut, surprising me. The mushroom remained outside of it, planted in the cliff, the purple cap a beacon in the dim light.

"People are going to be able to see that from a ways off," I muttered.

Though maybe that wasn't true. It might be hard to see once we got down from the cliff. I could *sense* the artifact and its power, however.

Duncan growled, looking like he wanted to stalk over and punt the case *and* the artifact off the cliff.

I rested a hand on his taut arm. "I think it's doing something to help our people."

He made a grunt of inquiry.

"I'm not sure exactly what, but would a vision in a weird cave that manipulated us into having sex lead us astray?"

He tilted his furry head.

I laughed softly and shrugged. "Mom thought it wouldn't. We'll have to see."

Despite the drizzle and clouds, the clifftop perch offered an appealing view of the brightening forest. On a sunny day, or maybe a moonlit night, sometime after I found Jasmine and Izzy, I would return and enjoy the vista more thoroughly.

Another text from Bolin reached me. *Rue said she'll make the potion. Also, Ivan MacGregor is here, looking for you.*

I grimaced, again feeling guilty that I wasn't actively searching for his sister. But if Izzy was with Jasmine, Rue's potion ought to lead us to them. Remembering how awful the dreadful things tasted, I said, "I hope I can talk Bolin into taking this one."

Duncan grunted.

"Can you change back into you? It's time to go back to the city, and I need a driver."

A second grunt may have been agreement, but some critter rustled down the slope, and he loped off in that direction.

I picked up the case and gathered his clothes, glad his car keys jangled in the pants pocket. "Looks like *I* might be the driver."

Before following him down the slope, I once more looked back at the view, the mushroom cap glowing a soft purple near the edge of the cliff, the forest stretching away beyond it. It felt like placing it had been a funeral of sorts, as if, in carrying out Mom's last wish, I was saying goodbye to her. I hoped the artifact did indeed offer some protection for our people and that this had been worth it.

20

By the time I reached the van, Duncan had finished his quick hunt and met me there, returning to his human form. I handed him his keys, and he dressed and took the wheel. Weary from being up all night, I dozed off a few times on the way back, only waking when updates from Bolin came in. He had to be standing on Rue's doorstep, pacing as she worked on the potion. That belief was verified when *she* called and complained about him.

"*You* are kind enough to leave me in peace when I work," she said. "Your intern is insufferable."

"He's in love."

"*Insufferable.* I had no idea that you were an ideal client, at least in comparison to this one."

"Does that mean you'll give me a discount on future potions?"

"My ingredients are expensive. I cannot give *discounts* if I wish to remain in business as a successful entrepreneur. I will, however, give you double stamps on your card the next time you purchase a potion."

"Thoughtful."

"Yes. I am not giving your intern a stamp card at all. No freebies for him." Rue made a disgruntled *harrumph*, then informed me that the order would be completed by the time we arrived.

Duncan took the freeway exit for Shoreline. "Are you going to be able to convince Bolin to consume that potion?"

"I think so. He's in love, after all."

"Was it love that convinced you to consume such a dreadful liquid to find *me*?" He lifted his hand from the steering wheel to touch his chest.

My first instinct was to say something snarky, possibly about having his van towed, and the smile on his lips suggested he expected it. But I thought about all we'd been through together, how many times he'd come to my aid, and that I might even now have the beginning of his child—*our* child—within me.

"Yeah," I said.

His eyebrows raised in mild surprise but only for a moment before he said, "I love you too."

"Yeah," I said again, smiling.

He pulled into the parking lot of Sylvan Serenity, and it would have been a great moment for a kiss, but Bolin stood on the sidewalk, waiting for us. He wore a backpack, a flak vest, and... was that a bandolier? It looked like it held vials rather than bullets, but that didn't keep him from looking like a slender Rambo ready to tramp into a jungle to fight bad guys.

"Love drives men to do interesting things," I observed.

A few kids of eight or ten were up early, playing on the lawn. Digging up earthworms drawn out by the rain, perhaps. I remembered encountering that crew before and that they'd been daring each other to eat such things.

"Oh, it certainly does." Duncan might have said more, but Bolin jogged up to his window.

"Rue said she would have the elixir soon," Bolin said when Duncan rolled it down. "Then we can go. But I need to be within ten miles of Jasmine before drinking it. Do you want to drive? Or I could. But... I don't have any idea where the kidnappers took her. Do you?"

"We do have an idea. I need to go to the bathroom and grab something to eat before we take off again, but we can all go together." I also wanted to see if I could sense my relatives, but that wouldn't take long. I tilted my thumb toward the back of the van in an invitation to Bolin.

"Okay. I have a few more supplies to load." Bolin held up a finger, then ran to his SUV, throwing open the back door.

"Do you think he might have stopped for grenades?" Duncan asked. "I haven't had a chance to replenish my reserves."

"I have no idea what kind of *supplies* a geeky, spelling-bee-competing, violin-playing druid might bring." I opened the door to slide out. "When Jasmine said she would bring provisions for one of our adventures, it was a bag of Doritos."

"Did the chips keep you sated?"

"They at least let me wash the taste of that potion out of my mouth. I'd better bring something along for Bolin to do the same." I was relieved that it sounded like *he* intended to take the elixir himself. Of course, he didn't have previous experience with the loathsome liquid to know how awful it was.

"I have a few chocolate-covered espresso beans left, but I'd intended to save those for you."

"I do like to caffeinate myself before storming an enemy compound."

"We all do. Is that... a Howitzer?"

I followed Duncan's gaze. Bolin was levering something large and metal out of the back of his SUV.

"Probably not," I said, "but it does look awkward."

"I'd better help him." Duncan hopped out. "And make sure he doesn't load anything that might be dangerous to my van."

"Good idea."

I strode toward my apartment, thinking fondly of my espresso maker as I yawned for the thousandth time that morning. Distracted by my longing for coffee, I almost missed sensing a werewolf in the woods.

It wasn't someone from my pack but Lykos. Uneasy, I stopped behind a lamppost and peered toward the trees, then looked toward the parking lot to make sure Duncan wasn't in a potentially vulnerable position.

He was helping Bolin carry some kind of tripod with a barrel on it—I decided it probably wasn't a weapon—to the van. Duncan must have sensed me looking because he met my gaze, tilted his head toward the woods, and nodded. Of course. With his superior senses, he must have already detected the kid out there.

Laughter came from the boys holding worms and, for who knew what reason, a hockey puck aloft.

Though Lykos was good at camouflaging himself in those woods, I got the sense from his position that he might be looking at the kids instead of at Duncan. Because he intended them some harm?

It was hard for me to imagine a clone of Duncan having a malevolent streak, but Lykos *was* apparently here on an assassination mission.

After taking care of biological needs and turning on the espresso maker to warm up, I grabbed ham out of the fridge and a bar of the caramel-truffled chocolate. So armed, I took a roundabout way to the woods, using one of the back apartment buildings to hide my approach. Lykos would sense me as easily as Duncan would, but maybe he'd be distracted by observing his prey and wouldn't have time to run off.

Taking a side trail, I veered into the woods and tried to sneak up behind Lykos. Not surprisingly, he sensed me and, soon after coming into my view, turned away from the kids to look at me.

His brown hair hung in his eyes, he wore torn, dirt-stained clothing, and he didn't have any shoes. My heart ached for him. I knew Abrams had been a shitty guardian, but things must have gotten worse lately. The memory of the scars on Duncan's wrists always haunted me, a testament to how Abrams had treated him in his youth.

"Hey, Lykos." I forced a smile and offered a friendly wave, rustling the bag of deli ham.

If he'd been a dog, familiar with the ways of humans and kitchen items, Lykos would have known to come running at the sound. His head cocked with curiosity, but he also lowered into a crouch, ready to spring off to run in any direction.

I stopped several steps away so I wouldn't appear threatening. "Do you want something to eat? Or did you come to see Duncan? I know he enjoyed teaching you about magnets. Have you gone fishing with him yet?"

Duncan had said Lykos could speak, but he'd yet to say anything to me, and he didn't respond to my burbling now. Instead, he looked toward the parking lot where Duncan and Bolin were gesturing near the open door of the van. He also glanced at the boys again, though they were heading toward a rack where their bicycles were chained, probably on their way out.

I didn't know where my family had gone but was glad they weren't loitering here. Maybe they were on the trail of the missing werewolves? Jasmine, at least, they knew well. But she'd been taken in a van, so I questioned if the pack would be able to track her. If it were easy to trail someone in an automobile, Duncan or I could have done it ourselves.

The wistful gaze on Lykos's face as he watched the group of children made me realize he hadn't been contemplating *hurting* them, the first thought that had come to my mind.

"Those kids all live here," I told Lykos. "If you lived with... Duncan, you could play with them." I'd almost said *lived with us*, but it wasn't as if Duncan and I had moved in together. Unfortunately, I still had no idea where I would be living in the future. "One problem at a time," I murmured.

Lykos met my gaze again. "I must kill him to take his place as the chosen wolf."

His tone was quiet and earnest. I couldn't tell from his eyes if he wanted to do that or didn't like the idea of it.

"Is that what Abrams said?" I asked. "He's an asshole and a liar."

"You killed Radomir."

"He was an asshole too."

"Is that ham?"

"Yeah, black forest. It's delicious." I waved the baggy again. "Do you want me to leave some?"

"You keep bringing food, as if you think I'm a hound that can be won over with treats."

I might have been comparing him to a dog scant moments before, but I refused to feel embarrassed. "Yeah, it's how I won over Duncan, so I figured I'd try it. You're mini Duncan, after all."

Lykos squinted suspiciously at me. "You earned his loyalty with ham?"

"Ham and chocolate. And bacon, though I guess that's similar to ham."

"That's it?"

"He likes my boobs too." Okay, that wasn't the most age-appropriate topic to bring up with a kid, but Lykos had the soulful eyes of someone who'd never had a childhood and wouldn't be fazed by anything adults discussed.

"He is your mate."

As of last night, I could finally say, "Yes, he is."

"Then you will say anything to keep me from killing him."

"I guess I would, but I'm not that concerned about you being able to pull that off. Not for some years anyway. He's full-grown and pretty badass."

Did Lykos look offended? The young never liked being told they were just kids. Maybe I'd done better with him before he'd started talking.

"He is powerful," Lykos said. "I will be too one day."

"Definitely. And you don't need to be the *chosen wolf* for that. Abrams is telling you stupid shit to manipulate you."

"You are also attempting to manipulate me."

The kid wasn't a dummy, was he? Nor that young and naive.

"Every chance I get," I said, opting for honesty instead of denying it. "Like I said, Duncan is my mate. And I'm watching out for him, the way he watches out for me. I also don't want to see one of his relatives killed. It would hurt him." I pointed at Lykos, assuming he understood the cloning thing and that he and Duncan were siblings, however great their age difference.

"When I succeed in slaying him, will you attempt to exact revenge?" Lykos touched his chest.

"You're not going to slay him."

"It is my duty, but it is regrettable that it would leave you without a mate."

"Your *duty* is to think for yourself. Abrams is a dick, and he's not even a werewolf. Not a pack leader. You don't need to *obey* him."

"I... must obey him."

"Why? Is he magically compelling you somehow?" I eyed the kid's forehead, but he didn't have a scar to indicate a link to a control device. I did, however, remember magic flowing into him when we'd been together before. It had seemed to force him to attack me.

"When I mature, I can become your mate, if you wish," Lykos said. "As a replacement for the one who I will slay."

"Sorry, kid. I'm not a cougar."

He blinked in confusion. "You are a wolf."

"I know. I meant— Never mind. Duncan is a good guy. He'd

like to be your *friend*, not your enemy. Not your *assassination* target."

Lykos's head swiveled around.

At first, I thought Duncan had done something to draw his attention, but Lykos was looking toward the woods to one side, not toward the parking lot.

Had one of my relatives returned? I sensed... not a magical being, but I did detect a magical item. A mundane human carrying an artifact?

A branch snapped, and a man in a cowboy hat stepped into view. His face grim, he carried a revolver in one hand, a small metal device in the other, and he wore a bracelet on his left wrist, the golden edge visible below the sleeve of a suit jacket.

"Ivan?" I asked, though maybe I shouldn't have been surprised. He'd called twice, looking for his sister.

He'd been scrutinizing Lykos—guided to him by whatever that device was?—and blinked in surprise when he spotted me. "Luna?"

"Yeah. We're about to head out to look for Izzy and my niece, Jasmine. She's missing too. We had to gather a few things to help us find them, but we think they might be located in the same spot."

"The ransom letter I received said they were kidnapped here and that a brown-haired wolf boy was helping identify the targets." Jaw clenching, Ivan strode toward Lykos.

He didn't point the gun at the kid, but his finger flexed on the trigger, as if he were thinking about it.

Lykos sprang behind a tree for cover, then ran deeper into the woods. Ivan started after him, but I surged forward to intercept him. I grabbed his arm in case he got a dumb idea about firing that gun. I had no idea if Lykos had anything to do with those kidnappings, but I couldn't let Duncan's little brother be hurt.

The kid glanced back, meeting my eyes, before disappearing from view—and my senses.

"He wasn't responsible," I told Ivan. "And what letter? If it was from Abrams, it can't be trusted. If it was a *ransom* letter—isn't that what you said?—it certainly can't be trusted."

"No. I know." Ivan looked down at my grip on his arm.

I released him. I didn't know if he'd activated that bracelet—when we'd first met, he'd said it could temporarily give one the strength and regenerative power of a werewolf—but he hadn't tried to shove me away. He'd also seemed conflicted about attacking a kid. I *hoped* he was.

"I actually came to give you something and implore you to help find Izzy."

"I'm working on it. Honest. I had to get some advice first." I left out that the *advice* had come from a magical cave in the form of a vision. Just because Ivan believed in werewolves didn't mean he would buy that. "We've got a pretty good idea where they're being kept now."

"Izzy is a pain in the ass," Ivan said, "but she's still my sister. And I can't let Olivia lose her mother."

"I understand."

"Can you get her back? Can I help?" Ivan raised his wrist, the sleeve falling back to show the whole bracelet.

"I'm going to get them back, yes. And I've already got a druid and a werewolf to help. I think that'll be sufficient."

He mouthed, "*Druid*," having probably never encountered one. At least not that he knew about.

"We'll get them," I promised and stepped back, intending to leave him and head for the van, but I paused. "Did the letter say anything useful? What ransom did Abrams want? That's who sent it, right?"

Maybe I shouldn't have assumed that. The real estate developers were still possible culprits behind everything, though all the magical potions that had been hurled about the premises continued to make me think Abrams the more likely antagonist.

But why would Abrams have thrown Lykos under the bus? Or had he believed his young werewolf assassin would *take care of* Ivan? I grimaced.

"For me to get that from you." Ivan pointed at the chain around my neck, though the medallion itself lay under my shirt. "And also another one from a werewolf living here in a van." He pointed to the parking lot.

"I guess that solidifies it. It *must* have been Abrams."

Chad had been interested in werewolf artifacts too, but I doubted he'd masterminded the kidnapping of Izzy and Jasmine.

"There wasn't a name on the letter," Ivan said. "I was to get the medallions and mail them to an address, and then the kidnapper would send Izzy to me."

"Do you have the address?"

"Yes." Ivan withdrew a folded paper from his back pocket and showed me the letter.

The address was familiar. I took a photo so that I could check later, but I was fairly certain that was one of the locations that Jasmine's father had come up with as being related to Radomir's business. Another piece of evidence to link this to Abrams.

"It crossed my mind to try to bribe you for those items." Ivan shook his head ruefully as he withdrew an envelope folded in half. "But, even if you'd agreed to sell them, which I doubted from the beginning, mailing priceless artifacts to a random address did not seem like a surefire way to get my sister back."

"No. You're supposed to do an in-person exchange when you're trading for a kidnap victim. Or so Hollywood informs us."

Ivan nodded his agreement, then offered the envelope. It was stuffed thickly enough that hundreds of dollars could be inside.

I held up my palm. "You were right that the medallions aren't for sale."

"This is for finding my bracelet and returning it. I did promise a reward."

"That's okay. I was looking for something else when I happened across it."

Ivan raised his eyebrows. "Are you going to be too proud to accept my offering? It's not a hand-out. I'm sure you don't need that."

"I'm not proud, but I'm also not a treasure hunter or anything like that. I'm a property manager."

"Let me at least reimburse you for the postage you spent mailing the bracelet."

"Okay."

Without taking any of the money inside out, Ivan held the envelope toward me again.

"The price of stamps hasn't gone up *that* much."

"Are you sure?" he asked. "Inflation has been particularly profound in that area."

As I shook my head, a call came from the lawn.

"Luna? Are you out there?" Rue stood in the grass, holding up a potion in a vial. "I have something for your intern, but he's not in the leasing office."

"I need to go," I told Ivan. "That might help us find your sister."

Without letting him make another attempt at foisting the money on me, I waved and jogged toward Rue.

With my future uncertain, maybe I was a fool not to take every coin, dollar, and *postage reimbursement* offered, but I felt guilty that Izzy had been captured because of me. Okay, she wouldn't have been captured if she hadn't been here *harassing* me, but still. It was hard not to feel that I had, all those years ago when I'd lost it with Raoul, set in motion the events that had led to her being taken. I might never stop feeling guilty over Raoul's death. Some regrets accompanied one to the grave.

"He's helping Duncan load up the van for the storming of an

enemy lair we're hoping to find today," I told Rue when I reached her.

"Here." She handed me the vial. "I trust you can instruct him on its use. Tell him that I put the invoice under the windshield wiper of his vehicle. If you are taking him to assail an enemy lair, I must insist that he pay for the elixir before you leave."

"He's the wealthy son of the wealthy family who owns this place." I waved to encompass all of Sylvan Serenity. "He's good for it."

"His credit worthiness is not my concern. That he might *die* before paying the debt is."

"Ah. I guess that's valid."

"Certainly. Did you know that an entire *pack* of werewolves came through here this morning?"

"That was my family."

"How dreadful. And there's been a young one lurking around the area for more than a week." Rue peered into the woods. "When I moved from the urban core of the city to this suburb, I expected life to be quieter and calmer."

"It hasn't been? I haven't noticed any graffiti on your door here. Werewolves rarely carry cans of spray paint when in their lupine forms."

"Yes, but the power of their auras is distracting when they cruise through. It interferes with my reading."

"Your life sounds difficult."

"It's very often fraught."

Duncan hopped out of his van, met my gaze, and waved. Were they ready to head off? Was I?

No, I thought, but I waved back, acknowledging that I would join them.

"I'll let Bolin know about the invoice," I told Rue before heading toward the van.

Duncan looked past me and into the woods, but if Lykos was

out there, I couldn't sense him. He'd either been scared away by Ivan, or he was off to enact some plan to kill Duncan.

I shook my head grimly, hoping the kid wouldn't show up at Abrams's Seattle compound. Duncan's determination to befriend him—be*father* him?—made me think he'd already started caring about what happened to Lykos. As someone who'd battled a loved one and won, I could attest to how that was as bad as losing.

21

I gave Duncan an address downtown near the Space Needle, though I had no idea where our real destination was. What the vision had given me... hadn't been a spot that existed. I'd been positive of that even before my internet map search.

Whether that garden was symbolic or an enlarged version of a yard or park that did exist, I didn't know. My hope was that if we started in the area the vision had shown, Bolin would be able to take the elixir and guide us to Jasmine. He was in the back of the van now, fretting about her and asking every five minutes if he should swallow it yet.

"Are you going to open that?" Duncan pointed to Ivan's envelope on the dash as we navigated traffic on I-5.

"No. I tried to reject it." I didn't even know where the envelope had come from. It had simply been in the van after I'd accepted the elixir from Rue.

"So, I should have objected when MacGregor slipped it in through my open window?" Duncan asked.

"Yes. I would have."

"He said he owed you postage money. The envelope looked

rather thick for that, but Bolin and I were busy stuffing a few items under the bed, table, and into already-full cabinets, and I didn't think much of it."

"Ivan's trying to reward me for returning his bracelet."

"Oh, well that's acceptable, isn't it? We *did* have to battle poison-vapor-exhaling robot bugs in order to get that. You're deserving of a reward."

"We were there anyway. For other reasons." I pointed at him.

Seeking a way to lift his curse had been my primary motivator in infiltrating that laboratory.

"You say that like it's a reason to decline reward money. Luna, if you want to get rich in this world, you can't turn down money that's granted to you in a rightful manner."

"It seems wrong to take money from some wealthy guy, especially when his sister was kidnapped on the grounds of the apartment complex I manage."

"That's *her* fault for being furry, surly, and all over your grounds."

I shook my head. Maybe he wouldn't understand. I probably wasn't articulating myself well.

"I don't want to *get rich*," I decided on as my counter.

"That's fine, but if you want to retire comfortably and not have to worry about having a roof over your head in your old age, then you can't turn down money."

That was... a legitimate argument. Maybe he was right.

"Did I mention that Ivan has seen me naked and suggested we hook up?"

"No." Duncan frowned at me.

"That means it would be extra weird to take his money. I wouldn't want him thinking... Well, he seems like an okay guy, but you know." I shrugged. "Weird."

Duncan took the exit for downtown Seattle, slowing for a red light before we'd gone far.

"You should take the money," he said, "and then show him a photo of us together, ideally with me looking sexy and irresistible and you gazing adoringly and lustfully at me."

"Ew," came a faint utterance from Bolin.

And here I'd thought he'd been too busy worrying about Jasmine to pay attention to our conversation.

"I don't have a photo like that," I told Duncan.

"No? How have we failed to properly document our burgeoning relationship, respect, and passion for each other?"

"It's a mystery," I said.

Duncan withdrew his phone, leaned toward me, stuck his arm out, and tapped selfie mode.

I rolled my eyes. He took a photo.

"Perfect." He glanced at it, tucking his phone away when the light turned. "I'll text it to you so you can send it along."

"I'm certain neither adoration nor lust was signaled by my expression."

"You're clearly unaware that you ooze those emotions in my direction all the time. Like pheromones."

That prompted another *ew* and also a sigh from the back.

Duncan turned onto a tight street with so many cars parked on either side that the van struggled to make it through. He slowed, and we peered down an alley lined by dumpsters and trash cans, with weeds growing up through cracks in the pavement.

"If this is the address, it looks... underwhelming." He looked at his phone's GPS map.

"I just gave you a starting spot. The location the vision suggested didn't have an address associated with it. Like I said, it didn't look like anyplace that actually exists in the city. I'm hoping we're close, though, and Bolin can lead us from here. Or wherever you can find parking." I waved vaguely.

"Okay." Duncan drove down a few more packed blocks before

parking in front of a fire hydrant, apparently not worried about the ticket police wandering through. "You're up, kid."

"Kid?" Bolin protested.

"You sighed and said *ew* twice as we discussed romance," I said. "*Kid* may be the right term."

"Funny." Bolin grabbed a pack—for this mission, he'd come with a backpack instead of his expensive leather messenger bag—and slung it over his shoulders before jumping out of the van.

I didn't know what he and Duncan had loaded into the van, but they must not have wanted to schlep around all of downtown Seattle with it. Duncan grabbed a pack, magnets clinking inside, and his magic detector, but that was it. I hadn't brought anything except a few snacks and the sword. Maybe I'd come underprepared. We would find out.

We gathered at the mouth of an alley that smelled of urine and held garbage bins and a couple of shopping carts with homeless people's belongings in them. I didn't see the owners. Nobody we could ask if there was an entrance to a secret garden nearby.

Duncan wrinkled his nose. "A lovely spot for the beginning of an adventure."

Bolin gazed down at Rue's vial in his hand. His expression was rightfully dubious, and I wondered if I should have warned him more thoroughly about how unpleasant the concoction was. But one of us had to take it, and I'd just as soon spread the delightful experience around.

"Do you think we're within ten miles now?" Bolin looked in the direction of the Space Needle, its tip visible over a building at the end of the street.

A breeze swept through, smelling of fish and seaweed. Better than urine, I supposed.

"If my vision was correct, we should be," I said.

"Vision," Bolin mouthed.

"We werewolves get them all the time. They're not weird." I looked at Duncan.

"Not weird at all," he agreed, though I doubted either of us had ever had many.

Until the medallion and these other magical artifacts had come into my life, I hadn't experienced any at all.

Since Bolin still looked dubious, I added, "The whole downtown area is less than ten miles across. Your odds of being close enough for the potion to work are good."

"Okay." Bolin removed the cork.

"How'd you talk him into taking the elixir instead of doing it yourself?" Duncan asked. Since he'd been there when I'd taken the last one, he had a notion of how distressing it was.

"True love," I told him.

"A feeling that he doesn't direct toward his esophagus?"

"Toward Jasmine."

"Ah, she is a comely girl."

"I think she'll be offended if she hears you use that word to describe her," I said. "Or any other word that peaked in popularity in the fifteenth century."

"It's a perfectly normal word that's still in use," Duncan said.

"In historical books and films." I looked at Bolin, certain he would know all about the word and its popularity over time, but he was holding his nose and tilting his head back.

With a shudder, he swallowed the elixir.

Duncan offered him one of the to-go coffee cups we'd brought. Bolin's face contorted, and he bent forward, making gagging sounds. Maybe we should have stopped at an espresso stand for something more potent—and laced with a lot of chocolate syrup.

Hoping he wouldn't throw up, I eyed the overcast sky as another chilly breeze swept through. The warm weather earlier in the week had broken, and I wondered if winter would make a reappearance.

"It'll be a full moon tonight," Duncan said quietly, noticing the direction of my gaze.

"Oh? That should favor us, right? If we find our way in and have to battle bad guys."

"Depends if the bad guys are also werewolves."

I started to shake my head but thought of Lykos. There'd also been a lupine assistant with the building inspector that Radomir had hired when they'd been pretending an interest in buying Sylvan Serenity. It wasn't as if Abrams didn't have access to werewolves.

More gagging sounds came from Bolin.

"It might not work if you throw it all up," I told him, though I was sympathetic. I well knew how dreadful that potion was.

"You warned me," Bolin rasped, "that drinking the Elixir of Locus would be unpleasant... but I didn't realize it would *hurt* so badly." He clutched his chest and staggered about. Tears leaked from his eyes, and his lips rippled with discomfort. "I may need an ambulance. Someone to like, I don't know, vacuum pump this out of me."

"Jasmine needs you to rescue her."

"I'll tough it out." His contorted face suggested otherwise. "But I think I'm dying. You said there'd be some heartburn and tingling."

"The tingling comes after the heartburn."

Bolin put his back to the brick wall and groaned and writhed.

"Maybe Rue made this one stronger," I said, starting to grow worried for him. Could something have gone wrong with the brewing of the elixir?

"Probably not." Not appearing as concerned, Duncan offered Bolin a bottle of water, then fished out some chocolate-covered espresso beans. Similar items that he'd given to me to help wash the taste out of my mouth, but Bolin looked like more than his tongue was protesting the stuff. "Men aren't as good at dealing with pain as women, you know. It's a proven fact."

"Is that so," I murmured.

"Yup. On account of ladies having to endure childbirth."

Bolin took the water and chugged it, threw the empty bottle at a dumpster, and then tossed back coffee from the cup.

"It makes them tough," Duncan added. "Candy, Bolin?"

"I'd choke and die if I tried to eat those." His words continued to come out raspy, and he shook his head. "The next potion I need to find people, I'll learn how to make myself. There has to be a druid equivalent." He drained the coffee cup. "A less painful druid equivalent." He massaged his chest through his shirt and groaned again. "I can't tell if it's starting to tingle or that's the feeling of my esophagus disintegrating. Do you think I might die before we can find Jasmine?" He writhed further against the wall.

"What's the origin of the word esophagus?" I asked.

Duncan arched his eyebrows at the topic shift.

"It's Greek." Bolin wiped tears from his eyes. "From *oiso*, which means *to carry*, and *phagos*, which means *to eat*."

"Phagos means that? Really? I can't think of anywhere else I've heard that used."

"Oh, please. It's in lots of words." Bolin bent double, gripping his knees.

Would he throw up? Our storming of a new compound wasn't off to the solid start I'd envisioned.

"Like what?" I asked. "I bet you can't name five."

"You're trying to distract me, aren't you?"

"No, I'm entirely ignorant when it comes to phagosry, and I need your help."

"That's *not* a word." Bolin gave me a scathing look. "Examples are phagophobia, phagocyte, necrophagous, oligophagous, and rhizophagous."

"Maybe you can define some of those for me so I can work

them into everyday conversations. I know you can at least *spell* them for me."

"I don't believe a wolf would wish to discuss necrophagy," Duncan said, "but a vulture certainly would."

Bolin wiped his eyes again and straightened.

"Do you know which way Jasmine and Izzy are yet?" I asked him.

"I think..." Bolin touched his chest and rotated toward the end of the alley. "That way."

"Good boy." Duncan offered the chocolate-covered espresso beans again.

This time, Bolin took a few. He drew a shuddering breath before chomping on them.

"Did you really take that potion more than once?" he asked me as we headed off, his face still damp from his tears and his hand on the brick wall for support.

"I had to help Duncan." I walked at Bolin's side, letting Duncan trail behind, waving his magic detector around. "Don't worry," I added to Bolin. "When we find her, I'll let Jasmine know about the sacrifice you're making."

"Will you?"

"Yeah."

"Thanks. She's not just cute. She's smart too. And we like the same kinds of coffee and snacks, and she doesn't care that I'm..." Bolin groped in the air with his hand.

"A big boffin?" Duncan suggested into the void.

Bolin scowled at him before looking back to me. "She doesn't care that my family has *money*. I don't think that matters at all to her. In the past, uhm." He glanced at Duncan again, then lowered his voice, apparently oblivious to how keen werewolf ears were. "I'm not the most suave."

"I hadn't noticed," I said blandly.

"Or hot or athletic or, you know." Bolin shrugged. "Sometimes,

I've convinced girls to go out with me because of my car and because I was willing to pay for everything. Jasmine doesn't let me pay for her half of things."

"She's more impressed by your ability to summon vines to grab the fenders of vans that are trying to smash into her," I said.

Bolin led us around a corner while he considered that. "That's okay. It's taken me a lot of studying and practicing to learn how to do that. I wasn't even sure I *could* learn. That's some old-school druid stuff." He lifted his chin. "My *dad* can't do anything like that."

"I guess you're getting pretty badass."

"Yeah." Bolin smiled a little, looking cheered. And determined.

"His badassery is impressive considering his esophagus was so recently disintegrated," Duncan said.

Bolin only scowled back briefly at him. With his hand on his chest again, he picked up the pace, turning down another street and heading for an alley, the brick walls half-smothered in ivy. After walking through the alley, we came to residential streets featuring old Victorian houses with small yards.

"Maybe we should have followed Bolin in the van instead of on foot." Duncan looked over his shoulder.

"Are you worried about being parted from your baby?"

"Worried that I parked in front of a fire hydrant. The bobbies give tickets for that here, don't they?"

"Yeah. And they pilfer any rusty treasures they find in the vehicles of offenders. Did you stash your Nabisco tin somewhere safe?"

"Of course." Duncan pointed. "There's parking on that side street. I'll move the van here and catch up with you."

"Okay." I hurried to keep pace with Bolin, who was striding along with determination, now cutting across lawns and down driveways to take the most direct route.

He walked down a cobblestone street that must have been built in the early days of the city. Since Seattle wasn't that old when compared to other metropolises around the world, or even in the country, such sights were rare.

"I feel..." Bolin touched his chest, then pointed toward a side yard on a lot larger than most on the street.

A flagstone path led around the house and into a garden, the raised beds fallow for the season. It had a pond with a fountain, a stone bench, and tiny ceramic frog houses, all tucked inside a fenced rectangular space with arches on either end, the wrought-iron frames covered in dormant vines, the leaves gone for the year.

Though it looked like a pleasant garden, there was no way it was the one in my vision. That had held lush and exotic foliage sprawled over hundreds of acres.

Bolin climbed over a low fence to gain access to the garden path.

"Uhm." I eyed the front of the house, expecting to find someone gawking out a window at this trespassing. Or maybe ready to unleash a guard dog.

"She's this way." Bolin stopped at one of the arches. The wrought-iron frame gleamed, as if it had been recently oiled.

"We can't traipse through someone's backyard." Lingering on the sidewalk out front, I pulled out my medallion and wrapped my fingers around it, silently asking it if we were on the right trail. *To save Jasmine*, I emphasized, hoping it cared about protecting members of the pack.

"I don't think we will be for long," Bolin said. "The pull is strongest here. It's almost as if... if we passed under this arch, we'll be taken into another realm or something."

Reluctantly, I climbed over the fence and joined him outside the garden.

While looking at the vines and wrought-iron support, Bolin passed under it. Nothing happened.

"Another realm, huh?" I couldn't keep from sounding skeptical, even though I'd also been thinking that our destination had to be camouflaged or hidden somehow.

"Something." Bolin shrugged and walked back and forth under it.

Fingers still wrapped around the medallion, I stepped closer to the arch. Did I sense the faintest hint of magic from it? Maybe from the garden in general.

A sense of curiosity wafted from my medallion, and it warmed slightly against my hand.

"Interesting?" I murmured to it.

Curious about the oily gleam on the metal, I ran a finger over an iron curlicue in the arch. A zing ran up my finger from what felt like a recently applied viscous coating of... something magical. Nothing familiar to me.

After wiping my finger on my jeans, I tried walking under the arch, thinking my blood, or maybe the medallion, might be more likely to activate a magical doorway than Bolin's presence. But his blood had a paranormal element too, so maybe that was an arrogant assumption. Regardless, nothing happened.

"We need Duncan," I said.

"Because he knows how to open magical doorways to other realms?"

"You'd think a treasure hunter would have to."

A distant howl sounded, and I lowered my hand. That had come from a rooftop back in the more industrial area, the neighborhood we'd left.

"Was that him?" Bolin asked.

'No. I think that was Lykos, the young werewolf who wants to slay him."

"Assuming that kid doesn't drive or take public transportation, he's a long way from where we saw him last."

"He's on a mission and full of determination," I said grimly.

"To kill Duncan?"

"Yeah." I looked back, hoping to spot the Roadtrek cruising down the street, but Duncan hadn't appeared yet.

"Do you think he's in trouble?" Bolin asked.

"I don't know."

Several long minutes passed before Duncan's van drove into view. I let out a sigh of relief. I'd been on the verge of running back to look for him.

Duncan spotted us—or maybe *sensed* us—and parked nearby. When he got out, he looked around, and I wondered if he'd heard the kid howling.

"Are we taking up gardening?" he asked when he joined us.

"We've found an arch with a magical vibe and thought you might have ideas about how to activate... whatever is here." I spread my arms.

"*Something* worthwhile must be in the area. My van was hijacked by a highway... wolf."

I blinked. "You saw Lykos?"

"He jumped on my roof. It quite surprised me since I didn't sense him until he was right above me. I admit my first thought was that it was one of your parking enforcers."

"They don't jump on your vehicle; they just put a ticket under your windshield wiper."

"Lykos wasn't interested in my wipers." Duncan stepped past us to consider the arch, then wrapped his fingers around the iron bars.

"What *was* he interested in?" I eyed him, looking for signs that he'd been injured.

"Scaring me away, perhaps? He didn't say anything when I rolled down the window and asked. Instead, he leaped onto a fire-escape ladder, climbed up to a rooftop, and disappeared." Duncan touched his medallion. "This senses something here."

"Mine does too."

We looked at Bolin.

"I don't have a medallion," he said.

"Is your esophagus still tingling?" I asked.

"Oh, yes." Bolin pointed at the archway. "It's pointing me right at that."

Duncan returned to his van, pulled out his magic detector, and brought it to the backyard garden.

While he waved it about, I looked at the windows on the back of the house, again expecting someone to notice our trespassing. It was late enough in the day that a homeowner might be returning from work.

Faint beeping came from the detector, verifying that there was something magical about the archway. Duncan continued to point the device around the garden, and its pair of long antennae quivered, picking up something else. He padded past the bench and fountain and pointed the device toward the frog houses.

"You hear something?" a man asked from the street.

"Some beeping," another guy replied. "The kid said they went this way."

The kid? Lykos?

I waved for Bolin and Duncan to hide. The house and trees in the yard blocked us somewhat from the street but not enough.

Duncan turned off the magic detector to stop the beeping and crouched next to us. Visible between the houses, two big men who emanated magical power walked up the center of the street. I couldn't tell if they were paranormal by birth or had chugged potions to enhance their abilities, but they looked like the sorts of people Radomir had employed.

My senses told me a werewolf was trailing them. Lykos. In his lupine form, he loped up the street to catch up with the men. Planning to guide them toward us?

I gripped the hilt of the sword. Duncan and I ought to be able to handle two men, even two men amped up on potions, but I'd hoped to find Jasmine and Izzy before alerting Abrams that we were in the area.

"They go this way, kid?" one of the men asked, unperturbed by the appearance of the wolf.

Of course not. They were all on the same team. Lykos had been spying on Duncan all week.

I looked at Duncan, wondering if that stung, if it bothered him that his attempts to befriend Lykos hadn't worked.

He was rubbing the green-painted top on one of the ceramic frog houses. Nothing happened. He delved into one of his pockets and pulled out a cylindrical magnet on a rope. I shook my head, certain *that* wouldn't do anything, but a faint clunk sounded within the frog house. Like... a switch being flipped?

Abruptly, great power emanated from the nearest side of the garden, and a silver-blue glow brightened the center of the arch. Startled, Bolin and I scrambled backward. My heel caught on an uneven paver, and I had to flail to maintain my balance.

"Over there!" one of the men barked.

"Jasmine is that way," Bolin blurted and surged toward the arch.

Light flashed, and sparks outlined him as he leaped through. He yelped in pain before disappearing.

I faltered, hesitating to follow him through. But an eager howl came from the street. Even knowing I had the power to defeat Lykos, his lupine cry raised the hair on the back of my neck.

"I'll go first, Luna," Duncan whispered, rushing toward the arch—the portal?—from the other side.

He sprang through. The two men who'd passed the house surged back into view, leaping the fence and running toward the garden. They carried rifles. Loaded with silver bullets?

I didn't stay to find out. As Lykos ran into view, jumping over the fence, I rushed through the archway.

22

BLUE-SILVER LIGHT BLINDED ME, AND A BUZZING JOLT COURSED through my entire body as the ground disappeared from under my feet. I fell, flailing in terror for long seconds, as if I'd leaped into a pit instead of through a portal. My sword flew out of my grip.

Finally, I landed hard on my side on grassy earth, momentum sending me bumping and rolling across it, my body battered until I came to a stop. Somewhere behind me, the brilliant light faded, replaced by a soft silver—moonlight flowing down from a clear night sky.

The strong scents of flowers as well as grass flooded my nostrils.

"Ouch," Duncan murmured from a few feet away. He'd come to a stop against a huge mossy log. "I might have activated the security system as well as opening the doorway."

Bolin groaned from another direction. Grass spread for hundreds of yards in all directions except one. There, a vast garden stretched away, pathways meandering among plantings, fountains, and statues of winged creatures that I wanted to call fairies, though they had animal faces more reminiscent of gargoyles. This was what I'd seen in my vision.

I looked back in the direction we'd come. There was no sign of an archway or portal on this side, but the Space Needle rose in the distance, visible over a forested area beyond the grass. The rest of the city had disappeared.

"Uhm, okay." I rose to hands and knees and peered around, hoping my sword had come through with me.

"Are we... still in Seattle?" Bolin had also fallen but pushed himself to his feet. He touched his chest. Was the potion still guiding him toward Jasmine?

"I've no idea," I said.

Was this some kind of alternate dimension? Did such things exist?

"Maybe we should have done more research before you waved your magnet over that frog house, Duncan," I added.

Ah-ha. My sword lay in the grass. I plucked it up, having a feeling I would need it.

"With enemies barreling down on us?" Duncan rose to his feet and faced in the direction we'd come from, probably reminded that those enemies might follow us through the archway. They had to know about this place.

But there remained no sign of the portal. If they appeared, it would be out of nowhere.

"I hope there's another way back," I said.

"Maybe you wave a magnet over another frog house." Duncan patted his pack.

"We'd better get out of here in case—"

"She's that way." Bolin pointed and headed toward one of the paths leading into the garden.

"Okay, then." I walked after him, waving for Duncan to follow.

He continued to eye the spot where we'd appeared. Expecting Lykos and those men to pop out at any moment?

They *had* been right behind us. Likely, they were waiting for the rest of whatever patrol had been put on duty to keep an eye out for us. Then, they could all come through together. With *rifles*. What was my sword supposed to do against those?

"Do you want me to stay here?" Duncan asked. "And—"

"No," I interrupted. "I'd pine terribly if you weren't at my side."

"Worried I'll get myself in trouble, eh?"

"Vastly." I walked back and gripped his hand to make sure he didn't intend to stay behind and buy us time while he risked his life.

Besides, we might face something more dangerous here. I would need Duncan.

Determined to find Jasmine before the potion wore off, Bolin was already dozens of yards ahead of us. So many of the garden beds had towering stalks and flowering bushes that rose well over our heads that it would be easy to lose track of him, and something told me we wouldn't have cell reception to send texts here.

Duncan and I jogged to catch up with Bolin, the night air crisp and cool on our skin as a breeze swept through, rustling the plants. When we started down a path that traveled between beds of what looked like bamboo, the length of the green shoots covered in purple flowers, I paused to look behind us. Just before we rounded a bend that would take the area out of view, an arch-shaped blue-silver light flared. The portal was activating again.

"They're coming through." I wondered how many men would arrive. For that matter, how many enemies were already here in this place? Hiding and waiting for us?

Duncan touched his hand to the small of my back, guiding me around the bend so that our enemies wouldn't see us as soon as they came through. Since Lykos would have no trouble tracking us by scent, did it matter?

Maybe not, but I let Duncan guide me away. Bolin was speed-walking, and I didn't want to lose him. Thanks to all the planters, raised beds, fountains, statues, and numerous paths meandering among them, the place was a maze.

"Have you ever heard of anywhere like this?" I asked Duncan, waving toward the distant Space Needle still visible between gaps in the plants.

"Oh, yes. There are artifacts that create pocket realms within our own world, and I've heard that powerful potions can allow people to access existing ones that are always there."

I remembered the damp viscous stuff on the wrought-iron archway. Had Abrams sprayed that on to convert someone's garden into a portal?

"These pocket realms are, however, rare," Duncan continued, "and I'd not heard of any on this continent. They're more frequent in the places where civilization existed in the times of stronger magic, back before it faded and those born with the ability to harness it and create artifacts grew fewer and fewer. On one of my treasure hunts in the Middle East, I once found an artifact that allowed me to visit a desert pocket realm. I almost died of thirst before finding a way back."

"So, they can be dangerous."

"Oh, certainly. Those who made them often left behind magical guardians." Duncan lifted a finger, then paused to clamber to the top of a fountain with a statue of what looked like a thorn-covered bear spitting water from its broad snout. From a perch on its back, Duncan looked behind us and also in the direction we were heading.

I didn't stop, not wanting to lose Bolin, who was not inclined to wait for us, but I did notice that Duncan's gaze snagged on the way behind us longer than on the way ahead.

"What did you see?" I asked when he rejoined me.

"There's a warehouse without any windows up ahead. It looks industrial and like it belongs in Seattle by the docks rather than in this realm, but it's surrounded by plants and birds from here. Wherever *here* is."

"And what's behind us?"

"Lykos and some men are coming."

"More than the two men we saw earlier?"

"Yes."

"That's what I was worried about."

We caught up to Bolin as he turned around a corner, pumping his arms in what looked like frustration that he couldn't go straight. Jasmine was probably in the warehouse Duncan had seen, but spiky green cactus-like plants barring the way kept us from taking a direct route.

Bolin started jogging toward a four-way intersection that offered an option to continue in the right direction. Before we reached it, an eight-legged metallic bug skittered into view. It rotated toward us, showing two glowing dots for eyes and a circular orifice for a mouth.

I groaned. "Not those guys again."

"Those aren't the magical guardians I had in mind," Duncan said.

"They must be Abrams's specialty."

"Since they're mechanical rather than alchemical, that's a touch surprising, but maybe he unearthed a stockpile of them someplace."

"Those vapors they spit are plenty alchemical." I well remembered the gaseous substance that could waft from their mouth-like orifices. During our previous encounter, the vapors had almost knocked out Duncan and me. Had we succumbed and continued to be exposed to the tainted air, they might have *killed* us.

In the intersection, another bug joined the first.

Duncan caught Bolin by the arm to keep him from charging toward it.

"They're not that large." Bolin pulled one of his spherical Orbs of Entanglement out of his pocket and fingered the vials on his bandolier.

"They exhale toxic gas," I told him.

"Fortunately, we came prepared," Duncan said.

"We did?" I grimaced as two more bugs skittered into view. Outside, the poisonous gas should dissipate more quickly, but I still wasn't eager to get close.

A questioning grunt from the path behind us suggested we might not have any choice. I could sense Lykos back there as well as magical weapons. The brute squad was getting close. *Herding* us.

Duncan tugged off his backpack and pulled out a nicer and newer version of the gas mask I kept in the leasing office. He handed it to me and drew out another one.

"I'm afraid I only brought two though," he said.

Bolin chopped his arm in an impatient motion. "I'm fine."

He chucked his sphere toward the center of the intersection. The Orb of Entanglement landed between the bugs, steaming as it lost cohesion and spread into what I well knew was a sticky puddle.

Not waiting to see how the mechanical constructs reacted, Bolin ran toward the intersection. He skirted the puddle to go around a cement planter marking the corner.

The bugs hissed out purple vapor, a cloud forming in the air above them. Though we were outside, the breeze had died down, and the stuff lingered.

I tugged the mask over my head, tightened the straps, and strode forward with Duncan. A glance back made me jump. Our wolf friend had appeared on the path behind us.

Eyes intent, Lykos watched us for a moment before looking back the way he'd come. He lifted his snout and howled.

"You might have to confront him," I said as Duncan and I ran around the corner after Bolin. My face was hot under the mask, the canister weighing down my jaw, but I trusted its filter would keep the air from poisoning us. Just in case, I held my breath.

"I'm going to confront *Abrams*," Duncan said, his voice muffled by his mask.

I didn't know if we would be able to reach Abrams without facing off against Lykos and the men.

Ahead of us, Bolin ran toward the warehouse Duncan had seen. The size of a football stadium, it was larger than I'd imagined. Its outer walls were a combination of cement and corrugated metal, and it had a flat roof with not a single window visible. As Duncan had said, it would fit into an industrial setting more than here in the strange garden.

At least the way was clear, a brick walkway surrounding the building on all sides and keeping the vegetation away from the walls.

We caught up to Bolin at a pair of solid metal doors with a keypad next to them. He tapped buttons, trying to guess the combination.

"That's not going to work." Duncan grabbed one of the metal handles, planted a foot on the opposite door, and heaved.

Bolin snorted. "That won't either. Maybe some vines could be summoned and coerced to slip underneath and open it from the other side."

As Bolin eyed the narrow crack under the doors, Duncan heaved, his muscles straining under his shirt.

"You didn't bring grenades this time?" I asked.

"*Of course* I did, my lady," Duncan said, his voice tight as he pulled. Something snapped. A metal hinge or one of his joints? "But we'll save them for the *hard* obstacles."

"There!" someone yelled from the path behind us.

Two of the men ran into view, lifting their rifles. Magic pricked at my veins, the full moon offering its power, promising I could turn into a wolf easily here.

But, with another snap, Duncan tore open the door. A broken hinge clattered onto the brick walkway, and Bolin uttered a startled oath and scrambled aside. With the door in his hands, Duncan whirled and heaved it at the men.

They weren't so startled that they didn't shoot, but their bullets went astray. Several struck the door as it flew end over end toward them. Those bullets left silvery streaks in the air, promising what my senses had told me. Their magic made them a threat to werewolves.

We leaped into the dark building and put our backs to the wall inside. Footsteps pounded as the men in heavy boots ran in our direction.

"If someone hadn't thrown the door away," I said, lifting my sword, "we could have locked them out."

"Tally ho!" Duncan called cheerfully as he leaned over and hurled something through the doorway. One of his grenades.

"Shit!" someone outside cried, the footfalls reversing direction.

Someone got off a shot, a bullet whizzing through the doorway and leaving a silver streak, but Duncan had already pulled back. The bullet clanged off one of many towering metal vats to either side of a walkway heading down the center of the building.

Outside, the grenade blew, a booming explosion in the previously still night. The cement floor under our feet reverberated, the walls trembling slightly, though they seemed sturdy and held. The whole building was sturdy. We didn't hear so much as a clunk to indicate something had fallen off a shelf.

Not that I saw any shelves anywhere. Twice as tall as us, and much wider, the vats blocked the view of much of the building, with darkness adding to the obscurity. Not seeing any bugs inside, I pushed my mask up for a better view. Duncan's already hung around his neck.

Inside, the air overwhelming with floral and chemical scents, the place reminded me a lot of the potion factory on the lavender farm where I'd first encountered Abrams. It was hotter, some of the open vats bubbling like molten ore, but the interior of the building had a similar look and maybe layout. In the dim lighting, that was hard to determine. The only illumination came from the glow of screens and panels on the sides of the vats. Just visible in the shadows of the high ceiling, metal catwalks ran along the walls and crisscrossed over the vats. Allowing access to the tops of them? A machine similar to a crane rose up from the center aisle —something that could lift giant barrels of chemicals to dump? Near the wall not far from us, plastic barrels were stacked, many of them emanating magic. A lot of the vats did too. More than one of those barrels glowed green even through its plastic sides.

"Wholesome ingredients, I'm sure," I muttered.

"She's in here, I think." Bolin touched his chest then pointed, not straight down the center aisle but toward a distant corner. Dozens of giant vats and who knew what else blocked the view in that direction. In *most* directions.

"So is he," Duncan said in a grim tone.

I followed his gaze to one of the catwalks, my senses telling me who he meant before I spotted the dark wolf in the shadows.

"How'd he get inside?" I glanced toward the doorway next to us—since Duncan had thrown the grenade, nobody else had tried to run in—but realized there had to be other entrances.

"You could ask him." Duncan waved as he held gazes with the kid.

Lykos was focused on him. I doubted he would answer my questions.

"I suppose I can't throw a salami outside and hope he'll run off and eat it."

"Probably not. He seems determined to... do as Abrams ordered." Duncan shook his head sadly. "As you pointed out, I'm going to have to confront him."

"I'll help you." I suspected Lykos didn't plan to leap into a one-on-one fight with the older, larger, and stronger Duncan. He had to have laid a trap.

Duncan turned toward a wall with a metal support post, rivets running up the sides. "I'll deal with him. You'd better keep an eye on Bolin."

I cursed. Bolin had already started down a walkway along the wall, doubtless hoping he could follow it to the corner that held Jasmine. Meanwhile, Duncan gripped the edges of the post and climbed toward the catwalk. Lykos padded back into the shadows, disappearing behind vats and machinery.

Luring Duncan away from me, my mind wanted to add, though it was possible the kid didn't care about me in the least.

"Help Bolin," Duncan called softly down to me. "I'll take care of Abrams and Lykos."

"Anyone think we should stick together and deal with our problems as a strong and cohesive group?" I called, the words both for Duncan and Bolin.

Neither man looked back at me. Duncan pulled himself over the railing of the catwalk, hazy blue-gray smoke that wafted from one of the vats obscuring his form. He trotted in the direction Lykos had gone, soon disappearing from my view.

"Men," I grumbled and jogged off after Bolin.

23

As I trailed Bolin down the shadowy walkway along the wall of the building, heat and magical energy radiating from the vats, distant *tink, tink, tink* sounds reminded me of the mechanical bugs. They would doubtless show up in here too. Other noises, I couldn't identify. Some of the vats gurgled ominously, and so many scents assailed my nostrils that something toxic could have been mixed among them, and who would have known?

Reminded of the mask, I touched it to reassure myself that wearing it was an option. Bolin passed an aisle that opened up perpendicular to the wall. He glanced down it but hurried past without slowing.

"It's getting harder to tell where she is," he whispered back to me. "I'm afraid the elixir is wearing off."

"We'll find her. She's in here somewhere." I kept glancing toward the catwalks, reminded that Lykos was in here too. And some of his rifle-toting allies? The grenade probably hadn't scared them off for long.

I couldn't sense Lykos up there anymore. I couldn't even sense

Duncan. There was too much other magic about. It was like trying to hear a pin drop in a room while rain hammered on the roof.

Since Bolin hadn't reacted to anything in the aisle, I didn't expect trouble when I reached it but glanced to double check. Two men jogged out of a gap between two vats. They were less than ten feet away, and I blurted an exclamation.

The men flinched, as surprised to find me as I was to find them.

Recovering quickly, one turned toward me, a rifle cradled in his arms. Maybe my instincts should have urged me to run, but I charged toward him with the sword instead, hoping to reach him before he could fire.

He aimed the weapon at my chest, finger on the trigger.

I whipped my blade toward the rifle, clipping the end of the barrel and deflecting it. To my surprise, the sword not only struck the gun but lopped off the last inch of the barrel.

My attack didn't keep the man from firing, but I'd knocked the rifle aside. Several bullets hammered into a nearby vat, and two struck his ally. The man screamed and reeled back, dropping his own weapon.

The guy who'd fired jerked his rifle back toward me and lunged in, trying to club me with it. I parried it as if it were a sword in a sparring match with Yuto in the dojo. Again, I knocked the rifle wide. This time, the man kept from accidentally firing, but I took advantage of the opening and kicked him in the gut. He stumbled back, bumping into his ally. The man had dropped to hands and knees, blood gushing from his neck. He gripped the wound, trying to staunch the flow, but it looked like a fatal wound.

My gut twisted—I hadn't wanted to cause anyone's death—but I forced myself to keep fighting. My other enemy remained on his feet, his rifle still in his hands. Again, he pointed it toward me.

Sword leading, I lunged in and stabbed him. He jerked his arm across to block me, and I struck his biceps instead of his chest. Even so, he cried out and dropped the gun.

I stepped back, thinking of ordering them to surrender, but what the hell would I do with prisoners? I hadn't brought rope to tie people up.

Thinking of Bolin's entangling magic, I opened my mouth to call to him to come back, but my foe wasn't ready to give up. Even as his ally groaned and flopped onto his side, blood puddling underneath him, the remaining man bent, reaching for his gun. I stepped on it so he couldn't pick it up and kicked him again.

"Surrender, you bastard," I ordered as he reeled back.

He slipped in the puddle of blood, pitched against one of the vats, and went down. A huge drop of a glowing blue liquid dripped off it and plopped onto him. Screaming, he rolled away from the vat. But more blue liquid spattered onto the cement floor and droplets struck him.

The sizzle of burning clothes and flesh invaded my nostrils, and I backed away, realizing one of the bullets had pierced a vat. The others had clanged off the sturdy material, but that one must have landed just right.

The man rolled about, swatting at his wounds and shrieking in utter pain. His ally had stopped moving and might already be dead.

I grabbed the rifle that hadn't been damaged and backed farther away, feeling far more horror than triumph.

These people brought it upon themselves, I told myself. They'd attacked *me*. Working for Abrams, they'd been attacking both Duncan and me for weeks.

That didn't keep me from hurrying around the corner, away from the screams of the dying man.

Back in the dark aisle that followed the wall, I wiped sweat from my brow. Bolin hadn't waited for me while I'd battled the men, and I cursed. He couldn't have failed to *notice* that gunshots were going off—and screams.

"The boy is obsessed," I grumbled, hurrying deeper into the building.

It was possible he'd heard something to suggest that Jasmine was in trouble. Abrams might use her as a hostage if necessary. Maybe that was the reason he'd kidnapped her in the first place.

"Who knows," I muttered, wincing at another scream, weaker this time. That guy didn't have much life left in him.

Whatever that blue gunk had been, it might have been worse —more *deadly*—than magical bullets.

I eyed the rifle in my grip, thinking of tossing it into a vat, but if I spotted Abrams across the building on a catwalk, it might come in handy.

Since I couldn't sense Bolin's aura, not with so many other magical items drowning everything out, I could only head deeper into the potion factory. Soon, ceiling-high stacks of crates and more white plastic barrels blocked the route I'd been following along the wall. I debated attempting to climb a support post up to the catwalk, as Duncan had done, but tried backing up to a perpendicular aisle instead.

It led me into the interior of the building, then turned to angle around giant metal mixing machinery. Sweat dripped down my face, the heat more intense farther from the walls.

Feeling overwhelmed by all the magic and the steamy air filled with chemical scents, my senses weren't at their sharpest. I jumped in surprise when I rounded a vat and stepped into an open area with two large cages on the floor surrounded by cabinets and counters littered with machinery and equipment.

One cage was empty, the gate ajar, but the other was not. A female wolf that I recognized—Izzy—lay tethered inside, chained to the bars so that she could barely move. Was some magic keeping her from shifting back into her human form? She lay on her belly, head between her forelimbs, eyes closed. Unconscious? Dead?

No, not dead. As I crept closer, I sensed her aura.

An IV ran from one of her limbs to a machine with a slight magical signature. My first thought was that Izzy was being drugged, but there was blood in the clear tubing. Maybe hers. A sample for Abrams's experiments? In his journal, he'd implied that he'd given up on needing werewolf blood, but with a ready supply available, maybe he'd decided to put it to use.

Broken tubing dangled in the empty cage as well, a few spatters of blood on the bottom. It was still damp. Jasmine must have been inside it recently. Bite marks on the mangled lock suggested she'd also been in her wolf form when she'd found a way to escape.

"Probably sensed Bolin coming and was moved by her love for him," I whispered. "Or her desire *not* to need rescuing."

The latter seemed more likely.

Where *was* Bolin, anyway? Guided by the Elixir of Locus, he should have found Jasmine before I had. Maybe *he'd* been the one to let her go? And then they'd gone...

"Where?" I looked all around and also up at the catwalks but didn't see anyone, neither enemy nor ally.

Izzy lifted her head, opening her eyes and looking at me. They were glassy—maybe she *was* drugged—but her lips parted, revealing her fangs. She recognized me... and still adored me.

It crossed my mind to leave her in the cage and stuck in another realm where she couldn't pester me further in the future, but she had a daughter. Besides, no werewolf deserved to be chained and experimented on.

"Do me a favor, and don't attack me when I let you go," I said.

A deep *bong* sounded elsewhere in the building, echoing from the walls and reminding me that we weren't alone. A nearby vat gurgled and bubbled.

The chains kept Izzy from rising to her feet. Fortunately, the cage wasn't locked from the outside, and all it took were human fingers to unlatch the door. Again, I wondered what power was keeping Izzy stuck in her lupine form. Had she shifted, she might easily have escaped.

Izzy stared at me as I swung the door open. She seemed... surprised? It was hard to tell with a wolf, but she cocked her head, a pointed ear flickering.

Glad I still had the sword—the magically *sharp* sword—I sliced through the chains securing her. I debated whether to cut the IV tube as well, but who knew what that would do?

Izzy rose to her feet, snarled, and lunged to the side. Her jaws snapped down on the tubing and she ripped it from her vein.

"Ouch," I murmured as a needle fell, blood flowing out and dampening her fur.

She padded out of the cage, then startled me by collapsing.

"Shit. I *knew* removing that wasn't a good idea." I glanced at the needle, as if I might stick it back in her leg to save her life.

But her aura rippled, and she shifted back into her human form. Blood continued to dribble down her limb—her *arm*—but she soon stirred.

"Thirsty," she rasped, looking at me.

Yeah, there was no sign of a water or food bowl. What if Abrams hadn't given her anything in the days since his thugs had caught her? I hurried to remove my pack and offer her a bottled water I'd brought.

She clawed it out of my hands, tore off the lid, and guzzled.

"He didn't give you anything to drink?" I asked. "What a bastard. How'd he expect to get good blood samples from your veins if you were dehydrated?"

"He got enough." Her hoarse voice made it sound like she hadn't spoken for days. If those bindings had magically kept her as a wolf, that might very well be the case. "That machine had no trouble pumping it out of me."

She drank more as she lifted a hand to look at it. Her fingers were shaking.

"Do you know where my friend Jasmine went?" I pointed to the other cage. "And was there a young man here too?" Remembering that Izzy had met Bolin at her brother's networking event, I added, "Bolin. Your daughter wanted him to turn into a bear."

"Is Olivia safe?" Izzy lunged forward and gripped my arm. "Nothing has happened to her, has it?"

"Nothing that I've heard about. Your brother is keeping an eye on her and searching for you."

"Thank the moon."

Izzy released me and dragged her bare arm over her face. As much sweat glistened on her skin as on mine, and her eyes remained glassy, showing the vestiges of whatever drug remained in her system.

"Bolin?" I prompted, though she might have been too out of it to notice if he'd come by. "And Jasmine?"

"I didn't see a man, but the other wolf—we were stuck in our lupine forms and never able to speak and share names. She escaped just a little bit ago. She was desperate. Drugged. We both were. When we heard gunfire, she must have thought the mad scientist was going to fulfill his promise."

"What promise?" I asked grimly.

"He kept saying…" Izzy groped in the air with her hand. "In my wolf form, I didn't grasp it all, but he kept saying he hadn't meant to take us but that he could use our magical blood, and he was keeping us alive instead of just… exsanguinating us because *they* were coming. That was what he said again and again. He wanted *them* to come, to be lured by his bait, and had a plan all worked out. But I wasn't the bait." Her mouth twisted. "I was an accident."

"You shouldn't have been hanging out at Sylvan Serenity, peeing on my bushes."

Izzy surprised me by looking ashamed by that. "I thought... I wanted you to know..."

"You were irked with me and planned to kill me?"

"I felt obligated to avenge Raoul."

A howl came from a far corner of the building. From up on one of the catwalks? The echoes in the vast space made it hard to tell, but I thought the voice sounded young, that it belonged to Lykos.

Had Duncan caught up with him? Or was Lykos trying to *lure* Duncan to him? Into his trap?

"Do you still feel that way?" I didn't want to linger and chat further but also didn't know what to do with Izzy. Would she help me find my allies? Or club me in the back of my head when I was distracted?

"I..." Izzy looked from me to the cage and back. "You could have left me there."

"Yeah."

"Whatever this place is..." She looked toward a distant wall in the direction where the Space Needle had been visible in the night sky. "Even if I'd escaped from the cage somehow, which didn't look likely after however many days I was stuck in there, I don't think I could have escaped *this* place."

"Maybe not." I shrugged, realizing I had no idea how to get back either. I didn't even have a magnet to wave at frog houses if we found one in the garden.

Maybe when I rejoined Duncan, we could find Abrams and wring the location of the exit portal out of his throat.

"My daughter needs me." Izzy's gaze slid to me. "I can't... vendetta right now. Maybe, as a responsible mom, I never should have taken up that mission."

Had time in here to think about it, had she?

"Being a responsible parent is tough sometimes." I knew that well.

"Yes."

A distant accented voice reached our ears, raised to carry throughout the building. "Show yourself, Drakon! Come up here to face me, or I'll kill the female wolves. I'll kill *your* female. We have her, you know."

"The hell he does," I growled.

Abrams sounded like he was at the far end of the building, back in the direction we'd entered from, but in the maze of vats and machinery, it was hard to tell.

Wherever Duncan was, he didn't answer.

"Will you help me find my friends and get out of here?" I asked Izzy.

Whether it was wise or not, I offered her the rifle. Right now, she couldn't likely turn back into a wolf, and without her fangs and claws, she was little more than a naked human woman.

"Yes," Izzy said firmly, taking the weapon. "I'd *love* to shoot someone."

"As long as it's not me."

"I've learned my lesson on that. Just being near you is trouble." She grimaced, probably having figured out along the way that she'd only been kidnapped because Abrams's men had been after me. "If anything, I should stay far, far away from you."

"Isn't your home in Arizona? I hear it's nice."

Izzy snorted. "Aside from getting cactus thorns in your paw pads and melting under the unrelenting summer heat."

A clang and a muffled grunt floated to our ears, just audible over the gurgling of a nearby vat. Had that been Bolin?

"Follow me." I would have to trust Izzy at my back and hope I wasn't being a fool.

Heading in the direction of the noises, I turned down an aisle I'd already visited, but I halted after only a step. Two of those awful bugs were in the center. They swiveled toward me, vapor puffing out of their orifices.

I reached for the gas mask hanging around my neck, but Izzy didn't have any such protection. And who knew what drugs already bogged down her system.

"We'll go that way." I pointed toward another aisle that ran between hulking machinery and vats linked by thick pipes.

The bugs skittered toward us. Izzy eyed them and didn't argue, jogging off after me.

Not far down the aisle, we reached another open area with counters filled with computer monitors and keyboards as well as lab equipment. The spot also held the first ladder I'd encountered, metal rungs leading up to a section of the catwalk, a railing running along only one side of it.

"This place can't be OSHA approved," I muttered.

"What?" Izzy asked.

"We'll go that way." I pointed my sword at the ladder.

From the catwalk, we ought to be able to see much more— maybe even Duncan and Lykos.

Izzy paused to look into a couple of cabinets and grab a white lab coat.

When I reached the top of the ladder, that portion of the catwalk deep in shadow, I crouched and peered about, hoping to spot Duncan. Though the view was more open than below, some of the vats and machinery rose higher than the railing, so I couldn't see the whole building.

A soft clank sounded, the rifle bumping the metal ladder as Izzy climbed.

"That's quite a look," I noted as she joined me, her borrowed white lab coat cinched about her waist, her feet and most of her legs bare, and the rifle in her hands.

"No need to take a photo. My daughter would be highly embarrassed if it appeared on social media."

"Isn't embarrassing one's children a staple of parenthood?"

"Well, yes, but *I* might be embarrassed about this too."

"Fair." Staying low, my instincts promising that more danger lurked up here, I crept toward a perpendicular catwalk, one that looked like it might run the length of the building. It had railings on both sides, but there were gaps in places, with tiny platforms sticking out to allow access to the open vats.

Another grunt came from the same direction we'd heard one from before. A *thud* followed. It sounded like a fight, and I thought I detected Jasmine's aura, but the magic all around us continued to make it hard to trust my senses.

As we crept along the catwalk, the area—the entire *building*—fell silent. Even the gurgling from the various vats seemed to soften.

I reached the intersection and peered around a crane at the corner, cables and mechanical arms partially but not entirely blocking the view. I froze to stare.

Halfway down the long building, on a platform with several catwalks attached to it, Duncan crouched as the bipedfuris. Faint light from below cast eerie shadows over his furry, muscular form, making him appear devilish and scary. Not far behind him, his clothes were draped over a railing along with a rope dangling down with a cylinder attached. One of his magnets.

Across the platform from him, Lykos also crouched. He was in his wolf form, hackles up and fangs on display as he looked at Duncan. But he also threw glances backward, toward someone egging him on.

Abrams.

24

Abrams wasn't alone. He stood at the back edge of the platform with two of his armed men, all three of them sheltered by a control panel that probably activated the machinery around the building. If he'd been more exposed, I might have grabbed the rifle from Izzy and fired at him. As it was, my grip tightened on the hilt of my sword. I wanted to put an end to Abrams. After all the torment he'd inflicted on young Duncan, and probably on young Lykos too, he deserved to have his stay on Earth—or wherever the hell we were—ended.

That platform would be a hell of a place for a confrontation. With gurgling vats on multiple sides and gaps in the railing, it looked far from safe. Not that Abrams was likely worried about anyone's *safety*.

Unlike his hired thugs, he wasn't armed with a weapon, but he gripped a flask in one hand, his thumb on the stopper. A dark liquid sloshed inside as he swirled it in agitation.

Izzy tapped my shoulder and pointed to something else. On a catwalk attached to ours and halfway between us and Duncan and Lykos, two more men with rifles stood, aiming their weapons at

Duncan. They had a clear shot and could have fired. Were they waiting for a command from Abrams? What, did he want *Lykos* to be the one to kill Duncan? To fight it out in some kind of test? Maybe the men were only there to protect Abrams if things got out of hand, if Lykos couldn't best his older brother.

Lykos hadn't even been a match for me, so I didn't know how Abrams expected that to happen, at least not in a fair fight.

But... maybe Abrams didn't intend for this to *be* a fair fight. Indeed, Lykos appeared larger than he had moments before. It was hard to tell from a distance, but his aura also seemed to have power that matched Duncan's. Had Abrams given him a potion? Tiger Blood or something else to enhance his abilities?

Though I didn't take my gaze from the standoff between Lykos and Duncan, I pointed at the gunmen nearest us and crept in that direction. Duncan hadn't attacked yet, and I didn't know what he planned, but it would be easier for him to win the confrontation without people taking shots at him from the side.

"*End* him," Abrams urged, his voice just audible across the distance and over the gurgling vats. "I gave you the power to do so." He lifted the flask in his hand. "Drakon has declared himself an enemy once more, and you'll never become the leader of a pack with *him* in the world."

What the heck did that mean? What lies had Abrams been telling the kid?

He took a step toward Lykos, and the greenish light of a glowing and gurgling vat to the side of the platform turned his face a dreadful shade.

Jaw clenched with irritation on Duncan's behalf, I continued toward the gunmen. With the butts of their weapons pressed into their shoulders and their cheeks to the stocks as they sighted down the barrels, they weren't looking at us. Their backs were almost entirely to us.

I picked up the pace, judging from Lykos's posture that he

might give in to Abrams and attack Duncan at any second. The last thing I wanted to see was the kid killed. I sure as hell didn't want to see *Duncan* killed either.

"He murdered Radomir and ended our plans for the distribution of my life's work," Abrams added. "You *will* end him, as I've commanded."

Abrams pointed at something on the platform behind Lykos. Even with my lupine heritage giving me keen eyesight in the poor light, it was hard to identify from such a distance. Something made from glass? An empty vial?

Neither Lykos nor Duncan looked back at Abrams. Their gazes were locked on each other.

Since Izzy and I were deep in a shadowy section of the vast building, I didn't think Abrams saw us creeping along the catwalk. The gunmen at his side were poised like the other two, weapons trained on Duncan.

I groaned to myself. Had Duncan not been worried about us— probably about *me* specifically—he wouldn't have let himself be lured into this situation.

The bipedfuris growled, clawed fingers flexing. His gaze shifted to Abrams, and he crouched, looking like he wanted to rush past Lykos and attack the man. But Lykos hunched and growled back. In the glow from the control panel, the whites of his eyes were visible. He was afraid. Afraid but determined. He didn't look like he would back away. If Duncan attacked Abrams, Lykos would attack *him*.

One of the gunmen closest to us stirred, his finger tightening on the trigger in anticipation. I resumed heading toward him, picking up the pace. We risked being spotted or heard, but I dared not delay. This was coming to a head.

To my surprise, the air rippled around Duncan, and he shifted back into a man. A naked and nearly defenseless man, at least compared to the powerful bipedfuris.

At first, I thought Abrams had thrown an alchemical concoction or used a magical artifact to force Duncan to change, but when Duncan spread his arms wide, hands open, I realized he might also have decided Lykos would attack if he threatened Abrams. But what if Duncan *didn't* threaten him?

"*Kill* him." Abrams thrust a finger toward Duncan's bare chest. "Now's your chance."

Lykos stiffened, as if magic compelled him to obey. It probably did.

"Really, now, old chap," Duncan said to Abrams, though he watched Lykos. "Given all the things we've been through together, I'm aghast that you're trying to arrange my death."

"You tried to kill *me*," Abrams snarled. "All those years ago. And you destroyed my *library*."

"I do regret that. I adored the library."

Lykos looked hesitantly back and forth between them. My heart went out to the kid for being caught in the middle of this.

"And then you destroyed my *laboratory* in Maple Falls." Pure hatred filled Abrams's eyes, as if that was the greatest crime of all.

"I don't regret that," Duncan drawled. "In truth, I helped you out. It was completely infested by huge insects."

"*Kill* him, Lykos," Abrams growled.

Earlier hesitation evaporating, Lykos jerked into a low crouch, ready to spring.

"I've a better idea," Duncan said, addressing Lykos now. "Why don't you change out of that form as well, and we'll go for a fish, eh?" He backed off the platform and to the railing on the catwalk where his clothes draped. Keeping his movements slow, he waved at the magnet. "Maybe we can find some more of those tins. Or even a bicycle. Have you ever ridden one? I had to teach myself as an adult. Abrams didn't grasp the importance of showing a child how to ride a bicycle."

Lykos didn't rise from his crouch, but he cocked his head, as if trying to understand. As if... curious?

Abrams turned toward one of his guards. To order them to fire?

I'd almost reached the other gunmen but paused, movement on the ground to the right of my catwalk drawing my eye. A man I hadn't seen before writhed about, a firearm several feet away. Not only did his clothes appear to be stuck to the floor but a thick green vine stretching out from between two vats had secured his ankle like a shackle. Slumped against one of those vats, another man bled profusely from fang puncture marks in his neck. Had Jasmine done that? While still in her wolf form? She and Bolin must have found each other.

"It'll be a right fun time," Duncan added. "*Much* more fun than taking orders from that dusty old git."

I was only five feet from the gunmen when one heard or somehow sensed me and glanced back. He cursed and spun toward me.

I leaped, hoping to knock the rifle out of the way with my sword, the same as I'd done below. The crack of a firearm sounded right behind me, almost startling me into dropping my blade. The second man, who'd also been turning to aim at me, flew backward as something slammed into his chest. A bullet.

As he pitched backward, I struck the rifle in the other man's hands. It clanged as it hit the railing and went off. The bullet flew wide, streaking toward a wall and striking it. I sprang upon the man, punching him in the nose before he could recover his equilibrium. He stumbled back, and I kicked him in the gut. When he lurched forward, I pointed the tip of the sword between his eyes.

He whirled, climbed over the railing, and jumped down of his own accord. Behind me, Izzy stood with the gun I'd given her. She nodded at me, then pointed it toward the platform.

I expected the two men who'd been guarding Abrams to have

heard us—how not?—and be preparing to fire. But a green vine had snaked up from the floor below, wrapping around the waist of one of the gunmen. It lifted him from his feet, and he kicked Abrams in the back as he flailed and shouted.

"Couldn't happen to a nicer guy," I muttered.

The second gunman turned, not toward me but toward the floor and where that vine was coming from. He leaned over and fired.

"Shit." I sprinted down the catwalk, not sure if he was aiming at Bolin or Jasmine. *Neither* was an acceptable target.

"I'm not the threat, brother," Duncan said calmly, as if the chaos going on all around him was of no consequence. His arms were still out as he stood naked, his focus on Lykos. "Abrams is. Until he's out of our lives, we'll never truly be free."

"*Kill* him, boy!" Denied his bodyguards, Abrams rushed toward Lykos with the flask.

To do what? Throw more of a coercion potion on the kid?

Whatever he intended, Lykos, in his wolf form, must have seen it as a threat. Even as I reached Duncan, leaping to his side with my sword at the ready, Lykos turned on Abrams. He charged straight at the man and sprang.

Eyes bulging, Abrams backpedaled but not fast enough. The wolf, made bigger and stronger by his own alchemical potions, slammed into his shoulder. Lykos didn't bite him, but his weight was enough to pitch Abrams backward. He tumbled through a gap in the railing and landed with a great splash in the bubbling vat of green liquid.

Abrams screamed and flailed, utter pain and horror contorting his face. Only as his flesh burned and his screams worsened did I realize what should have been obvious all along from the gurgling noises coming from the vats. Those liquids were *boiling*.

Lykos stared for a moment, then turned his back on Abrams. Duncan set his jaw and didn't move to help. I took a half step, so horrified that I wanted to pull Abrams out, but Duncan gripped my arm and shook his head once.

Before I could decide if I wanted to argue—even if Abrams deserved to die, surely this was too awful to inflict on anyone—the screams ended. Scalded to death, Abrams slipped under the surface and disappeared.

"Damn," I muttered and glanced back to see if Izzy was still with us.

She'd stayed back but had seen it all. Her only response was to toss the rifle she'd used to shoot the gunman into the same vat that had swallowed Abrams. Destroying the evidence that she'd been involved. I had a feeling the police wouldn't show up at the door to arrest us, but I couldn't blame her. I felt... less than wholesome after the night's events.

On the catwalk a few feet in front of us, Lykos sat on his haunches. His aura rippled, and he shifted from a wolf to an eight-year-old boy. Wrapping his arms around himself, he put his head between his knees and cried.

Duncan grabbed his clothes and went to him, resting a hand on his back. I started to join them, but an uncertain call of, "Aunt Luna?" floated up from below.

Reminded that those men had shot at Bolin and Jasmine, I ran to the railing on the other side of the control console and looked down.

Hair tousled and face red from whatever exertion creating vines took, Bolin stood beside Jasmine, offering her support. Somewhere along the way, she'd turned back into her human self. Her face was twisted with pain, and she gripped her left arm as blood leaked between her fingers.

"I want to go home." Jasmine's eyes weren't as glassy as Izzy's had been when I'd pulled her out of the cage, but she also looked rough.

"We will," I promised and turned back toward Duncan and his

little brother. "Lykos? Do you know the way back to Seattle? Can you take us home?"

After wiping his eyes, the boy rose. He looked numb and haunted by his choice, but he didn't push Duncan away. If anything, he appeared glad to have someone standing with him.

He took a shaky breath, then nodded. "Yeah."

"I say we take our leave then." Duncan also nodded as he looked around at the potion factory and our ragtag team. "Let's find a place with fewer bodies of enemies."

"And more clothes," Jasmine said firmly.

"There were some more lab coats in the cabinet I checked," Izzy said.

Jasmine couldn't have seen her from her position on the floor below the platform, but she must have heard the words, because she responded with a firm, "I'm not wearing anything that the freaks working in this place wore."

"You can have my shirt," Bolin offered. "And my pants if you want. Anything I've got. And when we get back, I've got a first-aid kit in my SUV."

"Thanks," she said. "I could really use a mocha."

"Me *too*," Bolin said.

Maybe he still needed to wash the taste of that potion out of his mouth.

Lykos didn't speak as he led us to a ladder heading down toward an exit out of the building. I leaned my shoulder against Duncan's while we walked, wondering if Lykos would be willing to stay with him now that his... whatever Abrams had been to him was gone. I could hardly call the old scientist a father or guardian. Creator and captor. That was what he'd been.

"I'm surprised I didn't have to change and lose my clothes too," I said, certain Duncan would also have offered me his shirt if I needed it.

"That's a shame," Duncan said as we walked outside after

Lykos, the rest of our group trailing us. "It's always more romantic to be nude as a couple instead of alone."

"I've not noticed that being nude alone ever bothers you."

"Oh, I'm not *bothered*. Certainly not. But I do enjoy the experience more when I'm with you."

"And your hand is on my boob?" I murmured.

"*Naturally.*"

Lykos glanced back at us, and I remembered his keen ears would have no trouble catching murmurs. Fortunately, Duncan refrained from flirting or commenting on nudity for the rest of the walk. In the gardens, on the far side of the building from where we'd originally arrived, an arch-shaped glowing portal waited for us. Thank the moon. I was more than ready to leave this place.

EPILOGUE

THE END OF THE WEEK BROUGHT AN UNSEASONABLY WARM SUNNY day, one that made me think of spring. As I finished repairs to the siding on one of the buildings and headed for the leasing office, I looked around, spotting all the perennials that would bloom and thinking wistfully of how much I enjoyed that time of year at Sylvan Serenity.

A few tenants using one of the barbecue grills on the grounds waved to me, the smoky smells of charcoal-cooked hamburgers and kebabs drifting to my nose. My two ghost hunters were with the group, none of their paranormal-sensing equipment in view. I supposed they wouldn't employ it during the middle of the day, but I hoped its absence meant that they'd retired from that hobby. These past few nights, I hadn't noticed them lurking in the parking lot. Maybe their encounter with irate business owners with tire irons had convinced them it wasn't the healthiest of pastimes.

Before I reached the leasing office, a car pulling into one of the staff spots made me pause and raise my eyebrows, waiting to see if the person turned around and left. If not, I would have to shoo him or her off with acerbic comments. Duncan was supposed to come by later, and I'd left that spot open for him, no longer threatening to tow him for loitering in my parking lot. We'd been through a lot, and I wanted him here.

My hand strayed to my abdomen. It had only been a couple of days since the showdown with Abrams—and my night in the cave with Duncan—so it was too soon for pregnancy tests and doctor visits, but thanks to the magic that I could sense within our kind, I knew. Barring complications, I would once again become a mother. And Duncan would become a father. Hopefully, his resolution with Lykos would make him more comfortable with the idea that he could handle that. I had no doubt that he could. Besides, what kid wouldn't *love* learning to magnet fish and pull rusty treasures from the bottoms of lakes?

When the driver turned off the car and got out, I lowered my hand in surprise. It was Cameron.

Immediately, I peered through the windshield toward the passenger seat, expecting Chad to be with him. That wasn't the Toyota my ex-husband had been driving around earlier in the week, but maybe they'd switched rental cars.

Cameron hesitated, then lifted his hand in a tentative greeting.

I returned it in kind and headed over, unsure whether to be wary or hopeful. When last we'd met... he'd seen me turn into a wolf and attack his father. And Duncan, as a great and powerful bipedfuris, had scared him and taken the wolf-lidded case that Chad had tried to get Cameron to run off with. That *couldn't* have left Cameron feeling warmly inclined toward wolves. Or... toward me.

Even so, something about his expression and the fact that he was here alone made me hopeful.

"Hi, Mom." Cameron lingered near the car as I approached.

I stopped a few paces back, as if he were a skittish wild animal that I didn't want to scare away. "Hi."

"Is the, uh, scary one around?" Cameron peered at the myriad cars in the lot. Looking for Duncan's Roadtrek?

"Is that Duncan? Or me in my other... incarnation?" I touched my chest.

"The shaggy beast that was eight feet tall and slavering as he leaped into my path and snatched your purse from me."

"I just call him Duncan."

"*Killer* would be more apt."

"I can see if he's up for that, but he picked Duncan for his name, so I think he's partial to it."

More partial than he'd been to Abrams's choice of *Drakon*—dragon—anyway.

Cameron considered me. "You weren't *un*scary, but I guess I was more ready for that after what Aussie said. At first, I didn't believe any of that story, but then I talked to Dad, and I guess... well, he'd always known, it sounded like."

"Yes."

"He said Aussie and I probably don't have any cool powers or anything though." Cameron looked sad about that, and I thought of Ivan, who'd possibly been driven to acquire his fortune out of a desire for artifacts that could grant him the power that his little sister had, however temporarily.

"Sorry. Being a werewolf comes with a lot of downsides too. You're better off being normal, I suppose." I didn't know if he would agree, so I shrugged. "I always wanted that for you. Normalcy."

Cameron shrugged back. "Anyway, that's not what I came about. I wanted to let you know that Dad took off after, you know." He waved vaguely in the direction of Monroe. "He said he's not messing with you ever again or taking any job offers in Seattle, and the hell with werewolves too. He's going to leave the country again."

The words filled me with glee—would it be inappropriate to

dance around, rejoicing?—but I didn't know how Cameron felt, so I attempted to keep my face neutral.

"It's for the best," I said. "The artifact he wanted had a greater use."

Even now, I didn't know exactly what that use was, but I'd heard from Emilio that it could be seen glowing at night on that cliff overlooking the pack's properties.

"And it has a giant shaggy werewolf protector." Cameron shook his head. "Good reason to leave it alone."

"I would think so. Where will *you* go next?"

"Before Dad called, I'd decided to come back to the area. I was going to tell you earlier, but things got a little weird when he got here. I've been saving a bit, doing some jobs while on the road, and I enrolled for the spring semester at U-Dub."

"Oh." My heart soared. One of my sons was coming *home*? "That's good news." I struggled for that neutral expression again. If I pounced on him with a hug or an overabundance of exuberance, it might scare him away as surely as a wolf nipping at his heels.

"Yeah. Aussie said he'll try to get leave this summer, and maybe we can all hang out and do something." He waved to me.

He wanted to *do* things with me? *Both* of my sons did? That urge to pounce returned, but Cameron spoke again before I could think of a cool and collected way to do so.

"I, uh. I wanted to let you know that..." Cameron studied the sidewalk at his feet. "I didn't realize Dad is such a... Well, he's kind of a loser, isn't he?"

"Yes," I said without hesitation.

Cameron snorted. "When he was bitching about you, I asked him straight-up about the college money. I remember you kind of implied it was his fault, but you didn't say he *stole* it. I hadn't realized. I mean, he didn't say as much now, either, but I read between the lines from some other comments he made. And when he asked *me* to pay for dinner a couple of times. Like *I* was the mature adult."

"Oh, you were. Trust me."

"Yeah?" Cameron's eyebrows rose as he seemed surprised and maybe pleased by the pronouncement.

"Yes." I nodded firmly. "I'm delighted that you'll be starting school. And I'm proud of you."

"It's no big deal." He shrugged and looked at the sidewalk again.

"It's a very big deal. I'd like to hug you."

"Oh, geez." He looked around, spotting a couple of tenants climbing out of their car. "You're not going to do it *here*, are you?"

"Would it be less weird and awkward if I dragged you into the bushes for it?"

"I don't know. Is that where you go to turn into a wolf?"

"Sometimes. The rhododendrons keep their leaves year-round, so they're handy."

Cameron rolled his eyes and hugged me. He stepped back before I could grip him for more than two seconds, but I grinned hugely anyway. After his near silence for the last two years, it was enough. More than I'd expected.

Bolin's gleaming blue SUV rolled into the lot. After parking, he and Jasmine climbed out with mochas from their favorite coffee shop in hand, whipped cream drizzled with caramel filling the clear dome lids.

Jasmine waved vigorously and headed straight for us. Cameron took that moment to slink away, probably deeply and emotionally scarred by our public embrace. But he'd instigated it, so it couldn't have been *that* bad. As the mature mother that I was, I resisted the urge to text him a chain of *hug* emojis.

Besides, Jasmine's arrival distracted me.

"Guest what, Aunt Luna?" she blurted.

"You and Bolin have fallen deeply in love and you're eloping?"

"Of course not. My mom and dad would kill me if I eloped. They've already told me I'm getting married at their house when that day comes. They have a big yard and gazebo, so apparently that qualifies it as a wedding venue."

"A gazebo?" Bolin asked, walking up in time to hear her words.

"Sure. Dad grows his wine-making grapes on it." Jasmine eyed him. "Where do rich people get married?"

"Uhm, my parents' neighbors' daughter and new husband did it in Italy. The whole extended family went for two weeks."

Jasmine pursed her lips.

"My parents weren't rich when they got married," Bolin said. "I think they were wed at a local park. There might even have been a gazebo."

"Hah, they're romantic," Jasmine said.

"Some kind of covered pavilion or something anyway," Bolin said. "There's a picture of Mom sitting in Dad's lap on a swing."

I blinked at the notion of the always-stern Kashvi Sylvan being moved to swing on Rory's lap.

"Are you going to tell her the news?" Bolin asked.

"Oh, yes." Jasmine spun back toward me. "My mom told me something this morning, and I talked to Rosaria, and she confirmed it."

Bolin lifted a finger.

Jasmine waved him down. "Let me tell her this first. *She'll* think it's more important. Trust me."

Bolin lowered his arm.

I sensed Duncan and Lykos approaching from the direction of the woods. They'd gone off to magnet-fish that morning, and I imagined them returning with a cluster of rusty twentieth-century tins hooked and hanging on lines like a bouquet of trout.

At some point during the day, Lykos had gotten a haircut and new shoes and clothes. I trusted Duncan hadn't fished them out of a pond.

"The road going out to your mom's property—*all* the werewolf properties back there—has disappeared." Jasmine gestured expansively. "I mean, we can still see it and drive up there, but we've learned that the road seems to be altogether gone to the outside world. To people who *aren't* werewolves. It's still on existing maps, but the latest satellite imagery doesn't show it. Look." Jasmine showed me a map app on her phone, including an earlier attempt to program in the address for my mother's cabin. All that came up was the road itself, outlined as a mere stub rather than the miles-long gravel and eventually dirt route that had led back to the properties.

"That's... odd," I said.

"It's *magic*. That's what Rosaria said."

I thought of the mushroom artifact on the cliff.

"Why would it have hidden the werewolves?" I mused, waving to Duncan when he came into view, ambling out of the woods.

Lykos saw our group and must have decided there were too many strange people, because he slunk back into the trees. It might take Duncan a while to fully tame the kid—and indoctrinate him into society.

"The artifact's whole reason for being created," I continued, "at least as far as we could figure was to protect people *from* werewolves. From being bitten by them, specifically."

"Yeah, I know, but if people can't find the werewolves, then they won't likely be bitten by them, right?" Jasmine shrugged. "It's not like any of our pack can turn others into werewolves anyway, but we all mostly want to be left alone. We don't want to wantonly go out and make more werewolves."

Duncan, who'd gotten close enough to hear the conversation, lifted his eyebrows.

"If people can't find the pack properties," Jasmine said, "they're not going to be bothered by werewolves at all."

"That's true, though not how I would have expected that

problem to be solved. Maybe the medallions had something to do with it. They could have communicated with the artifact, I suppose, and come to an agreement."

"That sounds kind of weird," Jasmine said.

"Weirder than roads disappearing?"

"I guess not." She wrinkled her nose in Bolin's direction.

He merely spread his arms.

"Anyway, our people can still find the way back there," Jasmine said, "and the whole area seems really serene now. It's hard to describe. You'll have to go up there when, you... oh." Her shoulders slumped, as if she'd remembered something unpleasant. "Lorenzo came back this morning and let people know... maybe he already reached out to you? But if not, your mom passed. Sorry, Luna."

"Oh." Now, it was my shoulders that slumped. Even though I'd expected to hear that news any day, it weighed me down.

"Lorenzo said she was content in the end, that what she'd wanted to see pass had come to pass."

I met Duncan's gaze. "Yes, I think that's true."

He came over and wrapped an arm around my shoulders, and I leaned against him.

"My mom says you're the heir to your mother's property too," Jasmine added. "You'll inherit all those lush acres, including the hot springs."

"You mean the lukewarm mud holes?"

"They were enough to entice those developers."

"Those guys were kind of weird."

"I won't disagree with that. Anyway, you'll be able to go up there anytime you want to hunt. Speaking of that, the elders are planning to invite you two out for that." Jasmine waved to include Duncan. "It'll be a chance for Duncan to meet the whole pack and for everyone to celebrate your mom's life and memory. They also want to get to know Duncan better. Some of the pack have been pushing, on account of the medallions and the artifact protecting everyone, for you two to lead the Savagers."

"I..." I didn't know what to say. Even though Mom had implied that when she'd given me the medallion—an artifact that usually passed down from one alpha female to the next—I hadn't thought anything about it. What did I know about leading a pack of wolves? I leaned even more heavily against Duncan.

Fortunately, he was unfazed and unflappable, and accepted my weight without shifting.

I felt daunted and sad, still regretting that I'd spent so much of my life away from the pack and my mother, and hadn't gotten to know her as well as I should have as an adult. But if she'd been satisfied in the end... that was something. Maybe that was more than most people got.

"Thanks for letting me know, Jasmine," I finally managed to say.

"Of course."

"And your news?" Bolin prompted her.

"Oh, I got a job in Kirkland at a real estate start-up that's doing these cool, modern tiny homes in cottage communities. They managed to snag some land by the waterfront near Saint Edward State Park and get the zoning and everything approved for sixteen of them. I was originally just asking about purchasing one because they look *so* much cooler than the dingy sixty-year condos that are on the market and all that I might otherwise have been able to afford, but it turned out they needed someone with my qualifications. It helped that I had an impeccable résumé with great references." She gestured toward me.

"I hope *I* wasn't your best reference."

"No, I put Ivan MacGregor down too. His sister said I could also add her. Even though we were wolves the whole time, we kind of bonded over being tortured prisoners."

"I'm sorry you had to go through that." I wished we'd gotten there sooner.

"I'm not. With references like that, I'll have whatever jobs I wish for the rest of my life." Jasmine sipped from her mocha, leaving whipped cream smearing her upper lip, and looked satisfied, if not smug.

I forced a smile onto my face, though it wasn't easy for me to put aside the news of my mother's passing. "Congratulations."

"Thank you. I'll have a house-warming party and invite you all when I get my new home."

"Will we all fit?" Bolin asked. "In a tiny home? Aren't they under five-hundred square feet?"

"Yeah, but to some people here, that has to be palatial." Jasmine smirked at Duncan. "No offense, Duncan, but the shower in your bathroom looks like it hits the toilet seat."

"It does," he said. "You can have a seat while you bathe. I believe in this country that makes my bathroom handicap accessible."

"The correct term these days is *accessible* or *barrier-free*," Bolin said.

"Palatial," Jasmine said again, smiling as she no doubt envisioned her future home.

"I'm sure you'll enjoy it," I told her. "That's a much trendier location for a young person than the alley- and freeway-adjacent condo you were musing about in Everett."

"Tell me about it." Jasmine pointed at Bolin. "You've got news for Luna too, right?"

I stood straight and took a breath to brace myself. I didn't know if I could handle any more news this morning.

"Yes." Bolin cocked his head as he looked at me. In curiosity? Puzzlement? His expression was hard to read. "It's about someone buying Sylvan Serenity."

"Oh." I slumped against Duncan again and wondered if I should ask Jasmine about the availability of other tiny homes in her new community.

Surprisingly, Bolin looked at Duncan.

"Ah yes," he said, "I believe this is the part where I have a private conversation with Luna."

Bolin nodded at him. "I think so. If it helps, my parents would be delighted if it works out."

"If what works out?" I looked back and forth between them.

"Ivan MacGregor offered to buy the place, too, and keep Luna on as the property manager," Bolin said, "but the other option would be even better. We all agree."

Jasmine nodded at Bolin.

"What other option?" I propped a fist on my hip, feeling more left out than mysteriously intrigued.

"My lady, if you'll permit me a private moment with you?" Duncan bowed and stretched an arm toward the leasing office.

"Fine, but if you irk me, just know that my sword is in there."

"I... hope you won't be irked, but I don't know. I haven't *signed* anything yet or even said... Well, it would be completely up to you. I don't want to be presumptuous."

I followed him into the office, shutting the door behind us. "Presumptuous about what?"

"You'll recall that I brought up the idea of *you* buying Sylvan Serenity."

"I believe I quashed that idea due to a lack of funds or backers with funds."

"Yes, but not a lack of interest in the idea on your part? You've spoken numerous times of one day owning rental property, right?"

I started to shake my head, but it was more a reflex, not because I wouldn't love to stay where I was as a partial owner of the property I'd dedicated so much of my life to maintaining.

"Why?" I asked instead. "You didn't find a bunch of rich backers, did you?"

Ivan MacGregor was the only person I knew, besides the Sylvans themselves, with the kind of money that could purchase a place this large.

"Well, I've all along known a possible backer with the available funds," Duncan said, "but until we... became a *we*..." He gestured not only toward me but toward my abdomen and his own chest. "Being a rather nomadic sort, I hadn't originally considered settling down at all. Certainly not *investing* in this area. But it's not as if an investor would have to stay on the premises or even be in the country all that often. Nor an owner for that matter. And you have mentioned that you might be willing to travel some with me."

"You're rambling, Duncan." I couldn't get a grasp on what he meant either.

"I'm trying to say that if you're interested, *I* would be willing to back the project." He rested a hand on his chest. "I've had plenty of time to learn that you're more than capable of running the place and making it profitable."

"You. You want to put up the down payment for an apartment complex with *hundreds* of units? Duncan, you paid for coffee and light-rail fare with coins stolen from a koi pond."

"I am frugal. Even more so now that you've introduced me to experienced clothing."

"You can't *possibly* have the money for this. Did you—"

"Get the pro forma from Bolin and his parents? I did. Besides, it's just the down payment we need to come up with."

"*Just.* As if that isn't millions and millions of dollars alone."

"It is, yes. But because it's you, the Sylvans are willing to owner-finance you for the first ten years, until you've got the experience and track record to show a bank that you're a solid bet for a loan. Of course, with the profit you've allowed this place to make, you might well be on your way to having it paid off by then. When you're the owner, will you continue to install the toilets yourself?"

"Of *course* I would, but Duncan. You can't possibly have that kind of money."

"Sure I can. I've had it for a while. I even told you about it. You'll recall the story of me diving a wreck off the coast of Africa some time back and finding a wee bit of treasure."

"What I recall is that a killer whale wearing a salmon hat was there watching you."

"Yes." Duncan snapped his fingers and beamed with pleasure that I remembered. "As I said, I bought her some salmon to celebrate, but that didn't cost much. The rest of the gold and silver... Well, it's been sitting in a vault. I daresay, it would do much better invested in a particular piece of profitable real estate here." He tilted his head, watching my face. "Is it presumptuous of me to make the offer?"

I sat at the desk. "Yes."

"Are you secretly delighted?"

I blew out a slow breath. Was this... the answer to all the problems that had plagued me of late? Or at least, *one* of the problems? I, or rather *we* together, had solved most of the rest of them.

"More than I should be," I admitted numbly.

"Oh, good. I've wondered for some time if I should mention that I'm well-endowed in more than the particular area that you know about."

"You mean your ego?"

"Please, I only think as highly of myself as is justified by my many fine attributes and talents." Duncan tilted his head. "Do you mind? That I'm a... rather well-off bloke?"

"Of course I don't mind. And you didn't owe me any explanations about your financial status. It's not like, until recently, we were even..." I waved vaguely. "Mates."

"I *wanted* to be mates. The world kept conspiring to keep us apart."

"True."

"I will point out that if you inherit all that land, you could probably use it as collateral and get a loan even without my assistance." Duncan touched his chest.

"Land that is magically hidden so that nobody but a werewolf can find it? What's the value on that, do you think?"

"Ah, it might be hard to assess. You'd better accept my offer."

"There would have to be a contract with everything legal and legitimate to protect us both."

"Naturally." Duncan didn't appear offended by the idea. "That would be romantic *and* practical."

"After all I've experienced in my life, I am much comforted by practical."

"Yes, I can see why that would be true." He offered me a hug.

I leaned into his embrace and looked around at the grounds with new hopeful eyes. "This would mean... I wouldn't have to move. We could stay here."

We might need a three-bedroom apartment instead of two, especially if we ended up adopting Lykos, but that was doable. In fact, there was a nice unit in the back coming up next month. It had a view of the woods. Lykos, in particular, might appreciate that.

"And you'll let my van and me stay free of rent?" Duncan smirked as he waved to the parking lot. "It won't be towed, and you won't bill me if I hook up the hose for water?"

"I was thinking you might move in with me."

"Goodness, what would I do with so much space? An entire apartment? I might get lost in it."

"You're kind of an odd well-off bloke."

"As we've established often in the past."

"Yes."

Duncan smiled, bent his head, and kissed me. I wrapped my arms around him and returned it.

THE END